KT-372-471

April Lady

Author of over fifty books, Georgette Heyer is one of the best-known and best-loved of all historical novelists, making the Regency period her own. Her first novel, The Black Moth, published in 1921, was written at the age of seventeen to amuse her convalescent brother; her last was My Lord John. Although most famous for her historical novels, she also wrote twelve detective stories. Georgette Heyer died in 1974 at the age of seventy-one.

Also available by Georgette Heyer

Georgette Heyer
April Lady

arrow books

19 20

Arrow Books
20 Vauxhall Bridge Road
London SW1V 2SA

Arrow Books is part of the Penguin Random House group of companies
whose addresses can be found at global.penguinrandomhouse.com.

Penguin
Random House
UK

First published in the Great Britain by William Heinemann in 1957
First published by Arrow Books in 2005
This edition reissued by Arrow Books in 2020

www.penguin.co.uk

A CIP catalogue record for this book is available from the British Library.

Typeset by SX Composing DTP, Rayleigh, Essex

Penguin Random House is committed to a sustainable future for
our business, our readers and our planet. This book is made from
Forest Stewardship Council® certified paper.

MIX
Paper from
responsible sources
FSC® C018179

Printed and bound in Great Britain by Clays Ltd, Elcograf S.p.A.

April Lady

One

There was silence in the book-room, not the silence of intimacy but a silence fraught with tension. My lady's blue eyes, staring across the desk into my lord's cool gray ones, dropped to the pile of bills under his hand. Her fair head was hung, and her nervous hands clasped one another tightly. In spite of a modish (and very expensive) morning-dress of twilled French silk, and the smart crop achieved for her golden curls by the most fashionable coiffeur in London, she looked absurdly youthful, like a schoolgirl caught out in mischief. She was, in fact, not yet nineteen years old, and she had been married for nearly a year to the gentleman standing on the other side of the desk, and so steadily regarding her.

'Well?'

She swallowed rather convulsively. The Earl had spoken quite gently, but her ears were quick to catch the note of implacability in his voice. She stole a scared look up at him, and dropped her eyes again, colouring. He was not frowning, but there was no doubt that he meant to obtain an answer to the quite unanswerable question he had put to his erring bride.

Another silence fell, broken only by the ticking of the large clock on the mantelpiece. My lady gripped her fingers so tightly together that they whitened.

'I asked you, Nell, why all these tradesmen –' the Earl lifted the bills and let them fall again – 'have found it necessary to apply to me for the settlement of their accounts?'

'I am very sorry!' faltered the Countess.

'But that doesn't answer my question,' he said dryly.

'Well – well, I expect it was because I – because I forgot to pay them myself!'

'Forgot?'

Lower sank her golden head; she swallowed again.

'Under the hatches yet again, Nell?'

She nodded guiltily, her colour deepening.

His expression was inscrutable, and for a moment he said nothing. His gaze seemed to consider her, but what thoughts were running in his head it would have been impossible to have guessed. 'I appear to make you a very inadequate allowance,' he observed.

The knowledge that the allowance he made her was a very handsome one caused her to cast an imploring glance up at him and to stammer: 'Oh, no, no!'

'Then why are you in debt?'

'I have bought things which perhaps I should not,' she said desperately. 'This – this gown, for instance! Indeed, I am sorry. I won't do so any more!'

'May I see your paid bills?'

This was said more gently still, but it effectively drove the flush from her cheeks. They became as white as they had before been red. To be sure, she had any number of receipted bills, but none knew better than she that their total, staggering though it might seem to the daughter of an impoverished peer, did not account for half of that handsome allowance which was paid quarterly to her bankers. At any moment now my lord would ask the question she dreaded, and dared not answer truthfully.

It came. 'Three months ago, Nell,' said the Earl, in a measured tone, 'I forbade you most straitly to pay any more of your brother's debts. You gave me your word that you would not. *Have* you done so?'

She shook her head. It was dreadful to lie to him, but what else was to be done when he looked so stern, and had shown himself so unsympathetic to poor Dysart? It was true that Dysart's recurring difficulties were all due to his shocking luck; and it seemed that Cardross couldn't understand how unjust it was to blame Dysart for his inability to abandon gaming and racing. That Fatal Tendency, said Mama, with resignation, ran in the family: Grandpapa had died under a cloud of debt; and Papa, with the hopeful intention of restoring the fortunes of his house, had still more heavily mortgaged his estates. That was why Papa had been so overjoyed when Cardross had offered for her hand. For Cardross was as well-born as he was wealthy, and Papa had previously been obliged to face the horrid necessity of giving his eldest daughter to the highest bidder, even (dreadful thought!) if this should prove to be a rich merchant with social aspirations. He had done so with great fortitude, and he had had his reward: in her very first season – indeed, before she had been out a month – Cardross has not only seen the Lady Helen Irvine, but had apparently decided that she was the bride for whom he had so long waited. Such a piece of good fortune had never even occurred to Lord Pevensey. It was certainly to be supposed that Cardross, past thirty, and with no nearer relation than a cousin to succeed him, must be contemplating marriage in the not too distant future, but such was his consequence that he might have had the pick of all the damsels faithfully presented by their mamas at the Queen's Drawing-rooms, and thereafter exhibited by them at Almack's Assembly Rooms, and all the ton parties. Moreover, to judge by the style of the lady who was pretty generally known to be his mistress, his taste was for something older and by far more sophisticated than a child fresh from the schoolroom. Never had Papa thought to see his little Nell do so well for the family! In the event, her success, and Cardross's generosity proved to be rather too much for him: hardly had he led his child to the altar than he suffered a stroke. The doctors assured his lady that he had many years of life before him, but the visitation had rendered him so far incapable that he had had to abandon his usual pursuits, and to retire to the seclusion of his ancestral home in Devonshire, where, it was the earnest if unexpressed hope of his wife and son-in-law, he would be obliged to remain.

3

Nell did not know just what Cardross had done to earn her parents' gratitude. It all came under the vague title of Settlements, and she was not to bother her pretty head over it, but to take care always to conduct herself with dignity and discretion. Mama, declaring herself to be deeply thankful, had made quite plain to her what her duty henceforward would be. It included such things as always showing my lord an amiable countenance, and never embarrassing him by asking ill-bred questions, or appearing to be aware of it if (perhaps) he was found to have formed a Connection outside the walls of that splendid house of his in Grosvenor Square. '*One* thing I am sure of,' had said Mama, fondly patting Nell's hand, 'and that is that he will treat you with the greatest consideration! His manners, too, are so particularly good that I am persuaded you will never have cause to complain of the sort of neglect, or – or indifferent civility, which is the lot of so many females in your situation. I assure you, my love, there is nothing more mortifying than to be married to a man who lets it be seen that his affections are elsewhere engaged.'

Mama should have known, for this had been her fate. What Mama did not know, and no one must ever guess, was that her carefully instructed daughter had tumbled headlong into love with my lord at their very first meeting, when Lady Jersey, one of the Patronesses of Almack's, had brought him across the room to be introduced to her, and she had looked up into his eyes, and had seen them smiling down at her. No, Mama had no suspicion of that. Mama was all sensibility, but she knew that marriage had nothing to do with romance. It had been her dread, she confided, that Nell would be married to a man whom she could not like, but she was quite sure that Nell must like so charming and so handsome a gentleman as Cardross. And, what was more, there could be little doubt that he was disposed to hold his bride in considerable affection. He had actually desired Lady Jersey to present him to her, on that memorable evening; and what he had said later to Papa, when he had made his offer, had quite soothed a mother's anxiety. Nell would meet with nothing but courtesy and consideration at his hands.

It hadn't seemed possible to Nell, lost in love, that Cardross could have proposed to her only because she was pretty, and well-born, and rather more pleasing to him than any of the other young ladies who met his critical eye, but Mama had been right. When Nell had met my lord's half-sister and ward, a vivid brunette, not then out, but hopeful of being presented by her sister-in-law, that impetuous damsel had exclaimed, warmly embracing her: 'Oh, how pretty you are! Prettier by far than Giles's mistress! How famous if you were to put her nose out of joint!'

It had been a dreadful shock, but Nell had not betrayed herself, which was some small consolation; and she was thankful to have been made aware of the truth before she could render herself ridiculous by showing her heart to the world, or have become a tiresome bore to my lord by hanging on him in the doting way which one short season had taught her was con-sidered by the modish to be not at all the thing. As for putting Lady Orsett's nose out of joint – it had not taken her long to discover the identity of my lord's mistress – that ambition probably belonged, like her earlier dreams, to the realm of make-believe, and certainly seemed very far from achievement today, when my lord was commanding her to account for her debts.

'Tell me the truth, Nell!'

His voice, quite kind, but unmistakably imperative, recalled her from her hurrying, jumbled thoughts. But it was impossible to tell him the truth, because even if he forgave her for having disobeyed him he was very unlikely to forgive Dysart, for whom, in his eyes, there could be no excuse at all. And if he refused to rescue Dysart from his difficulties any more, and made it impossible for her to do so either, what would become of Dy, or, for that matter, of poor Papa? Not so long ago he had said, a trifle grimly, that the best turn he could render Dysart would be to buy him a pair of colours, and pack him off to join Lord Wellington's army in the Peninsula; and it was all too probable that this was precisely what he would do if this fresh disaster came to his ears. Nor was there much doubt that Dysart would jump at the offer, because he had always hankered after a military career. Only Papa, with his next son a schoolboy still at Harrow, had refused even to discuss the matter; and Mama, at the mere thought of exposing her beloved eldest-born to the dangers and discomforts of a military campaign, had suffered a series of distressing spasms.

No, the truth could not be told, but how did one account for three hundred pounds with never a bill to show? There was no need for Lord Pevensey's daughter to cudgel her brains for more than a very few moments over that problem: few knew better than an Irvine how money could vanish without leaving a trace behind. 'It wasn't Dysart!' she said quickly. 'I am afraid it was me!' She saw his face change, an arrested look in his eyes, a hardening of the lines about his mouth, and she felt suddenly frightened. 'Pray don't be angry!' she begged rather breathlessly. 'I promise I will never do so any more!'

'Are you telling me you lost it at play?'

She hung her head again. After a pause he said: 'I suppose I should have known that it would be in your blood too.'

'No, no, *indeed* it isn't!' she cried, with passionate sincerity. 'Only it seemed stupid and prudish not to play, when everyone else did so, and then I lost, and I thought that perhaps the luck would change, but it didn't, and —'

'You need say no more!' he interrupted. 'There was never yet a gamester who didn't think the luck must change!' He looked frowningly at her, and added in a level tone: 'I should be very reluctant, Nell, to take such steps as must put it wholly out of your power to play anything but silver-loo, or a pool at commerce, but I give you fair warning I will not permit my wife to become one of faro's daughters.'

'Well, I am not perfectly sure what that is,' she said naïvely, 'but indeed I won't do it again, so *pray* don't do anything horrid!'

'Very well,' he replied. He glanced down at the bills on his desk. 'I'll settle these, and any others that you may have. Will you bring them to me, please?'

'Now?' she faltered, uneasily aware of a drawer stuffed with bills.

'Yes, now.' He added, with a smile: 'You will be much more comfortable, you know, when you have made a clean breast of the whole.'

She agreed to this, but when she presently rendered up a collection of crumpled bills she did not feel at all comfortable. There could be no denying that she had been woefully extravagant. The allowance Cardross made her had seemed so enormous to a girl who had never had anything to spend beyond the small sum bestowed on her with the utmost reluctance by her papa for pin-money that she had bought things quite recklessly, feeling her resources to be limitless. But now, as she watched my lord glance through the appalling sheaf, she thought she must have been mad to have spent so much and so heedlessly.

For some moments he read with an unmoved countenance, but presently his brows knit, and he said: 'A two-colour gold snuffbox with grisaille paintings?'

'For Dysart!' she explained apprehensively.

'Oh!' He resumed his study of the incriminating bills. With a sinking heart, she saw him pick up a document headed, in elegant scroll-work, by the name of her favourite dressmaker. He said nothing, however, and she was able to breathe again. But an instant later he read aloud: 'Singing-bird, with box embellished turquoise-blue enamelled panels – What the *devil* – ?'

'It was a music-box,' she explained, her voice jumping. 'For the children – my sisters!'

'Ah, I see!' he said, laying the bill aside.

Her spirits rose, only to sink again an instant later when the Earl exclaimed: 'Good God!' Peeping in great trepidation to see what had provoked this startled ejaculation, she perceived that he was holding another scrolled sheet. 'Forty guineas for one hat?' he said incredulously.

'I am afraid it *was* a little dear,' she owned. 'It – it has three *very* fine ostrich plumes, you see. You – you said you liked it!' she added desperately.

'Your taste is always impeccable, my love. Did I like the other eight hats you have purchased, or haven't I seen them yet?'

Horrified, she stammered: 'N-not *eight*, Giles, *surely*?'

He laughed. 'Eight! Oh, don't look so dismayed! I daresay they were all quite necessary. To be sure, forty guineas seems a trifle extortionate, but it is certainly a charming confection, and becomes you delightfully.' She smiled gratefully at him, and he took her chin in his hand, and pinched it. 'Yes, very well, ma'am, but that is only the sop that goes before the scold! You've been drawing the bustle disgracefully, my dear. You seem not to have the smallest notion of management, and I should doubt whether you have ever kept an account in your life. Now, I am going to settle all these bills of yours and I am also going to place a further hundred pounds to your account. That should – indeed, it must! – keep you in reasonably comfortable circumstances until the quarter.'

She exclaimed: 'Oh, thank you! How *very* kind you are! I will take the greatest care, I promise!'

'I trust you won't find it necessary to exercise any very stringent economies,' he said, with a touch of irony. 'But if you have any more bills laid by, give them to me now! I won't scold, but I warn you, Nell, it won't do to keep your money safely in Childe's while you run up debts all over town! There are to be no bills outstanding at the quarter, so if you are concealing any from me now, make a clean breast of them! If I found that you had deceived me, then, indeed, I should be angry with you, and do much more than scold!'

'What – what would you do, if – if I did happen to owe any money at the quarter?' she asked, looking frightened.

'Give you only enough money for such trifling expenses as must occur from day to day, and arrange that all your bills are sent to me for payment,' he replied.

'Oh, no!' she cried, flushing.

'I assure you I should dislike it as much as you, and feel as much humiliated. But I have seen something of what such reckless spending as you appear to delight in may lead to, and I am determined it shall not happen in my household. Now, think, Nell! Have you given me all your bills?'

The consciousness of having already deceived him, as much as his treat, coupled as it was by a certain look of inflexibility in his face, almost overpowered her. In suppressed agitation, which rendered calm reflection impossible, she said hurriedly: 'Yes – oh, yes!'

'Very well. We shan't speak of this again, then.'

The flurry of her heart subsided; she said in a subdued voice: 'Thank you! Indeed, I am very much obliged to you! I did not mean to be such an extravagant wife.'

'Nor I such a tyrannical husband. We could deal better than this, Nell.'

'No, no! I mean, I never thought you so! You are most kind – I beg your pardon for being so troublesome: pray forgive me!'

'Nell!'

His hand was outstretched to her, but she did not take it, only smiling nervously, and saying again: 'Thank you! You are very good! Oh, how late it is! M-may I go now?'

His hand fell; he said in quite a different voice: 'I am not a schoolmaster! Certainly go, if that is your wish!'

She murmured something, in disjointed phrases, about his sister, and Almack's and fled out of the room. That gesture, coming as it did at the end of a scene during which he had indeed seemed to be more schoolmaster than husband, seemed to her rather the expression of kindness than of any warmer emotion, and, with her nerves already overset, she had not been able to respond to it as, in general, she had forced herself to respond to any advance made by him. That her retreat might offend him she knew; that it could wound him she had no suspicion, having, from the start of her married life, seen in his love-making only a chivalrous determination not to betray to her that although he had bestowed his name on her his heart belonged to another.

As for Cardross, he was left with some rather bitter reflections to bear him company, and the growing suspicion that all the well-wishers who had begged him not to marry Nell had been right after all: no good could come of an alliance with an Irvine. One of his cousins, that Pink of the Ton, Mr Felix Hethersett, had put the matter to him with brutal frankness. 'Nothing to say against the girl, dear old boy, but I don't like the stable,' had said Mr Hethersett.

Well, he had not liked the stable either. Nothing had been further from his intention than marriage with an Irvine; and nothing had seemed more improbable than a love-match. It was his duty to marry, but for some years he had enjoyed an agreeable connection with a fashionable lady of easy morals and skilful discretion, and that he should succumb to a pair of blue eyes and a mischievous dimple had been an event quite outside his calculations. But so it had been. He had first seen his Nell in a ballroom, and he had instantly been struck, not so much by her undeniable beauty as by the sweetness in her face, and the innocence of her enquiring gaze. Before he well knew what had happened, his heart was lost, and every prudent consideration thrown to the winds. She sprang from a line of expensive profligates, but he had been ready to swear, looking into her eyes, that she had miraculously escaped the Irvine taint.

She had been less than eighteen when he had married her, fourteen years younger than he, and when he found himself with a shy, elusive bride he handled her very gently, believing that tenderness and forbearance would win for him the loving, vital creature he was so sure lived behind the nervous child.

He had caught glimpses of that creature – or so he thought – but he had never won her; and the fear that he had deceived himself was beginning to grow on him. She was dutiful, even submissive; sometimes an entrancing companion, always a well-mannered one; but although she never repulsed his advances she never courted them, or gave any sign that she could not be perfectly happy out of his company. Once installed in Grosvenor Square she entered with apparent zest into every fashionable amusement, took her young sister-in-law into society, rapidly acquired a court of her own, and was by no means the sort of wife who constantly demanded her husband's escort. She was extravagant; he had today discovered that, like the rest of her family, she was a gamester; and what affection she had she appeared to lavish on her little sisters, and on her scapegrace of a brother. There had been plenty of people to tell Cardross that Nell had accepted him for the sake of his wealth. He had not believed them, but he was beginning to wonder. In her precipitate retreat from his book-room he saw only a spoilt child's desire to escape from a disagreeable schoolmaster, and never dreamed that she had fled because her feelings threatened to overcome her.

She made for the shelter of her own apartments, hoping, since she needed a little time in which to compose herself, that she would not find her dresser already there. She did not. She found her sister-in-law instead, blithely engaged in trying on one of those eight – no, *nine*! – modish hats.

The young Countess's apartments consisted of a spacious bedchamber, and an adjoining room, known to the household as her dressing-room but partaking more of the nature of a boudoir. My lord had had both rooms redecorated on the occasion of his marriage, nesting his bride in a tent-bed with rose-silk curtains upheld by Cupids and garlands, and hanging her dressing-room with blue and silver brocade. In this frivolous bower, of which she was frankly envious, the Lady Letitia Merion was parading between various mirrors, very well-pleased with her appearance, but unable to decide on the precise tilt at which the hat should be worn. She hailed her sister-in-law light-heartedly, saying: 'Oh, I am glad you are come! I have been waiting for ever! Nell, I do think this is a *ravishing* hat, only should one wear it? Like this, or like *this*?'

'Oh, don't!' begged Nell involuntarily, unable to bear the sight of what had contributed to her late discomfiture.

'Good gracious, what's the matter?' demanded Letty.

'Nothing, nothing! I have the headache a little, that is all!' She saw that Letty was staring at her, and tried to smile. 'Pray don't be concerned! It is only – I only –' She could not go on, her voice being totally suspended by the tears she was unable to control.

'Nell!' Letty flung off the ravishing hat, and ran across the room to put her arms round her sister-in-law. 'Oh, pray don't cry! Has something dreadful happened?'

'No, no! That is – I have been so wickedly extravagant!'

'Is *that* all? I collect Giles has been giving you a scold. Don't regard it; he will come about? Was he very angry?'

'Oh, no, but very much displeased, and indeed it was unpardonable of me!' Nell said, drying her eyes. 'But that was not the worst! I was obliged –' She broke off, flushing, and added in a hurried tone: 'I can't tell you! I shouldn't have said that – pray don't regard it! I have been sadly heedless, but I shall hope to go on better now. Did you wish to speak to me particularly?'

'Oh, no! Only to ask you if I may wear your zephyr scarf this evening, if you shouldn't be needing it yourself – but if you are in a fit of the dismals I won't tease you,' said Letty handsomely.

'Oh, yes, do wear it! In fact, you may have it for your own, for I am sure *I* can never bear to wear it again!' said Nell tragically.

'Never bear – Nell, don't be such a goose! Why, you went into transports when they showed it to you, and it cost you thirty guineas!'

'I know it did, and he saw the bill for it, and never spoke one word of censure, which makes me feel ready to sink!'

'For my part,' said Letty candidly, 'I should be excessively thankful for it! May I have it, indeed? Thank you! It will be just the thing to wear with my French muslin. I *had* meant to try if I could persuade Giles to purchase one like it for me.'

'Oh, no, do not!' exclaimed Nell, aghast.

'No, I shouldn't think of doing so now that he has taken one of his pets,' agreed Letty. 'I'm sure I never knew anyone so odious about being in debt! What shall you wear tonight? You haven't forgotten that Felix Hethersett is to escort us to Almack's, have you?'

Nell sighed: 'I wish we need not go!'

'Well, there's not the least occasion for you to go if you don't choose,' said Letty obligingly. 'You may send a note round to

Felix's lodging, and as for me, I daresay my aunt Thorne will be very willing to take me with her and my cousin.'

This airy speech had the effect of diverting Nell's mind from her own iniquities. Upon his marriage, the Earl had removed his young ward from the care of her maternal aunt, and had taken her to live in his own house. Mrs Thorne was a goodnatured woman, but he could not like the tone of her mind, or feel that she had either the desire or the power to control his flighty half-sister. He had been startled to discover how casual was the surveillance under which Letty had grown up, how improper many of the ideas she had imbibed; and he was still more startled when she disclosed to him that young as she was she had already formed what she assured him was an undying attachment. Jeremy Allandale was a perfectly respectable young man, but although well-connected he could not be thought an eligible husband for the Lady Letty Merion. He was employed at the Foreign Office, and although his prospects were thought to be good his present circumstances were straitened. His widowed mother was far from affluent, and he had several young brothers and sisters for whose education he considered himself to be largely responsible. The Earl thought this fortunate, for although the young man conducted himself with the strictest propriety he was plainly infatuated with Letty, and no dependence whatsoever (in her brother's opinion) could be placed on her discretion. Could she but gain control of her fortune she was quite capable of persuading her lover to elope with her. In the event, he was wholly unable to support her, so that that contingency seemed unlikely. Mr Allandale received little encouragement to visit in Grosvenor Square, but, whether from wisdom or from a dislike of enacting the tyrant, the Earl had never forbidden his sister to hold ordinary social intercourse with him. She could incur no censure by standing up for two dances with Mr Allandale; but Nell was well aware that under the careless chaperonage of her aunt she would not stop at that. She guessed from Letty's ready acquiescence in her own desire to remain at home that evening that Mr Allandale would be at Almack's, and she at once shook off her megrims, and said that of course she would take Letty there.

Mr Allandale was indeed at Almack's, and for the fiftieth time Nell found herself wondering why it was that Letty had fallen in love with him. He was a well-made man, he was even good-looking; but his manners were too formal for ease, and his conversation was painstaking rather than amusing. He was certainly solid: Nell found him a little dull. Mr Felix Hethersett, not mincing matters, said: 'Fellow's a dead bore. Shouldn't think the affair would last.'

'No,' agreed Nell, 'but I must own that she has shown the greatest constancy, in spite of having been very much made up to, ever since she came out. I did venture once to suggest to Cardross that perhaps it would not be such a very bad match after all, but – but he cannot like it, and will only say that if she is still of the same mind when she is a few years older he will not then receive Mr Allandale in an unfriendly spirit.'

'Throwing herself away,' said Mr Hethersett disapprovingly. 'Dash it, cousin, very taking little thing! Besides being an heiress. Not but what,' he added, as a thought occurred to him, 'very understandable you should wish to see her safely tied up to someone! I daresay she's the deuce of a charge.'

'Oh, no, indeed she is not!' Nell said, quite distressed. 'How could you think I wished to be rid of her? I am only too happy to have her companionship!'

Much abashed, he begged pardon. His earlier strictures on her family notwithstanding he was one of her more faithful admirers, and was generally recognized to be her cicisbeo-in-chief. She had other and more dazzling followers, but he was certainly her favourite: a circumstance which presented an enigma to the worldlings who never dreamed that the beautiful young Countess had no taste for dalliance, but smiled on Mr Hethersett because he was her lord's cousin. She treated him much as she treated her brother, an arrangement which suited him very well, since he was not, in fact, much of a lady's man, but attached himself to the court of some lady of rank and beauty as a matter of *ton*. A high stickler, Mr Hethersett, precise to a pin, blessed with propriety of taste, an impeccable lineage, and a comfortable fortune. He was neither handsome nor articulate, but his dress was always in the first style of elegance; he could handle a team to perfection; was generally thought to be up to every rig and row in town; and had such obliging manners as made him quite the best liked of the Bond Street beaux. The gentlemen thought him a very good fellow; the ladies valued him for two very excellent reasons: to be admired by him added to any female's consequence, and to possess his friendship was to enjoy not only the distinguishing notice of a man of the first stare of fashion, but the willing services of one whose good-nature was proverbial. For the more adventurous ladies, the dashing chippers who damped their muslins to make them cling revealingly to their exquisite forms, painted their toe-nails with gilt, and lived perpetually on the brink of social disaster, there were many more attractive blades; but young Lady Cardross was not a member of this sisterhood, and, while she naturally did not wish to be so unfashionable as to own no devoted admirer, she took care not to encourage the pretensions of any of the notorious rakes who courted her. Mr Hethersett could be depended on to gallant one uncomplainingly to quite the dullest party of the season; and there was no need to fear that the abandonment of formality would lead him to encroach on his position. He was neither witty nor talkative, but a certain shrewdness characterized him, his bow was perfection, and his grace in a ballroom unequalled. Even Letty, who said that his notions of propriety were quite gothic, did not despise his escort when she went to Almack's. Almack's was abominably slow, of course, and its haughty patronesses by far too high in the instep; but any lady refused a voucher of admission to its sacred precincts must consider herself to be socially damned. To attend the Assemblies gallanted by Mr Hethersett ensured for one the approval even of censorious Mrs Drummond Burrell, and had been known to win for a perfectly insipid damsel a condescending smile from that odious Countess Lieven.

Nell was as much astonished as she was delighted to perceive, on arrival in King Street, that her graceless but beloved brother was rather inexpertly dancing the boulanger, with a quiet-looking girl for his partner. He explained to her presently that he had never been so taken-in before. 'Ay, you may well stare!' he said, his angelic blue eyes kindling with indignation.

She could not help laughing, but she said: 'Oh, Dy, what a wretch you are, when you wouldn't come with *me*, and said wild horses couldn't drag you here!'

'It wasn't wild horses,' he replied darkly. '*They* couldn't have done it! It was old Mother Wenlock! Beckoned to me to come up to that antiquated landaulette of hers in Bond Street this morning, and said I must dine in Brook Street to meet her niece. Of course I said I was engaged with a party of friends, but I might as well have spared my breath. Of all the devilish things, Nell, these shocking old hags who are hand-in-glove with Mama are the worst! Mind, if I'd known she meant to drag me to Almack's she could have said what she chose, I wouldn't have budged! I ain't a dancing man, you can't get a thing to drink but lemonade and orgeat – and of the two, damned if I'd not as lief drink lemonade! – and this precious niece, whom she swore was a ravishing girl, is nothing but a dowdy!'

'Ought to have known she would be,' said Mr Hethersett, from the depths of his worldly wisdom.

'Why?' demanded the Viscount.

In other company Mr Hethersett would have answered him with brutal frankness, but under Nell's innocently enquiring gaze his courage failed, and he said he didn't know. After all, one couldn't tell an adoring sister that no chaperon in her senses would invite Dysart to gallant a ravishing girl to a party. If the damsel in question seemed likely to attract his roving fancy she would be much more likely to forbid him the house. He might be the heir to an Earldom but it was common knowledge that his noble father (until he had the good fortune to catch Cardross for his daughter) was all to pieces, having, in vulgar parlance, brought an abbey to a grange; and no one who had observed his own volatile career could place the slightest dependence on his setting the family affairs to rights by more prudent conduct. So far from being regarded as an eligible bachelor, he was considered to be extremely dangerous, for he combined with decidedly libertine propensities a degree of charm which might easily prove the undoing of the most delicately nurtured female. He was also very goodlooking, and although his critics unequivocally condemned the carelessness of his attire, it could not be denied that his tall person, with its fine shoulders, and its crown of waving golden hair, inevitably drew all eyes. He had an endearing smile, too, at once rueful and mischievous. It dawned now, for he was no fool, and he knew very well what Mr Hethersett had meant.

'Craven!' he said challengingly.

But Mr Hethersett refused to be drawn; and since Letty came up at that moment, under the escort of Mr Allandale, Dysart allowed the matter to drop. He greeted Letty with the easy camaraderie of one who was in some sort related to her, and at once begged permission to lead her into the set which was just then forming. However unalterably devoted to Mr Allandale Letty might be, she was by no means impervious to the Viscount's charm, and she went blithely off with him, leaving her swain to exchange civilities with Nell.

Her cousin Felix watched these proceedings with a jaundiced eye. It would have been hard to have found a greater contrast than that which existed between Lord Dysart and Mr Jeremy Allandale. The one was a rather thick-set young man, whose grave eyes and regular features were allied to a serious mind, and solid worth of character; the other was a tall, handsome buck, bearing himself with careless arrogance, laughter never far from his lips, and in his gleaming blue eyes a reckless light which sprang from a disposition which was as volatile as Mr Allandale's was dependable. But in one respect they were blood-brothers: as prospective bridegrooms each in his way was wholly ineligible. Mr Hethersett, watching the start of a promising flirtation between Letty and his lordship, was much inclined to think that he had grossly failed in his duty towards Cardross. A quicker-witted man, he gloomily reflected, would have intervened before Letty had had time to accept Dysart's invitation.

Nell, too, was watching the couple on the dance-floor, not with misgiving (for although she knew that Cardross had no great liking for Dysart she also knew that Letty had no great liking for anyone but her Jeremy), but a little wistfully. When she had seen Dysart she had known an impulse to confide her troubles to him. She had no expectation of his being able to give back to her the money she had so blithely bestowed on him, but at least she might have warned him not, in future, to depend on her.

There was no further opportunity offered her for speech with Dysart. Her own hand was claimed; her place in the set was far removed from Dysart's; and by the time she left the floor he had restored Letty to Mr Hethersett's protection, and had returned to his own party.

He left it, on the flimsiest of excuses, ten minutes later: a circumstance of which she was soon made fully aware by his hostess, who sailed across the room for the express purpose of favouring her with her opinion of his manners and upbringing. Mr Hethersett could do nothing to spare her this ordeal, but when one of his and Cardross's more formidable aunts conceived it to be her duty to censure Nell for her thoughtlessness in permitting Letty to dance with Mr Allandale he came out strongly in her support, even recommending Lady Chudleigh to address her criticisms to Cardross himself.

'Let me assure you, Felix,' said the lady in quelling accents, 'that nothing is further from my intentions! Far be it from me to seek to make mischief!'

'Just as well,' responded the intrepid Mr Hethersett. 'Very likely to give you one of his set-downs!'

Nell was quite overcome by such a display of heroism on her behalf, but Mr Hethersett disclaimed heroism. Having watched through a quizzing-glass which hideously magnified his eye the retreat of the dowager, he assured Nell that he had spoken nothing more than the truth. 'No need to fear Cardross would listen to *her* tales,' he said. 'What's more, he must know you couldn't stop Letty dancing with anyone. Doubt whether he could do it himself.'

It seemed as though the Earl shared this doubt. He had not returned from a dinner given by the Sublime Society of Beefsteaks when the ladies were set down in Grosvenor Square sometime after midnight, but he visited his bride later in the morning. He found her with a breakfast-tray across her knees, the curtains of her bed drawn back in billowing folds of rosy silk. She was engaged, between sips of coffee and nibbles at a slice of bread-and-butter, in reading her correspondence. This seemed, from the litter on the counterpane, to consist largely of gilt-edged invitations, but there was a letter, crossed and recrossed, from her mama, which she was trying to decipher when Cardross came into the room. She put it down at once, and tried to tuck back the ringlets which had strayed from under her becoming night-cap of muslin and lace. 'My lord! Oh, dear, I did not think you would be coming to see me so early, and I am dreadfully untidy!'

'Don't!' he said, capturing her hand, and kissing it. 'You look charmingly, I assure you. Was it amusing, your party?'

'Yes, thank you. That is – it was just one of the Assemblies, at Almack's, you know.'

'Not very amusing, then,' he remarked, seating himself on the edge of her bed, and picking up one of the invitation cards. 'Nor will this be, but we shall be obliged to accept it, I suppose. She is Letty's godmother. Did Letty behave with propriety last night, or did she hang on that fellow Allandale the whole evening?'

'No, indeed she did not! She stood up only twice with him.'

'I am astonished to learn that she had as much moderation – and I make you my compliments: it must surely be your doing!'

'Well, of course, I should *try* to dissuade her from doing what you don't like,' said Nell doubtfully, 'but it wasn't at all necessary. Mr Allandale's scruples are so *very* strict that I am persuaded he would never ask her to do anything that might set up people's backs.'

'Good God!' said his lordship. 'What a slow-top! My dear, what *does* she see in him to hit her fancy?'

'I can't think!' said Nell candidly. 'Though I am sure he has many excellent qualities, and a most superior understanding.'

'Superior fiddlesticks! I never found him to be anything but a dreadful bore. I wish to God she would recover from this greensickness! It's quite impossible, you know: he has neither fortune nor expectation, and I'll swear I never saw a couple less suited to one another. I should be a villain to countenance such an attachment. If his scruples are as strict as you tell me I collect I've no need to fear he may run off with her to Gretna Green?'

'Good gracious, no!' Nell exclaimed, startled.

'So much, then, for my aunt Chudleigh's croakings!'

'Your aunt Chudleigh! Oh, Giles, she was at Almack's last night, and she gave me a terrible scold for permitting Letty to dance with Mr Allandale!'

'What impertinence!'

'Oh, no! Though that is what Felix said. And also he told her to make her complaints to you, which was not very civil of him, but excessively brave, I thought!'

'I wonder what she imagines I can do to stop Letty? Short of incarcerating her at Merion – By the by, I must go to Merion next week. Useless, I suppose to ask you to go with me?'

She showed him a face of sudden dismay. 'Next week! But the Beadings' masquerade – !'

He raised his brows. 'Is it so important? For my part, masquerades at Chiswick –'

'No, indeed, but you did promise Letty she should attend it! It is the first she has ever been to, and she has had the prettiest domino made, and – and I must own I think it would be dreadfully shabby to tell her now that she cannot go!'

'Hang Letty! Can't she – No, I suppose not. Very well: I won't tease you to go with me.'

'I wish I might,' she said wistfully.

He smiled at her, but rather quizzically, and picked up another of the invitation cards. 'A quadrille ball at the Cowpers'!

How dashing! It will be a horrible squeeze: must we go?'

The post had brought her ladyship a polite reminder from Mr Warren, Perfumier, that a trifling account for scent, white nail-wax and Olympian Dew, was outstanding. It had lain hidden by Lady Cowper's invitation, and was revealed when the Earl picked this up. Only a few guineas were involved, but Nell instinctively put out her hand to cover it. The movement caught his eye; he glanced down, and she at once removed her hand, flushing, vexed with herself.

'What other delights are in store for us?' he asked, picking up another card. 'Assemblies and balls seem to be in full feather: you will be knocked up by all this raking! Don't drag me to *this* affair, I beg of you!'

'That? Oh, no! It is to be a petticoat-party. You – you will be present at our own dress-party, won't you?'

'Of course.'

There was a short silence. After that one glance the Earl had not again looked at Mr Warren's account, but it seemed to his guilty wife imperative to divert his attention from it. She said a trifle breathlessly: 'Cardross, what a very elegant dressing-gown that is! I think I never saw you wear it before.'

'Ah, I hoped you would be pleased with it!' he replied blandly. 'And with me for letting you see it.'

'How absurd you are! It is certainly most handsome.'

'Yes, and wickedly dear – as dear as your feathered bonnet, though not, I fear, as becoming. You see how I lay myself open to strong counter-attack!'

'Oh, Giles!'

He laughed, and tickled her cheek. 'Foolish little Nell! Is it *very* shocking?'

She heaved a sigh of relief, smiling shyly at him. 'No, indeed it isn't! Only it – it does chance to be a bill I had forgotten, and I was afraid you would be angry with me.'

'What a disagreeable husband I must be!' he murmured ruefully. 'Shall I pay that bill with the rest?'

'No, please! It is a *very* small one – look!'

She held it out to him, but he did not look at it, only taking her hand in his, the bill crushed between his fingers, and saying: 'You mustn't be afraid of me. I never meant to make you so! I'll pay this bill, or any other – only don't conceal any from me!'

'Afraid of you? Oh, no, no!' she exclaimed.

His clasp on her hand tightened; he leaned forward, as though he would have kissed her; but her dresser came into the room just then, and although she quickly withdrew, the moment had passed. Nell had snatched her hand away, vividly blushing, and the Earl did not try to recapture it. He got up, his own complexion rather heightened, feeling all the embarrassment natural to a man discovered, at ten o'clock in the morning, making love to his own wife, and went away to his dressing-room.

Two

hortly before four o'clock that afternoon young Lady Cardross's barouche was driven into Hyde Park by the Stanhope Gate. It was a very stylish vehicle, quite the latest thing in town carriages, and it had been bestowed on her ladyship, together with the pair of perfectly matched grays that drew it, by her husband, upon her installation as mistress of his house in Grosvenor Square. 'Slap up to the echo,' was what Dysart called it: certainly no other lady owned a more elegant turn-out. To be seen in Hyde Park between the hours of five and six on any fine afternoon during the London season, driving, riding, or even walking, was de rigueur for anyone of high fashion; and before her marriage, when she had sat beside her mama in an oldfashioned landaulet, Nell had frequently envied the possessors of more dashing equipages, and had thought how agreeable it would be to sit behind a pair of high-steppers in a smart barouche, with its wheels picked out in yellow. She had been delighted with the Earl's gift, exclaiming naïvely: 'Now I shall be all the crack!'

'Do you wish to be?' he had asked her, amused.

'Yes,' she replied honestly. 'And I think I ought to be, because although Miss Wilby – our governess, you know – says that it is wrong to set one's mind on worldly things, *you* are all the crack, which makes it perfectly proper, I think, for me to be fashionable too.'

'I am persuaded,' he said, his countenance admirably composed, 'that Miss Wilby must perceive it to be your *duty*, even.'

23

She was a little dubious about this, but happily recollecting that she was no longer answerable to her governess she was able to put that excellent educationist out of her mind. 'You know how people talk of Lord Dorset on his white horse, and Mrs Toddington with her chestnuts?' she said confidentially. '*Now* they will talk of Lady Cardross, behind her match-grays! I should not be astonished if my barouche were to draw as many eyes as hers!'

'Nor should I,' agreed his lordship, grave as a judge. 'In fact, I should be much astonished if it did not.'

Whether it was the smart turn-out which drew all eyes, or its charming occupant, Nell had soon experienced the felicity of attracting a great deal of attention when she drove in the Park. She became a noted figure, and never doubted that she owed this triumph to her splendid horses until her more knowledgeable sister-in-law remarked chattily, as she stepped into the carriage that day: 'Isn't it a fortunate circumstance, Nell, that you are fair and I am dark? I don't wonder at it that everyone stares to see us: we take the shine out of *all* the other females! Mr Bottisham told Hardwick so, and Hardwick says it is a compliment well worth having, because Mr Bottisham is in general quite odiously censorious. I think,' she added, dispassionately considering the matter, 'that you are prettier than I am, but, on the other hand, I have a great deal of countenance, besides being dark, which is more in the mode, so I don't *excessively* mind your being beautiful.'

Nell could not help laughing, but, with Miss Wilby's precepts in mind, she ventured to suggest to Letty that such candour was a trifle improper.

'That is the sort of thing Aunt Chudleigh says,' observed Letty, unabashed. 'For my part, I see nothing improper in speaking the truth. And you can't deny that it *is* the truth!' She made herself comfortable beside Nell, and unfurled a pink sunshade. 'We make a perfect picture,' she said complacently.

'I collect Lord Hardwick told you so!'

'*Everyone* tells me so!'

'Well, take care they don't next tell you that you are abominably conceited,' recommended Nell.

'They won't,' asserted Letty, with confidence. 'No one I care a fig for, at all events. I daresay Felix might, for I never knew anyone so stuffy!'

However, when they presently saw Mr Hethersett strolling in the Park there was nothing to be read in that stickler's countenance but critical appreciation. Nell directed her coachman to pull up his horses, and when Mr Hethersett came up to the carriage leaned forward to give him her hand. 'How do you do? I hoped we might see you. Do you mean to go to the Beadings' masquerade next week? Cardross has been obliged to cry off: isn't it infamous of him? Will you dine with us, and give us your escort in his stead?'

He looked regretful, and shook his head. 'Can't,' he said mournfully. 'Excused myself to Mrs Beading. Told her I had another engagement. Not the thing to go there after that. Pity!'

She smiled. 'You cannot hoax me into believing that you think so! Confess! You dislike masquerades!'

'Not trying to hoax you: happy to escort you anywhere! Not but what it ain't the sort of party I like. If I were you I'd cry off, because you won't enjoy it. Not just in your style.'

'I declare, you are the stupidest creature, Felix!' Letty broke in. 'Why shouldn't we enjoy it? It will be rare mummery, for we are all to wear masks, and –'

'Yes, a vast rout of people, and rompings!' interrupted Mr Hethersett, in a tone of deep disapproval. '*You* may enjoy it: I never said you wouldn't. All I said was, Lady Cardross won't. Do you want a piece of advice, cousin?'

'No,' said Letty crossly.

'Mistake,' he said, shaking his head. 'Not saying that ain't an elegant gown: it is. Not saying that hat don't become you: it does.' He left an ominous pause, during which Letty eyed him uneasily. She might despise him for what she considered his antiquated notions of propriety, but no aspirant to high fashion could afford to ignore his pronouncements on all matters of sartorial taste. He delivered his verdict. 'I don't like those pink ribbons. Or the feather. Insipid.'

'*Insipid?*' she exclaimed indignantly. She cast a glance down at the double row of pink knots which ornamented her dress of delicate fawn-coloured muslin. They exactly matched the feather that hung down on one side of a little straw hat which was turned up on the other side, and worn at a dashing angle on her glossy black ringlets. French kid gloves of the same pink completed a toilette which she had thought to be, until this painful moment, in the first crack of the mode. Doubt now entered her soul; she turned her anxious gaze upon her cousin. 'It isn't! You are saying it to vex me!'

'No wish to vex you. Just thought you wanted to be up to the knocker.'

'I do – I *am* up to the knocker!'

'Not with those pink bows,' said Mr Hethersett firmly. 'Quite pretty, but dashed commonplace! Ought to be cherry. Give you a new touch!'

With these words he made his bow to both ladies, and proceeded on his way, leaving his cousin torn between wrath and a growing conviction that he was right, and Nell a good deal amused.

'If Felix were not related to me I should cut his acquaintance!' said Letty, glaring vengefully after him. 'He is prosy, and uncivil, beside placing himself on *far* too high a form! And now I come to think of it I didn't above half like his waistcoat!' She transferred her gaze to Nell, as Mr Hethersett's exquisitely tailored person receded in the distance. 'If he thinks my ribbons insipid I am astonished that he hadn't the effrontery to say that *your* dress was commonplace! Depend upon it, he thinks you would look more becomingly in purple, or puce, or scarlet! *Odious* creature!'

'Oh, he couldn't say that to me, when he told me weeks ago never to wear those strong colours!' said Nell, whose gown of Berlin silk was just the colour of her eyes. 'That was when I was wearing that maroon pelisse. I promise you, he was quite as odious to me. Don't regard it!'

'I never pay the least heed to a word he says,' replied Letty, in a lofty voice. She relapsed into thoughtful silence while the barouche proceeded on its way, but said after several minutes: 'Do you think I should tell my woman to dye this feather, or purchase a new one?'

'Dye that one,' responded Nell. 'And also the ribbons. I wish he might have gone with us to the masquerade: it would have been much more comfortable! I suppose . . .' She hesitated looking doubtfully at Letty. 'I suppose you would not like to go to Merion with Cardross instead?'

'Nell!' almost shrieked Letty, an expression of scandalized dismay on her countenance. 'Go to Merion in the middle of the season? You must be out of your senses! And if that is what Giles wishes us to do I think it is the shabbiest thing I ever heard of, when he *promised* I should go to the masquerade! Yes, and after fobbing me off with this, when I particularly wanted to go to the Covent Garden masquerade!' she added indignantly. 'Saying it was not the thing, and we should go to the Beadings' private masquerade instead! Just like him! I daresay, if I only knew –'

'It is *not* just like him, and I wish you will not fly into a pet for nothing!' said Nell, firing up. '*If* you only knew, he said not another word to persuade me to go with him to Merion when I reminded him that you particularly wished to go to the masquerade! And if Felix hadn't failed –'

'But, Nell, it's of no consequence!' Letty urged. 'I am sure quite fifty of our friends are going to it, and even if we found ourselves amongst strangers it still wouldn't signify, because Mrs Beading is your cousin! I own, it would be more comfortable to take some gentleman along with us, but you may easily invite Westbury, or Sir George Marlow, or –'

'No!' said Nell emphatically. '*Not* to a masquerade!'

Letty uttered a tiny spurt of laughter. 'Are you afraid they wouldn't keep the line? For my part, I think it would be very good fun if they did flirt outrageously with us! But you are the oddest creature! Not up to snuff at all, in spite of having come out a whole year before I did. Why, at my very first ball –' She broke off, as Nell nipped her arm, directing her eyes to the servants on the box of the carriage. 'Oh, stuff! No, don't be cross: I won't say a word, I promise! How would it be if we took Jeremy with us? I daresay he would be very glad to go, and you may be sure he would conduct himself with all the propriety in the world, because even Giles owns that he is *perfectly* the gentleman!'

'Don't be so absurd!' begged Nell. 'He told you himself that he hadn't received an invitation, and I can readily believe that he has too much propriety to go to the party without one. Besides, you know very well I wouldn't invite him when it is what Giles would particularly dislike.'

Letty accepted this rebuff philosophically, saying in a resigned tone: 'No, I didn't think you would. Well, what is to be done! *Pray* don't say you cannot go if Giles does not, for of all the dowdy notions – !'

Nell flushed. 'No such thing! I mean, I haven't the remotest intention of saying such a thing! Only I can't immediately think of any gentleman whom I –' She stopped, as her troubled gaze alighted on two horsemen, riding easily towards them. Her eyes brightened; she exclaimed: 'Dysart!'

'The very man!' declared Letty enthusiastically. 'Now you may be easy!'

This optimism, however, seemed for several minutes to have been ill-founded. The Viscount, who was bestriding a nervous young blood-chestnut few men would have cared to exercise in the Park at an hour when it was thronged with traffic, responded readily enough to his sister's signal, bringing his reluctant mount up to the barouche, and holding it there with all the apparent ease of an accomplished horseman; but when she asked him if he had received an invitation to the Beadings' masquerade, he replied: 'Ay, but I don't mean to go.'

'Oh, Dy, you didn't refuse?' Nell said anxiously.

'No, I didn't *refuse* precisely,' admitted Dysart, whose careless practice it was to leave all but a few favoured invitations unanswered. 'Here, Corny! Don't have to introduce you to my sister, do I? Or to Lady Letitia?'

His companion, who had been holding coyly aloof, edged his horse forward, raising the low-crowned beaver from his head, and bowing slightly to both ladies. Mr Cornelius Fancot was a chubby-faced young gentleman, slightly junior to the Viscount, whose devoted follower he had been ever since the pair had met at Harrow. There, he had been privileged to lend his aid to his dazzling friend in various hare-brained exploits; later, he had been of invaluable assistance in disposing suitably of the statue of Mercury in the Quad at Christ Church; and if he had never, either when up at Oxford or since both had come down from that seat of learning, contrived to rival Dysart's more celebrated feats, which included putting a donkey to bed with a complete stranger in an inn, and leaping one of his hunters over a dining-table equipped with a full complement of plate, silver, glasses, and chandeliers, he had won for himself, besides the reputation of being one who never refused a wager, considerable fame for having walked the length of Piccadilly on a pair of stilts; and for having won a bet that he would journey to Dover and back again to London before his too-hopeful challenger had made a million dots on sheet after sheet of paper. Unlike his noble friend, he was possessed of a handsome fortune, and was unencumbered by any kin more nearly related to him than several aunts, to whose admonitions he paid no heed at all; and various cousins whom he had no hesitation in condemning as a parcel of slow-tops. His habit proclaimed the sporting man, but a hankering after dandyism was betrayed by buckram-wadded shoulders to his lavishly corded and tasselled Polish coat, and a Brummell tie round his rather short neck. The life and soul of a convivial party at Long's Hotel, or Limmer's, he was apt to be tongue-tied in the presence of ladies, and might be looked for in vain at Almack's Assembly Rooms. He was sufficiently well-acquainted with Nell to feel no particular alarm when she addressed him; but a quizzing glance from Letty's mischievous eyes threw him at once into stuttering disorder. Observing this, the Viscount, with his customary lack of ceremony, recommended that enterprising damsel to pay no heed to him. 'Not in the petticoat-line,' he explained. 'Are you going to this precious masquerade, Nell?'

'Yes, indeed we are, only we find ourselves in a little fix. Cardross has been obliged to cry off, you see, and it is so disagreeable to go to such affairs with no gentleman to escort one! And Felix cannot go with us either, so, if you please, Dy, will you be so obliging as to –'

'No, dash it, Nell!' interrupted the Viscount hastily. 'Not to a masquerade out at Chiswick! Ask Marlow, or Westbury, or another of your flirts! The lord knows you've plenty of 'em! Why choose me?'

'She is afraid they wouldn't keep the line,' said Letty demurely.

Before the Viscount could reply Mr Fancot rather unexpectedly entered into the discussion. 'Shouldn't wonder at it if she was right,' he said. 'Masquerades, you know! Ramshackle! Ought to go with her la'ship!'

'What the deuce do you know about masquerades, Corny?' demanded Dysart. 'You never went to one in your life!'

'Yes, I did,' asserted Mr Fancot. 'I went with you, Dy! Well, I wouldn't let *my* sister go to one alone. What I mean is, I wouldn't if I had one. Had a sister, I mean,' he added, becoming a little flustered, as Letty giggled.

'Covent Garden!' exclaimed Dysart scornfully. 'I should think not indeed! But this affair will be quite another thing. Pretty insipid, I should think. Why do you go to it?'

'You see, it is the first masquerade Letty has attended, and so she wishes particularly to go,' Nell explained.

'Yes, and, what is more, I am quite *determined* to go,' corroborated Letty. 'I collect you don't mean to be so obliging as to escort us, which doesn't surprise me above a very little, because of all imaginable persons I think brothers to be by far the most disagreeable!'

'Letty, that is not just!' exclaimed Nell. '*You* have no cause to say so, and I assure you I have none either!' She smiled lovingly up at the Viscount. 'Don't come, if you had rather not! At my cousin's party I can't need an escort, after all.'

However, the Viscount, either from perversity, or from a sense of obligation, said, with a darkling look at Letty, that if his sister was set on attending the masquerade he would certainly accompany her. He added, with an austerity which accorded ill with his rakish appearance, that if it suited Cardross's notions of propriety to allow Nell to go alone to such parties that was where he must join issue with his lordship. He then, most unhandsomely, rode off before either lady could counter this charge. Nell was merely distressed that he should think her husband neglectful, but Letty, who reserved to herself the right to criticize Cardross, was extremely incensed, and charged Mr Fancot, lingering to make his adieux in form, with a rude message to him.

'Though, to be sure, I don't know why I should put myself to the trouble of fighting Giles's battles,' she observed, as Mr Fancot left them, and Nell told her coachman to drive on. 'I am persuaded he would never fight *mine*!'

She encountered a very direct look from Nell's soft blue eyes. Nell said quietly: 'You must not say so. It is quite untrue, and you know it!'

Letty sighed. 'Well, I didn't mean precisely that, but you must own that no one was ever more unsympathetic than Giles. It is so unkind of him to take poor Jeremy in aversion! I had not believed he could be so proud, or care so much for consequence, or so little for my happiness!'

'It isn't that! Indeed, it is not, Letty! He doesn't dislike Mr Allandale, and as for caring about his consequence you know he has said that if you are still of the same mind in a – in a year or two, he will not then refuse his consent. It *is* your happiness which he thinks of. I don't say that he *likes* the match, for although Mr Allandale's situation in life is respectable, he is *not* your equal in station, and there is a disparity between your fortunes which makes the marriage even more ineligible.'

'That is just what I have no patience with!' Letty said quickly. 'If *I* were poor too it would be another matter! I don't mean to say that I shouldn't wish to marry Jeremy, for I should; but there would then be justice in Cardross's objection! It is a melancholy

31

reflection, Nell, but I fear I shouldn't be a very good wife for a man in straitened circumstances. Of course I should endeavour to learn how to manage, but it is useless to deceive oneself: I don't think I have any turn for economy!'

'No, alas, nor I!' agreed Nell, with a wry grimace.

'The thing is, we were not bred to it,' said Letty profoundly. 'But what does it signify, after all, when I shall be the mistress of a substantial fortune as soon as I come of full age?'

'I think the thing is that Cardross feels you are too young to be making up your mind just yet,' Nell said diffidently.

'Depend upon it, he would not say so if I wanted to marry a man of rank and fortune!' Letty said, her eyes kindling. 'He did not think *you* too young when he offered for you, and I dare swear your papa did not either!'

'No,' admitted Nell.

'No! But if he had *not* been Cardross, your papa *would* have said so, even though he came of a very good family, and was in all respects a most superior man! It is all pride and pretension, and for my part I think it is detestable!'

'No, no, not that – not *quite* that!' Nell said. 'I suppose he would wish you to make what is called a good match, but he has told me himself that if you are still of the same mind in a year or two –'

'He knows very well that in a year or two – and probably much sooner! – Jeremy will have been sent abroad. Indeed, Jeremy has the greatest hope, if all goes as he has reason to expect – But I mustn't tell you! Pray don't repeat it, Nell! He particularly desired me not to speak of it while nothing is yet settled.' She hesitated, and then slid an impulsive hand into Nell's, and whispered: '*One* thing I must tell you! I believe – I hope – that he will shortly be calling in Grosvenor Square, to see Cardross. You may guess for what purpose! I should not be mentioning it to you, but oh, Nell, you will stand our friend, won't you?'

'Well, I might,' said Nell, in whom a year's intimacy with her sister-in-law had engendered a good deal of caution. 'But not if you mean to do something outrageous!'

'Nothing of the sort!' declared Letty indignantly. 'Unless, of course, Cardross drives me to it, and that I depend on you to prevent!'

'Oh, pray don't!' begged Nell, alarmed. 'If he won't consent to your marriage, it is because he feels it would be wrong in him to do so, and how could I overcome such scruples, or – or even wish to overcome them? If only you will be a little patient! Once Cardross is satisfied that your affections are truly fixed –'

'When that day dawns, if ever it does, Jeremy may be thousands of miles distant!' Letty interrupted. 'I shall have nothing to do then but to continue in patience until he returns to England – if he does return!'

'But naturally he will return!'

'Yes, but would you wager a groat on his doing so alone?' Letty retorted. 'I would not! I don't mean to say that he does not love me as much as I love him, but if he does not set eyes on me for years, besides being made up to by I daresay a dozen girls, or more, it would be wonderful indeed if he escaped being snatched up into matrimony with another!'

Nell could find nothing to say. Her imagination boggled at the picture of Mr Allandale being courted by a dozen (or even half-a-dozen) girls, but she prudently kept this reflection to herself, only venturing to ask, after a slight pause: 'What made you fall in love with him, Letty? I don't mean to say that he is not very amiable and civil, but – but –'

'I know precisely what you mean,' said Letty, with unexpected cordiality. 'And I haven't the smallest conjecture! If he had been like – oh, like your brother! – no one would have wondered at in the least: I shouldn't myself! I assure you, I am quite as much surprised as anyone, for it is not as if I had never met any other gentlemen! When I lived with my aunt I met everyone who came to the house, for she was not at all stuffy, you know, and didn't even *try* to keep Selina and me in the schoolroom. We knew *all* Maria's and Fanny's beaux, and some of them were pretty dashing, I can tell you! Only I never had the smallest tendre for any of them, until I met Jeremy. I don't know how it was: it has

33

me quite in a puzzle!' She bestowed a dazzling smile upon a natty young gentleman in a sporting curricle who was trying to attract her attention. 'Now, if I had formed an attachment to *him* Cardross would have had cause to be cross!' she observed. 'In fact, when you consider, Nell, the *lures* that are for ever being thrown out to me by all the most shocking court-cards on the town, on account of my being an heiress, I think it astonishing that Cardross should not be thankful my interest has been fixed by a man of principle and character! And if he supposes that Jeremy loves me for my fortune he much mistakes the matter!'

Cardross did not suspect Mr Allandale of fortune-hunting, but when the promised visit was paid him, a few days later, he received his sister's suitor with a cool civility that gave little promise of a yielding disposition.

Mr Allandale was not a nervous man, but it was with considerable reluctance that he presented himself in Grosvenor Square. He prided himself on his level judgement, and although he did not set his own worth low every objection Cardross could raise to his pretensions was felt by him, and acknowledged to be just. His love for Letty bordered, in the opinion of his mother, on infatuation, but it had needed much persuasion from her to induce him to make Cardross a formal offer for her hand. The disparity between them of rank and fortune weighed heavily upon his spirit; he had felt from the outset that his suit was hopeless, and that his wiser course would be too keep out of Letty's way, and try to put her from his mind. Unfortunately, noble resignation was not a virtue which in any way attracted Letty. When he spoke of parting she first burst into tears, which unmanned him; and then accused him of wanting to be rid of her, which made him utter some very ill-advised vows of eternal fidelity. After that there was no more talk of renunciation. Mr Allandale did indeed speak sometimes of waiting, but with this plan also Letty was out of sympathy; and since he had never desired anything so passionately in the whole of his well-ordered life as to marry her he allowed himself to become infected with her optimism, and even began to think that perhaps Cardross might not prove so inimical to his suit after all, if he were approached in a manly and straightforward way.

This confidence, never very strong, waned as he trod up the steps of Cardross House, and wholly deserted him while he waited for the Earl in the book-room. His appearance was always characterized by a neatness and a propriety of taste which struck the happy mean between the man of fashion and the man of affairs, and he had spent more time than usual that morning on the arrangement of his neckcloth. But as the clock on the high mantelpiece rather aggressively ticked away the minutes he became convinced that the faint stripe in his toilinette waistcoat made him look like a park-saunterer, that his coat of sober blue cloth was too tightly moulded to his form, and that by brushing his mouse-coloured hair into the Brutus style affected by Mr Brummell he had committed a gross error of judgement: Cardross would probably suspect him of aping the fashions of the dandy-set.

However, when the Earl at last came into the room he did not appear to notice what by this time amounted in Mr Allandale's mind to the blatant vulgarity of his waistcoat. On the other hand, his handsome, impassive countenance betrayed no sign of pleasure at sight of his visitor, and his greeting was courteous rather than cordial. Overcoming the sudden realization that his errand would certainly be regarded as a piece of presumption, Mr Allandale opened the interview by saying with a stiffness engendered by his determination not to truckle to his siren's guardian: 'You may wonder, my lord, why I am here.'

'No,' said the Earl.

There was nothing particularly daunting about this calm monosyllable, but it threw Mr Allandale quite out of his stride. His carefully composed speech of explanation had to be abandoned, and he could not immediately decide what to say in its stead.

'Pray be seated, Mr Allandale!' invited his host, himself strolling towards a chair.

Mr Allandale hesitated. On the whole, he preferred to remain on his feet, but it was difficult to do so while the Earl sat at his ease, one leg, cased in an elegant Hessian boot, thrown over the other, and one hand even now raising his quizzing-glass to his eye. Mr Allandale sat down, and cleared his throat. 'I shall be brief,' he stated. 'It cannot, I fancy, be unknown to your lordship that I have been so fortunate as to engage the interest of Lady Letitia Merion.'

A flicker of amusement crossed the Earl's eyes. 'I understand that the violence of your mutual feelings is such as must melt all but the hardest of hearts. Mine, I am informed, is of marble.'

Colouring, Mr Allandale replied: 'I am aware, my lord, that the affection I bear Lady Letitia must appear to you in the light of an encroaching fancy.'

'Oh, no!' said Cardross. 'I am really not as high in the instep as you seem to think. I don't deny that I should prefer her to make what passes in the world for a good match, but, I assure you, if your affections stand the test of time you won't find me ill-disposed towards you.'

This very reasonable speech added nothing to Mr Allandale's comfort. He said heavily. 'I'm obliged to you, sir. I might remind you that the attachment between us was formed more than a year ago, and has but been strengthened by the passage of time, but I shall not do so.'

'As we see,' murmured Cardross dryly.

'The force of your objection is fully felt by me,' continued Mr Allandale, embarking on one of his rehearsed periods. 'It might well be thought that Lady Letitia is as yet too young to be permitted to follow the dictates of her heart. Moreover, no one is more conscious than I that in so doing she would be held, in vulgar parlance, to have thrown herself away.'

'Yes, well, do let us talk in vulgar parlance!' begged Cardross. 'Not to wrap the matter up in clean linen, my sister is a foolish chit with a turn for the high-romantical; and you, my dear sir, are not very much wiser! Her fortune apart – and you need not tell me that you wish for fortune at Jericho, because I acquit you of hanging out for a rich wife – I can conceive of few more unsuitable partners for a man in your position. You have your career before you: I wish you very well, and in proof of this can only advise you not to saddle yourself with an extravagant and shatterbrained little puss for a wife!'

Considerably taken-aback by this forthright speech, Mr Allandale could think of nothing better to say than: 'Am I to understand, then, that you refuse your consent to our betrothal, sir?'

'For the present, most certainly you are!' returned the Earl. 'You look to be a man of sense, so you will not, I hope, accuse me of cruelty. I have not said, nor shall I, that I will never give my consent; I don't even say that you must wait until Letty comes of age. But do, I beg of you, consider *my* position in this! Can you feel that I should honourably have fulfilled my charge if I allowed a chit who has not yet reached her eighteenth year to tie herself up in matrimony to a young man in your circumstances?'

'No,' said Mr Allandale bleakly.

The Earl was conscious of an impulse to retract, even to bestow his blessing on the lovers. He quelled it, saying cheerfully: 'Of course you cannot! But if, in a couple of years' time, you are both still of the same mind, and you come to me again with this proposal, I must be hardhearted indeed to refuse my consent.'

'I do not anticipate being in England in a couple of years' time,' said Mr Allandale, more bleakly still. 'It was my intention to have explained to your lordship at the outset that I was emboldened to come to you today by the circumstance of my having been appointed to a very advantageous post. I owe this advancement in part to the kind offices of Lord Roxwell, who was formerly much attached to my father; and I have every reason to expect that it will lead, should I acquit myself creditably, to more rapid promotion than has hitherto seemed probable.'

'I am sure you will acquit yourself admirably, and must beg leave to congratulate you on your good fortune. I collect that you are to join one of our embassies?'

'Yes, sir. I am appointed – that is to say, I shall, within the next three months be appointed to the staff of our minister at the Court of the Regent of Portugal.'

'The Regent of Portugal?' repeated Cardross. 'But he is in Brazil!'

Mr Allandale inclined his head. 'Just so, sir,' he agreed.

'Good God!' ejaculated Cardross. 'Were you proposing in all seriousness to take Letty to South America? You must be mad!'

'She assures me,' said Mr Allandale earnestly, 'that she would like it above all things.'

'And what the devil do you imagine she knows about it?' demanded Cardross.

'I am credibly informed,' offered Mr Allandale, 'that the climate at Rio de Janeiro is salubrious.'

'Oh, take a damper!' said Cardross impatiently. 'Did this cork-brained notion come out of your head, or hers? Did she persuade you to come here today, or – No, of course she did! You at least cannot have supposed that there was the least likelihood of my consenting to such a preposterous scheme!'

'No,' said Mr Allandale. 'I must own that I had little hope of obtaining your lordship's consent. I am aware that in your eyes the scheme must seem preposterous.'

'And how does it seem in yours?' enquired the Earl curiously. 'You have been acquainted with my sister for more than a year, after all!'

'Were it not for your lordship's refusal to entertain my proposal, I should have no hesitation in asking Lady Letitia to accompany me, as my wife, to Brazil.'

'The devil you wouldn't!'

'I believe her to be equal to anything,' said Mr Allandale reverently. 'When I first learned of the appointment, I confess that the very natural feeling of delight I experienced was instantly tempered – I might almost say dissipated – by the same doubt of which your lordship is conscious. I could not believe that a delicately nurtured female – and one, moreover, of such tender years – could contemplate without dismay the several evils attaching to the appointment. The discomforts of a long sea-voyage! the going amongst foreigners! the separation from her relations! I promise you, sir, every disagreeable possibility that presented itself to my mind was at once communicated to her by me. But nothing was ever like her spirit! What inconveniences there may be she will not regard; and although I do not anticipate that there is any danger to be apprehended, *that* she would meet with the same trust and courage which she shows in being willing to bestow her hand upon one whose prosperity must depend upon his own exertions!'

The thought of this nobility overcame him so much that his voice thickened, and he was obliged to blow his nose. Its effect upon Cardross was to exasperate him into saying, with a snap: 'I suppose she told you so!'

'Yes,' replied Mr Allandale simply.

'Did she also work on you to come here today with your fantastic proposal?'

'She certainly thought that with my advancement now secured we might hope for some relenting on your part,' admitted Mr Allandale.

The Earl looked him over somewhat grimly. 'But you did not think so, Mr Allandale, did you?'

'Well –'

'It appears to me, my dear sir, that you are as wax in my sister's hands! It is a reflection which fills me with deep misgiving. I know Letty to be as headstrong as she is bird-witted, and what she may next bully or bewitch you into doing there is no saying – though I might hazard a guess!'

'If you mean, sir, that I might be tempted to elope with Lady Letitia you may be easy!' returned Mr Allandale, reddening. 'Even if I were not a man of honour, my circumstances must forbid me to embark on anything of a clandestine nature.' He drew a breath, and continued with a little difficulty: 'You were kind enough, my lord, to acquit me of hanging out (as you phrased it) for a rich wife. That is true, for, in fact, I had not, until I met Lady Letitia, any thought of marriage at all. My widowed parent, though possessed of a respectable jointure, is quite unable to support the expense of educating my younger brothers and sisters without my assistance; and until they are established creditably I must not – indeed, I cannot! – marry a female who has no fortune of her own. Just a genteel fortune, to match my own. I never contemplated marriage to a great heiress – and, to own the truth, it is not what I like! However, I daresay it may be possible to form some kind of a trust which would ensure that *I* should not benefit by anything more than a reasonable amount.'

'The matter is not of pressing importance,' said the Earl. 'Until she reaches the age of five-and-twenty my sister's fortune is in my hands, and her allowance is at my discretion. If I chose to do it, I could cut off every penny of it.'

'I cannot believe, sir, that you would be guilty of such inhumanity!' said Mr Allandale, in a voice of strong censure.

'There would be no inhumanity,' replied Cardross coolly. 'Letty would merely be obliged to continue living in my house, and her dress-bills would be paid by me. I may add that I already pay quite a number of them. I am afraid you would find her very expensive, for she never has a feather to fly with, you know.'

'I am aware that she has not been taught habits of economy,' said Mr Allandale stiffly. 'Indeed, she has told me so herself, and has regretted it. She is very willing to learn, and I hope to teach her to manage better.'

'Yes, in my more optimistic moments I too indulge that hope,' agreed Cardross. 'Go and take up this appointment of yours, and I'll engage to do my best to instil some small knowledge of economy into her head while you are away. Who knows? You may return to find her quite prudent!'

Mr Allandale rose, and walked over to the window. He said, staring out of it: 'I do not imagine that it will be of any use to return. Not, of course, that I contemplate passing the rest of my life in Brazil, but –' He stopped, and cleared his throat. 'I cannot flatter myself that I shall find her still unattached. So much sought-after – and by men of far greater address than will ever be mine – separated from me for a prolonged period, and by such a distance – No, it would be too much to expect of her! She will wed another.'

'The same fate may as easily overtake you, my dear sir,' remarked the Earl.

'No,' said Mr Allandale baldly. He added, after a pause: 'My feeling is unalterable. I am not subject to fits of gallantry, sir. I had even believed myself to be proof against – But from the moment when I first saw your sister, I knew myself lost! I struggled against it, for the unsuitability of the match was as plain to me as it is to you. It was to no avail. I shall never marry any other lady.'

'Ah!' murmured the Earl, looking amused. 'I remember that I said much the same thing myself – a good many years ago. She was ravishingly beautiful – at least, I know I thought so, though, to own the truth, I can now only vaguely recall her face to my mind.'

'I am happy to afford your lordship entertainment!' said Mr Allandale, in rather less measured accents.

'No, you are not,' replied Cardross, rising. 'You would like to plant me a facer, and I'm sure I don't wonder at it. Nothing is more exasperating than to be obliged to listen to advice based on experience which is necessarily wider than your own – particularly when you have an uneasy suspicion that it may be good!'

'I have no such suspicion,' instantly retorted Mr Allandale. 'I venture to think that my nature is more tenacious than your lordship's!'

'In that case,' said Cardross, with unimpaired good-humour, 'I shall expect to see you again upon your return from Rio de Janeiro. In the meantime, accept my best wishes for your success in that salubrious locality!'

'Do you forbid me to hold further communication with Lady Letitia, sir?' demanded Mr Allandale, somewhat reluctantly taking the hand that was being held out to him.

'My dear sir, do let me assure you that I am neither so gothic nor so cork-brained! I daresay you will meet Letty at any number

41

of parties. As for clandestine meetings, I am persuaded that your sense of propriety must be safeguard enough.'

'Anything of a clandestine nature is repugnant to me,' stated Mr Allandale. 'I can only beg of you, sir, to consider well before you blight, perhaps for ever, the happiness of two persons, one of whom is – or should be – dear to you! I reject – indeed, I scorn! – your suggestions of inconstancy, but too well do I know the arts that are employed in the world of fashion to detach from an unworthy object the affections of such as Lady Letitia! All is sacrificed to pride and consequence! If I were in more affluent circumstances, I believe no considerations of propriety could avail to prevent me – But it serves no purpose to continue talking!'

'None whatsoever,' agreed Cardross, leading the way to the door. 'It might even lead me to take you in dislike, and that, you know, would be fatal to your chances!'

Three

Any scheme of intercepting her lover on his way out of the house which Letty might have cherished was frustrated by the Earl's escorting him to the front-door, and seeing him safely off the premises. He strolled back to the library; and, after hesitating for a moment or two at the head of the stairs, from which post of vantage she had watched Mr Allandale's departure, Letty ran lightly down, and herself entered the library.

Cardross was engaged in mending a pen, but he looked up, and, when he saw his half-sister backed against the door, an urgent question in her speaking eyes, abandoned this task. A laugh quivered in his voice as he said: 'Letty, you goose! Did you really think that I should succumb to that unfortunate young man's oratory? Do forgive me! But surely he is a very dull dog?'

'I don't care for that,' she said, swallowing a sob. 'He is not dull to me. I love him!'

'You must do so indeed! I should have supposed him to be the last man to take your fancy, too.'

'Well, he is not, and even if you are my guardian I won't submit to having my husband chosen for me by you!'

'Certainly not. It's plain I should make a poor hand at it.'

Hope gleamed in her eyes; she moved towards him, and laid a coaxing hand on his arm. '*Dear* Giles, if you please, may I marry him?'

He gave her hand a pat, but said: 'Why, yes, Letty, when you are older.'

'But, Giles, you don't understand! He is going away to Brazil!'

'So he informed me.'

'Are you thinking that perhaps it might not suit me to live there? I believe the climate is *perfectly* healthy!'

'Salubrious,' he interpolated.

'Yes, and in any event I am never ill! You may ask my aunt if it's not so!'

'I am sure it is. Don't let us fall into another exhausting argument! I have already endured a great deal of eloquence today, but it would take much more than eloquence to make me consent to your marriage to an indigent young man who proposes to take you to the other end of the world before you are eighteen, or have been out a year.'

'That doesn't signify! And although I own it would be imprudent to marry Jeremy if I were indigent too I am *not* indigent, so that's of no consequence either!'

'I promise you I shan't refuse my consent on that head, if, when he returns from Brazil, you still wish to marry him.'

'And what if some odious, designing female has lured him into marrying her?' she demanded.

'He assures me that his nature is tenacious, so we must hope that he will be proof against all designing females,' he replied lightly.

'You don't hope that! You don't wish me ever to marry him!'

'No, of course I don't! Good God, child, how could I wish you to throw yourself away so preposterously, far less help you to do it when you are hardly out of the schoolroom?'

'If he were a man of rank and fortune you wouldn't say I was too young!'

'If he were a man of rank and fortune, my dear, he would not be taking up a post as some kind of secretary in Rio de Janeiro. But if it comforts you at all I don't wish to see you married to anyone for a year or two yet.'

'Oh, don't talk to me as if I were a silly little child!' she cried passionately.

'Well, I don't think you are very wise,' he said.

'No, perhaps I'm not wise, but I'm not a child, and I know my own mind! *You* aren't very wise either, if you think I shall change it, or forget Jeremy! I shall remember, and be unhappy for two whole years, and very likely more! I daresay you don't care for that, for I see that you aren't kind, which I thought you were, but, on the contrary, perfectly heartless!'

'Not a bit of it!' he said cheerfully. 'With the best will in the world to do it, I fancy you won't fall quite into dejection. There will still be balls to attend, and new, and extremely expensive dresses to buy.'

'I don't want them!'

'I wish I might believe you! Do you mean to abjure the fashionable life?'

She threw him a smouldering look. 'You may laugh at me, but I warn you, Cardross, I am determined to marry Jeremy, do what you will to prevent me!'

He replied only with an ironical bow; and after staring defiantly at him for an instant, she swept from the room with an air of finality only marred by the unfortunate circumstance of her shutting a fold of her gown of delicate lilac muslin in the door, and being obliged to open it again to release the fabric.

Twenty minutes later Nell came softly into the room. The Earl looked up impatiently, but when he saw his wife standing on the threshold his expression changed, and he smiled at her, saying in a funning tone: 'How do you contrive, Nell, always to appear prettier than I remembered you?'

She blushed adorably. 'Well, I did hope you would think I looked becomingly in this gown,' she confessed naïvely.

'I do. Did you put it on to dazzle me into paying for it?'

This was said so quizzically that her spirits rose. It had taken a great deal of resolution to bring her to the library that morning, for a most unwelcome missive had been delivered by the penny post. Since the Earl paid five shillings to the General Post Office every quarter for the privilege of receiving an early London delivery Madame Lavalle's civil reminder to her ladyship that a court dress of Chantilly lace was still unpaid for had lain on Nell's breakfast-tray. It was not an encouraging start to the day. It had quite destroyed Nell's appetite, and had filled her with so much frightened dismay that for an unreasoning hour she could think of no other way out of her difficulties than to board the first mail-coach bound for Devonshire, and there to seek refuge with her mama. A prolonged period of reflection, however, showed her the unwisdom of this course, and convinced her that since it was extremely unlikely that a thunderbolt would descend mercifully upon her head there was nothing for it but to make a clean breast of the matter to Cardross, devoutly trusting that he would understand how it had come about that she had forgotten to give him Madame Lavalle's bill with all the others which he had commanded her to produce.

But the more she thought of it the less likely it seemed that he could possibly understand. She felt sick with apprehension, recalling his stern words. He had asked her if she was quite sure she had handed all her bills to him; he had warned her of the awful consequences if he found she had lied to him; and although he had certainly begged her, later, not to be afraid of him, it was not to be expected that he would greet with equanimity the intelligence that his wife had overlooked a bill for three hundred and thirty-five guineas. It even seemed improbable that he would believe she really had overlooked it. She herself was aghast at her carelessness. She was so sure that she had given the bill to Cardross with all the others collected from a drawer crammed with them that her first thought on seeing Madame Lavalle's renewed demand was that that exclusive modiste had erred. But an agitated search had brought the previous demand to light, wedged at the very back of the drawer. It was by far the heaviest single item amongst her debts, casting into the shade the milliner's bill which had staggered Cardross. What he would say she dared not consider, even less what he might do. At the best he must believe her to be woefully extravagant (which, indeed, she knew she had been), and he would be very angry, though forgiving. At the worst – but to speculate on what he might do at the worst was so fatal to resolution that she would not let herself do it.

With a childlike hope of pleasing him, she had arrayed herself in a gown which she knew (on the authority of that arbiter of taste, Mr Hethersett) became her to admiration. It had instantly won for her a charming compliment, and she was now able to reply, not without pride: 'No, no, it is paid for!' She added honestly, after a moment's reflection: '*You* paid for it!'

'It is a great satisfaction to me to know that I didn't waste my money,' he said gravely, but with laughter in his eyes.

This was a much more promising start to the interview than she had expected. She smiled shyly at him, and was just about to embark on a painful explanation of her new embarrassment when he said: 'Are you Letty's envoy, then? I own, I might listen with more patience to you than to her, but on *this* subject I am determined to remain adamant!'

Not sorry to be diverted from her real errand, she said: 'Of course, I do see that it would be throwing herself away quite shockingly, but I believe you will be obliged, in the end, to consent. Well, I thought myself that it was just a fancy that would pass when she had seen more of society, and had met other gentlemen, but it isn't so, Cardross! She hasn't swerved from her devotion to Mr Allandale, even though she has been made up to by I don't know how many others – and all of them,' she added reflectively, 'of far greater address than poor Mr Allandale!'

'Nell!' he interrupted. 'Can you tell me what she perceives in that dead bore to dote upon?'

She shook her head. 'No, there is no accounting for it,' she replied. 'She doesn't know either, which is what makes me feel that it is a case of true love, and certainly no passing fancy.'

'They are totally unsuited!' he said impatiently. 'She would ruin him in a year, what's more! She is as extravagant as you are, my love!' He saw the stricken look in her face, the colour ebbing from her cheeks, and instantly said: 'What an unhandsome thing to say to you! I beg your pardon: *that* is all forgotten – a page which we have stuck down, and shan't read again. My dear Nell, if you could but have heard that absurd young man addressing me in flowing periods this morning! Do you know that he proposed in all seriousness to carry Letty off to Brazil?'

Her thoughts were very far from Letty's affairs, but she answered mechanically: 'Yes, she told me of his appointment.'

He regarded her with a slight crease between his brows. 'You are looking very troubled, Nell. Why? Are you taking this nonsense to heart?'

Now, if ever, was the moment to tell him that the page had not yet been stuck down. The words refused to be uttered. She said instead: 'I can't help but be sorry for them. I know it is a bad match, and indeed, Cardross, I understand what your sentiments must be.'

'I imagine you might! To be wishing Letty joy of a shockingly bad bargain would be fine conduct in a guardian! To own the truth, I wish I were not her guardian – or that I had never permitted her aunt to take charge of her. That woman wants both manner and sense, and, as far as I can discover, reared her own daughters as well as my sister in a scrambling way, encouraging them in every extravagant folly, and allowing them to set up their flirts when they should have been in the schoolroom!'

'Well, yes,' admitted Nell. 'I don't like to abuse her, for she is always very civil and goodnatured, but she does seem to be sadly shatterbrained! But I can't suppose that she encouraged Mr Allandale, for she doesn't at all wish Letty to marry him, you know. She talked to me about it the other evening, at the Westburys' drum, and she seemed to feel just as she ought.' She paused, considering this. 'At least,' she amended, 'just as *you* think she ought, Cardross.'

He was amused. 'Indeed! But not as *you* think, I collect?'

'Well, not precisely,' she temporized. 'I must say, it has me quite in a puzzle to understand how it comes about that such a lively girl should fall in love with Mr Allandale, for he is not at all sportive, and he doesn't seem to have more than common sense, besides having such very formal manners, – but – but there is nothing in his disposition to make him ineligible, is there? I mean, it isn't as if she wished to marry someone like Sir Jasper Lydney, or young Brixworth. And one wouldn't have felt the least surprise if she had, because they have both been dangling after her ever since she came out, and no one can deny that they have very engaging manners, in spite of being such shocking rakes! You would not have liked her to marry either of them!'

'I should not, but there is a vast gulf between Brixworth and Allandale, my love! As for eligibility, though there may be nothing in Allandale's disposition to dislike, there is nothing in his circumstances to recommend him. He has neither rank nor fortune.'

'Letty doesn't care for rank, and she *has* fortune,' Nell pointed out.

'Unequal marriages rarely prosper. Letty may imagine she doesn't care for rank: she doesn't know how it would be to marry a man out of her own order.'

Nell wrinkled her brow over this. 'But, Giles, I think she does know!' she objected. 'For it is not as if she had been accustomed all her life to move only in circles of high fashion. Mrs Thorne is perfectly respectable, but not at all exclusive, and you yourself told me that Letty's mama was not of the first rank.'

'You are a persuasive advocate, Nell! But I must hold to my opinion – and to what I conceive to be my duty. I have said that I won't withhold my consent, if both are of the same mind when Allandale returns from Brazil, and that must suffice them. I shan't conceal from *you* that I hope Letty, by that time, will have transferred her affections to some more worthy object.'

'You want her to make a *good* match, don't you?'

'Is that so wonderful?'

'Oh, no! Perhaps, if she doesn't see Mr Allandale for some years, she will do so. Only – only – it would be so very melancholy!'

'My dear child, why?'

She tried haltingly to express the thought in her mind. 'She loves him so much! And I cannot think that she would be happy if she married – only to oblige her family!'

His brows had drawn together. He said harshly: 'As you did?'

She stared at him almost uncomprehendingly. 'As – as *I* did?' she faltered.

A smile, not a very pleasant smile, curled his lips. 'Had I not been possessed of a large fortune, you wouldn't have married me, would you, Nell?'

She was conscious of a pain at her heart, but she heard him without resentment. She thought of her debts, and of those mysterious Settlements, and could only be thankful that she had not disclosed to him Madame Lavalle's bill. Its existence weighed so heavily upon her conscience that she found herself unable to utter a word. A deep flush stained her cheeks, and her eyes, after a hurt moment, dropped from his.

'You must forgive me!' His voice had an ironical inflexion that made her wince. 'My want of delicacy sinks me quite below reproach, doesn't it? I fancy it gave Allandale a disgust of me too.'

She managed to say, in a stifled tone: 'I didn't think – I didn't *know* about your fortune!'

'Didn't you?' he said lightly. 'How charming of you, my dear! *Your* manners make *mine* appear sadly vulgar. Don't look so distressed! I am persuaded no man ever had so beautiful, so polite, or so amiable a wife as I have!' He glanced at his watch. 'I must go. I don't know what nonsense Letty may have taken into her head, but I hope I may trust you not to encourage her in it. Happily, it appears to be out of Allandale's power to marry her without a substantial portion. She's under age, of course, but I'd as lief not be saddled with that kind of a scandal!'

A smile, a brief bow, and he was gone, leaving her with her brain in a whirl. There was little thought of Letty in it. For the first time in their dealings Cardross had hinted that he had looked for more than complaisance in his wife; and his words, with their edge of bitterness, had made Nell's heart leap. It was almost sacrilege to doubt Mama, but was it, in fact, possible that Mama had been wrong?

She went slowly upstairs, to be pounced on by Letty, bursting with indignation, and the desire to unburden herself. She listened with half an ear to that impassioned damsel, saying yes, and no, at suitable moments, but assimilating little of the molten discourse beyond the warning that her sister-in-law would be forced to take desperate measures if Cardross continued on his present tyrannical course. Before it had dawned on Letty that she had no very attentive auditor to the tale of her wrongs a message was brought up to the drawing-room that the Misses Thorne had called to take up their cousin on a visit to some exhibition.

Nell soon found herself alone, and at leisure to consider her own problems. These very soon resolved themselves into one problem only: how to pay for a court dress of Chantilly lace without applying to Cardross. If Cardross had offered for her hand not as a matter of convenience but for love, this was of vital importance. Nothing could more surely confirm his suspicion than to be confronted with that bill; and any attempt to tell him that she had fallen in love with him at their first meeting must seem to him a piece of quite contemptible cajolery.

No solution to the difficulty had presented itself to her by the time the butler came to inform her that the barouche had been driven up to the door, and awaited her convenience. She was tempted to send it away again, and was only prevented from doing so by the recollection that civility obliged her to make a formal call in Upper Berkeley Street, to enquire after the progress of an ailing acquaintance.

She directed the coachman, on the way back, to drive to Bond Street, where she had a few trifling purchases to make; and there, strolling along, with his beaver set at a rakish angle on his golden head, and his shapely legs swathed in pantaloons of an aggressive yellow, she saw her brother.

The Viscount had never been known to extricate himself from his various embarrassments, much less anyone else; but to his adoring sister he appeared in the light of a strong ally. She called to the coachman to pull up, and when Dysart crossed the street in response to her signal leaned forward to clasp his hand, saying thankfully: 'Oh, Dy, I am so glad to have met you! Will you be so very obliging as to come home with me? There is something I particularly wish to ask you!'

'If you're wanting me to escort you to some horrible squeeze,' began the Viscount suspiciously, 'I'll be dashed if I –'

'No, no, I promise you it's no such thing!' she interrupted. 'I – I need your advice!'

'Well, I don't mind giving you that,' said his lordship handsomely. 'What's the matter? You in a scrape?'

'Good gracious, no!' said Nell, acutely aware of her footman, who had jumped down from the box, and was now holding open the door of the barouche. 'Do get in, Dy! I'll tell you presently!'

'Oh, very well!' he said, stepping into the carriage, and disposing himself on the seat beside her. 'I've nothing else to do, after all.' He looked her over critically, and observed with brotherly candour: 'What a quiz of a hat!'

'It is an Angoulême bonnet, and the *height* of fashion!' retorted Nell, with spirit. 'And as for quizzes – Dy, I never saw you look so odd as you do in those yellow pantaloons!'

'Devilish, ain't they?' agreed his lordship. 'Corny made me buy 'em. Said they were all the crack.'

'Well, if I were you I wouldn't listen to him!'

'Oh, I don't know! Always up to the knocker, is Corny. If you ain't in a scrape, why do you want my advice?'

She gave his arm a warning pinch, and began to talk of indifferent subjects in a careless way which (as he informed her upon their arrival in Grosvenor Square) made him wish that he had not chosen to walk down Bond Street that morning. 'Because you can't bamboozle *me* into believing you ain't in a scrape,' he said. 'I thought you were looking hagged, but I set it down to that bonnet.'

Nell, who had led him upstairs to her frivolous boudoir, cast off her maligned headgear, saying wretchedly: 'I am in a *dreadful* scrape, and if you won't help me, Dy, I can't think what I shall do!'

'Lord!' said the Viscount, slightly dismayed. 'Now, don't get into a fuss, Nell! Of course I'll help you! At least, I will if I can, though I'm dashed if I see – However, I daresay it's all a bag of moonshine!'

'It isn't,' she said, so tragically that he began to feel seriously alarmed. She twisted her fingers together, and managed to say, though with considerable difficulty: 'Dysart, have – have you still got the – the three hundred pounds I gave you?'

'Do you want it back?' he demanded.

She nodded, her eyes fixed anxiously on his face.

'Now we *are* in the basket!' said his lordship.

Her heart sank. 'I am so very sorry to be obliged to ask you!'

'My dear girl, I'd give it to you this instant if I had it!' he assured her. 'What is it? A gaming debt? You been playing deep, Nell?'

'No, no! It is a court dress of Chantilly lace, and I cannot – *cannot!* – tell Cardross!'

'What, you don't mean to say he's turned out to be a screw?' exclaimed the Viscount.

'No! He has been *crushingly* generous to me, only I was so stupid, and it seemed as if I had so much money that – Well, I never took the least heed, Dy, and the end of it was that I got quite shockingly into debt!'

'Good God, there's no need to fall into flat despair, if that's all!' said the Viscount, relieved. 'You've only to tell him how it came about: I daresay he won't be astonished, for he must know you haven't been in the way of handling the blunt. You'll very likely come in for a thundering scold, but he'll settle your debts all right and regular.'

She sank into a chair, covering her face with her hands. 'He did settle them!'

'Eh?' ejaculated Dysart, startled.

'I had better explain it to you,' said Nell.

It could not have been said that the explanation, which was both halting and elusive, very much helped Dysart to a complete understanding of the situation, but he did gather from it that the affair was far more serious than he had at first supposed. He was quite intelligent enough to guess that the whole had not been divulged to him, but since he had no desire to plunge into deep matrimonial waters he did not press his sister for further enlightenment. Clearly, her marriage was not running as smoothly as he had supposed; and if that were so he could appreciate her reluctance to disclose the existence of yet another debt to Cardross.

'What am I to do?' Nell asked. 'Can *you* think of a way, Dy?'

'Nothing easier!' responded Dysart, in a heartening tone. 'The trouble with you is that you ain't up to snuff yet. The thing to do is to order another dress from this Madame Thing.'

'Order another?' gasped Nell.

'That's it,' he nodded.

'But then I should be even deeper in debt!'

'Yes, but it'll stave her off for a while.'

'And when she presses me to pay for that I buy yet another! Dy, you must be mad!'

'My dear girl, it's always done!'

'Not by me!' she declared. 'I should never know a moment's peace! Only think what would happen if Cardross discovered it!'

'There is that, of course,' he admitted. He took a turn about the room, frowning over the problem. 'The deuce is in it that I'm not in good odour with the cents-per-cent. I'd raise the wind for you in a trice if the sharks didn't know dashed well how our affairs stand.'

'Moneylenders?' she asked. 'I did think of that, only I don't know how to set about borrowing. Do you know, Dy? Will you tell me?'

The Viscount was not a young man whose conscience was overburdened with scruples, but he did not hesitate to veto this suggestion. 'No, I will not!' he said.

'I know one shouldn't borrow from moneylenders, but in such a case as this – and if you went with me, Dy –'

'A pretty fellow I should be!' he interrupted indignantly. 'Damn it, I ain't a saint, but I ain't such a loose-screw that I'd hand my sister over to one of those bloodsuckers!'

'Is it so very bad? I didn't know,' she said. 'Of course I won't go to a moneylender if you say I must not.'

'Well, I do say it. What's more, if you did so, and Cardross discovered it, there *would* be the devil to pay! You'd a deal better screw up your courage, and tell him the whole now.'

She shook her head, flushing.

'You know, it queers me to know what you've been doing,' said Dysart severely. 'It sounds to me as though you've had a quarrel with him, and set up his back. It ain't my business, but I call it a cork-brained thing to do!'

'I haven't – it isn't that!' she stammered.

'You must have done something!' he insisted. 'I thought he doted on you!'

Her eyes lifted quickly to his face. 'Did you, Dy? Did you *indeed* think so?'

'Of course I did! Well, good God, what would anyone think, when he no sooner clapped eyes on you than nothing would do for him but to pop the question? Lord, it was one of the on-dits of town! Old Cooling told me no one had ever seen him sent to grass before, no matter who set her cap at him. I thought myself he must be touched in his upper works,' said the Viscount candidly. 'I don't say you ain't a pretty girl, but what there is in you to make a fellow like Cardross marry into *our* family I'm dashed if I can see!'

'Oh, Dysart!' breathed Nell, trembling. 'You're not – you're not *roasting* me?'

He stared at her. 'Have you got windmills in the head too?' he demanded. 'Why the devil should he have offered for you, if he hadn't been head over ears in love with you? You aren't going to tell me you didn't know you'd given him a leveller!'

'Oh – ! Don't say such things! I did think, at first – but Mama told me – explained to me – how it was!'

'Well, *how* was it?' said the Viscount impatiently.

'A – a marriage of convenience,' faltered Nell. 'He was obliged to marry someone, and – and he liked me better than the other ladies he was acquainted with, and thought I should *suit*!'

'If that isn't Mama all over!' exclaimed Dysart. 'It was a dashed convenient marriage for us, but if he thought it was convenient to be obliged to pay through the nose for you (which I don't mind telling you my father made him do!), let alone saddling himself with a set of dirty dishes who have been under the hatches for years, he must be a regular cod's head!'

'Dysart!' she cried, quite horrified.

'Dirty dishes!' he repeated firmly. '*I* can't remember when my father last had a feather to fly with, and the lord knows I've never had one myself! In fact, it's my belief we should have been turned-up by now if you hadn't happened to hit Cardross's fancy. It's the only stroke of good fortune that ever came in our way!'

'I knew – I knew he had made a handsome *settlement*!'

Dysart gave a crack of laughter. 'Ay, and towed my father out of the River Tick into the bargain!'

She sprang up, pressing her hands to her hot cheeks. 'Oh, and I have been so *wickedly* extravagant!'

'No need to fret and fume over that!' replied Dysart cheerfully. 'They say his fortune knocks Golden Ball's into flinders, and I shouldn't be surprised if it was true.'

'As though that should excuse my running into debt! Oh, Dy, this quite overpowers me! No wonder he said *that*!'

He looked uneasily at her. 'Said what? If you mean to have a fit of the vapours, Nell, I'm off, and so I warn you!'

'Oh, no! Indeed, I don't! Only it is such an agitating reflection – I didn't tell you, Dy, but he said something to me which made me think he believes I married him for the sake of his fortune!'

'Well, you did, didn't you?'

'No!' she cried hotly. 'Never, never!'

'What, you don't mean to tell me you fell in love with him?' said the Viscount incredulously.

'Of course I did! How could I help but do so?'

'Of all the silly starts!' said his lordship disgustedly. 'What the devil should cast you into this distempered freak if *that's* the way of it? What have you been doing to make Cardross think you don't love him, if you do?'

She turned away her face. 'I – I was trying to be a *conformable* wife, Dy! You see, Mama warned me about not making demands, or – or hanging upon him, or appearing to notice it, if he should have Another Interest, and –'

'Oh, so the blame lies at Mama's door, does it? I might have known it! Never knew such a henwitted creature in my life!'

'Oh, Dysart, hush! Indeed, she meant it for the best! You will not repeat it, but she was so anxious I shouldn't suffer a mortifying disillusionment, as, I am afraid, she did!'

'Did she though?' said the Viscount, interested. 'I didn't know my father was pitching it rum in those days. I must say I should have thought even Mama could have seen that Cardross ain't a bird of that feather. Never been a man of the town from anything *I* ever heard. How came you to swallow all that humdudgeon, Nell? Dash it, you must have known he was in love with you!'

'I thought – I thought it was all consideration, because he is so *very* kind and gentlemanlike!' she confessed.

'*Kind and gentlemanlike?*' repeated Dysart, in accents of withering scorn. 'Well, upon my soul, Nell, seems to me you're as big a ninnyhammer as Mama! To be taken in by one of her Banbury tales, when there was Cardross making a regular cake of himself over you! If that don't beat the Dutch!'

She hung her head, but said in a faint voice: 'It was stupid of me, but there was more than that, Dy. You see, I knew about Lady Orsettt. Letty told me.'

'That girl,' said the Viscount severely, 'wants conduct! Not but what I shouldn't have thought you needed telling, because everyone knew she was his chère amie for years. And don't you put on any die-away airs to me, my girl, because, for one thing, it's no use bamming me you didn't know anything about my father's light frigates; and, for another, Cardross's way of life before you married him ain't your concern! Lady Orsett's got Lydney in tow now, so that's enough flim-flam about her!'

'*Has* she, Dy?' Nell said eagerly.

'So they say, *I* don't know!'

'Oh, if it were not for this dreadful debt how happy I should be!' she sighed.

'Nonsense! Make a clean breast of the whole to Cardross, and be done with it!'

'I'd rather die! Don't you *understand*, Dy? How could he believe me sincere, if I told him *now*, when I am in debt again, that I didn't care a button for his fortune?'

The Viscount checked the scoffing retort that sprang to his tongue. He did understand. After a thoughtful moment, he said: 'He'd think it was cream-pot love, would he? Ay, very true: bound to! Particularly,' he added, in a voice of censure, 'if you've been treating him with a stupid sort of indifference, which I've a strong notion you have! Oh, well! we shall have to think of some way of raising the blunt, and that's all there is to it!'

Too grateful for his willingness to come to her aid to cavil at his freely-worded criticisms, Nell waited hopefully, confident that he would be able to tell her how to extricate herself from her difficulty. Nor was she mistaken. After a turn or two about the room, he said suddenly: 'Nothing easier! I can't think why I didn't hit upon it at once. You must sell some of your jewellery, of course!'

Her hand went instinctively to her throat. 'The pearls Mama gave me? Her very own pearls? I *could* not, Dysart!'

'No need to sell them, if you don't care to. Something else!'

'But I haven't anything else!' she objected. 'Nothing of value, I mean.'

'Haven't anything else? Why, I never see you but what you're wearing something worth a king's ransom! What about all those sapphires?'

'Dysart! Giles's wedding-gift!' she uttered.

'Oh, very well! But he's always giving you some new trinket: you must be able to spare one or two of 'em. He'll never notice. Or if you think he might, you can have 'em copied. I'll attend to that for you.'

'No, thank you, Dy!' she said, with desperate firmness. 'I won't do anything so *odiously* shabby! To sell the jewels Giles has given me – to have them copied in paste so that he shouldn't know of it – Oh, how detestable I should be to deceive him in such a way!'

'Well, what a high flight!' said Dysart. 'It's no worse than going to a cent-per-cent – in fact, it ain't as bad!'

'It *seems* worse!' she assured him.

'I'll tell you what it is, Nell!' he said, exasperated. 'If you let this excessive sensibility of yours rule you, there will be no way of helping you out of this fix! If you don't care to have your trinkets copied, tell Cardross you lost them! I daresay you would not like to lose the sapphires, but you aren't going to tell me your heart would break for every one of the trinkets he's given you!'

'No, indeed it would not, if I really did lose them, but every feeling revolts from the thought of selling them for such a reason!'

She spoke with so much resolution that it seemed useless to persist in argument. The Viscount, never one to waste his time over lost causes, abandoned his promising scheme, merely remarking that of all the troublesome goosecaps he had encountered his sister bore away the palm. She apologized for being so provoking, adding, with an attempt at a smile, that he must not tease himself any more over the business.

But every now and then the Viscount's conscience, in a manner as disconcerting to himself as to his critics, cast a barrier in the way of his careless hedonism. It intervened now, just as he was congratulating himself on being well out of a tiresome imbroglio.

'Very pretty talking, when you know dashed well I can't help but tease myself over it!' he said bitterly. 'If there's one thing more certain than another, it's that if I hadn't borrowed that three hundred from you, you wouldn't be in this fix now! Well, there's nothing for it: I shall have to get you out of it. I daresay I shall hit on a way when I've had time to think it over, but I shan't do it with you sitting there staring at me as though I was your whole dependence! Puts me out. There's no saying, of course, but what I may have a run of luck, in which case the matter's as good as settled. I've got a notion I ought to give up hazard, and try how it will answer if I stick to faro.'

He then took his leave, bestowing an encouraging pat on his sister, and recommending her to put the whole business out of her mind. There were those who would have taken the cynical view that he would speedily put it out of his, but Nell was not of their number: it did not so much as cross her mind that her dear Dy, either from indolence or forgetfulness, might leave her to her fate. And she was quite right. There was an odd streak of obstinacy in Dysart, which led him, at unexpected moments, to pursue with dogged tenacity the end he had in view; and although his intimates considered that this streak was roused only by the most cork-brained notions, they were agreed that once such a notion had taken firm possession of his mind he could be depended on to stick to it buckle and thong.

Emerging from the house after a genial discussion with his brother-in-law's porter on the chances of several horses in a forthcoming race, he paused at the foot of the steps, considering whether he should summon a hackney, and take a look-in at Tattersall's, or stroll to Conduit Street, where, at Limmer's, he would be sure to encounter a few choice spirits. While he hesitated, a tilbury, drawn by a high-stepping bay, swept round the angle of the square, and he saw that the down-the-road-looking man in the tall hat, and the box-coat of white drab, who was handling the ribbons with such admirable skill, was Cardross. He had no particular desire to meet the Earl, with whom he knew himself to be no favourite, but he waited civilly for the tilbury to draw up beside him.

'Hallo, Dysart!' said the Earl, handing the reins over to his groom, and jumping down from the carriage. 'Are you just going in, or just coming out?'

'Just coming out,' replied Dysart, watching the tilbury being driven away. 'That's a nice tit you have there: looks to be a sweet goer. Welsh?'

'Yes, I'm pretty well pleased with him,' agreed Cardross. 'Very free and fast, and has a good knee action. Oh, yes! pure bred Welsh: I bought him from Chesterford last week. Do you care to come in again?'

'No, I'm bound for Limmer's,' said the Viscount. He eyed his brother-in-law speculatively. The Earl appeared to be in an amiable frame of mind; it was common knowledge that he was rich enough to be able to buy an abbey; and if there was the least chance of getting three hundred pounds out of him merely for the asking, the Viscount was not the man to let this slip. 'You wouldn't care to lend me three hundred, would you?' he suggested hopefully.

'Three hundred?'

'Call it five!' offered the Viscount, recollecting certain of his own more pressing obligations.

Cardross laughed. 'I'll call it anything you choose, but I shouldn't at all care to lend you money. And I'll thank you, Dysart, not to apply to Nell!'

'Nothing of the sort!' said the Viscount, repressing a strong inclination to tell him that the boot was on quite the other leg.

'Dipped again?' enquired Cardross. 'You ought to be tied, you know!'

'I see no sense in that,' returned Dysart. 'Wouldn't do me a bit of good! The only way to come about is to make a big coup. I don't doubt I'll do it, for it stands to reason the luck must change *one* day! However, I've been thinking seriously of devoting myself to faro, and I believe I'll do it. The devil's in the bones, and has been, this year past.'

The news that he was about to reform his way of life met with a disappointing lack of enthusiasm. 'What other entertainments have you in store for us?' asked Cardross. 'I didn't see you driving a wheelbarrow bindfold down Piccadilly last week, but I'm told you contrived to dislocate all the traffic for a considerable space of time. I must congratulate you. Also on your latest feat, of cutting your initials on all the trees in St James's Park.'

'An hour and fifteen minutes!' said Dysart, with simple pride.

'Very creditable.'

'Oh, lord!' Dysart said petulantly, 'what else is there to do but kick up a lark now and then?'

'You might see what can be done to put your estates in order.'

'They ain't my estates,' retorted Dysart. 'I fancy I see my father letting me meddle! What's more, if there's anything to be done old Moulton will do it far better than I could. He's been our agent for years, and he don't mean to let me meddle either. Not that I want to, for I don't.'

'I'll make you an offer,' said Cardross, scanning him not unkindly. 'I won't lend you three hundred pence to fling away at faro, but I'm prepared to settle your debts, and to buy you a commission in any serving regiment you choose to name.'

'By Jove, I wish you would!' Dysart said impulsively.

'I will.'

The Viscount's blue eyes had kindled, but that eager glow faded, and he laughed, giving his head a rueful shake. 'No use! The old gentleman wouldn't hear of it. God knows why he's so set on keeping me in England, for putting aside the fact that I'm not his only son it don't seem to be any pleasure to him to have me at home. Fidgets him to death! I did go down to Devonshire after he had that stroke, you know. Went to oblige my mother, but the end of it was she was obliged to own it didn't answer. But he wouldn't let me join for all that.'

'If you wanted it, I might be able to persuade him.'

'Grease him in the fist, eh? Take my advice, and fund your money! Or wait till I do something so outrageous he'll be glad to see me off to Spain on any terms!' said Dysart, pulling on his gloves.

'Don't be a fool! Come into the house: we can't discuss it in the road!'

'If you're so anxious to waste the ready, lend me a monkey!'

mocked Dysart. 'As for the rest – oh, lord, I don't know *what* I want, and it wouldn't be a particle of use if I did!'

He waited for a moment, and then, as Cardross made no reply, laughed rather jeeringly, and strode off down the flagway.

Four

*I*t was almost with relief that Nell, a few days later, bade her husband a polite farewell. When he had asked her to accompany him to Merion, she had wanted very much to do so (though not with an indignant Letty in her train); but from the moment that Madame Lavalle's bill had arrived to blacken her life she had dreaded that he might renew his persuasions. There was now nothing she wanted less than to be in his company, for the sense of guilt, which already weighed heavily on her spirits, almost crushed her when he was with her. If he smiled at her she felt herself to be a deceiving wretch; if there was a coolness in his manner she fancied he had found her out, and was ready to sink. It did not occur to her, in this disordered state of mind, that the scruples which forbade her to let him see her heart were prompting her to pursue a course that might have been expressly designed to confirm him in his suspicion that she cared for nothing but wealth, fashion, and frivolity. There was no lack of parties, at the height of the season, to fill her days; and no lack of eager escorts for the beautiful young Countess, if the Earl had engagements of his own. It seemed to him that he never saw her except on her way to a review, or a ball; and he could scarcely doubt that she preferred the company of even the most callow of her admirers to his. 'You know, my love,' he said to her once, mocking himself, 'I think fate must have thrown me in your way to depress my pretensions! Would you believe it? – I was used to think myself the devil of a fellow! I now perceive that I'm no such thing – almost a dead bore, in fact!'

She had not answered him, but the colour had flooded her cheeks, and as her eyes flew to his for a brief instant he thought that he caught a glimpse of the loving, vital creature he had once believed her to be. And a moment later she was gone, saying, with a nervous laugh, that he was absurd, that Letty was waiting for her, that she must not stay, because she had promised faithfully to attend Lady Brixworth's alfresco party out at Richmond.

Subjected to such treatment as this, it was hardly surprising that Cardross, far too proud to betray his hurt, retired behind a barrier of cool, faintly ironic civility, which effectually slew at birth Nell's impulse to fling caution to the winds, and all her doubts and difficulties at his feet.

To make matters worse, no word came from Dysart, and Letty, bent on achieving her own ends, wore her brother's temper thin by renewing her attacks every time she saw him. As she had been pledging his credit all over town for weeks past he was soon provoked into addressing a few shattering home truths to her, from which his unhappy wife, an unwilling third at this encounter, gathered that debt and dishonesty were, in his austere view, synonymous terms. Certainly no moment for the disclosure of her own embarrassments could be more unpropitious.

It was therefore with relief that she bade him farewell. He expected to be away for a se'ennight, within which time she thought it not unreasonable to suppose that Dysart must have discovered a means of discharging her debt to Madame Lavalle. By way of recalling it to his mind (just in case, in the press of his sporting engagements, he had temporarily forgotten its urgency) she sent round a note to his lodging in Duke Street, inviting him to dine in Grosvenor Square on the night of the masquerade. Well aware of the fatal results of importunacy she resisted a temptation to ask him what progress he had made towards settling her affairs, and was soon rewarded for her restraint. The Viscount not only sent back a note accepting her invitation, but added, in a postscript, that she need not trouble her head more over That Other Matter.

This cryptic message sent her spirits up immediately. It would have been more satisfactory, perhaps, if Dysart had told her what expedient he had hit upon but she knew him to be no ready letter-writer, and was content to trust that his third attempt at solving her difficulties would be more acceptable to her than his two previous suggestions. Except for one encounter in the Park, where it was impossible to hold private conversation with him, she did not meet him: a circumstance which led her to suppose that whatever plan he had evolved needed a good deal of preparation. This made her feel a trifle uneasy, but he nodded to her so reassuringly at the end of their once chance meeting that her misgivings were soothed. 'I shall see you on Thursday,' he said; and that, she thought, was his way of informing her that on Thursday, when he was to go with her to the masquerade, he would be able to tell her just what she must do to rid herself of her intolerable debt.

And then, on Thursday evening, when both the fair hostesses awaited his arrival in Grosvenor Square, he did not come.

Neither was surprised that he should be late in keeping his engagement, for his habits were known to be erratic; and for a full half-hour only the wizard belowstairs, with two capons roasted to a turn on the spits, fat livers in cases in imminent danger of becoming over-baked in the oven, and the caramel sugar spun over a dish of peu d'amours rapidly hardening, saw any cause for agitation. Letty, who had been in low spirits for days past, was wearing a new and extremely dashing ball-dress of white crape so profusely embroidered with silver spangles that when she stood in the light of the great chandelier in the drawing-room the effect was quite dazzling. Nell, less strikingly attired in satin and blonde lace, knew that if Lady Chudleigh should be at the masquerade she would unhesitatingly condemn this toilette as being totally unsuited to a young lady in her first season, for it was cut indecorously low, besides being worn over the most diaphanous of petticoats. Cardross would probably have insisted on its being changed for something more demure. He might even have considered that in his absence his wife should have done so, but Nell felt herself to be unequal to an exhausting and almost certainly losing battle; and assuaged her conscience with the reflection that the dress would be largely hidden by the domino of shimmering rose silk, which Letty had tossed across the back of a chair. Besides, Letty was so pleased with her appearance that it had put her into the sunniest of humours, which Nell, having endured a week of sulks and repinings, would not willingly upset.

'The worst of brothers is that they never think it is of the least consequence to keep one waiting,' remarked Letty, spreading open a fan spangled to match her gown. 'I only hope he may not be foxed when he does arrive! Look, do you think this is pretty?'

'Foxed! Why should he be?' demanded Nell rather indignantly.

'Oh! You know what men are, when they go off to watch a cock-fight!' said the worldly wise Letty. 'There was one at Epsom today, I fancy.'

'Good heavens, did he tell you he meant to go there?'

'No, but I heard Hardwick talking to Mr Bottisham about it, and he said something about Dysart's taking him up in his curricle.'

'Oh, dear!' said Nell, considerably dismayed by this most unwelcome intelligence. 'If that is so – Oh, I do hope he may not have forgotten he is to take us to Chiswick tonight!'

'What, you don't mean to say that you think he might?' exclaimed Letty, allowing her fan to drop into her lap. 'Oh, it would be too infamous!'

Certain sinister memories flitted through Nell's mind. 'Well, I trust he has not, but he – he does sometimes forget his engagements – particularly when he doesn't like them excessively!' she said.

Letty controlled herself with a strong effort, but when, at the end of another ten minutes, there was still no sign of the Viscount, she could contain herself no longer, but said bitterly: 'Even if he *is* your brother, Nell, I don't believe he ever meant to go with us, and he just said he would so that you shouldn't tease him!'

'No, no, he did mean to, for he said he would see me tonight when we met him in the Park that day! Besides, although I own he is shockingly careless, he wouldn't serve me such an unhandsome trick as that! I was wondering if I should perhaps send a note round to his lodging, to *remind* him. Only I daresay it would take my footman at least twenty minutes to reach Duke Street –'

'Yes, and ten to one he wouldn't find him at home when he did reach his lodging!' interrupted Letty. 'For my part, I don't care a button whether he comes or not, for I am persuaded we shall do very well without him!' She looked at Nell with sharp suspicion. 'You are *not* going to say we can't go to the masquerade unless he escorts us? Oh, Nell, you couldn't be so shabby!'

'No – that is, I know I need not scruple to go, when it is to my cousin's party, but I cannot like it! I wish you were not so set on it – and, to own the truth, I can't think why you should be, unless you have cajoled Mr Allandale to go, and mean to spend the evening in his pocket! And mask or no mask, Letty, I can't and I won't permit it!'

'I did try to make him go,' admitted Letty, quite unabashed, 'but he holds to it that it would be improper, even if he slipped away before the unmasking, so you needn't be in a fidget! The thing is that I have never attended a masquerade, and if I don't go to this one I may not have the chance to go to one for years, for there's no saying that they have them in Brazil, after all.'

Nell looked at her in concern. 'No, but – Dearest Letty, don't indulge your fancy with *that* thought! Cardross won't give his consent: it is useless to think he might!'

'I shall *compel* him!' Letty said, looking mulish.

'How could you possibly do that?'

'Well, I don't know that yet, but you may depend upon it that I shall do it! Recollect that he said I shouldn't be presented till I was eighteen, or act in the theatricals at Roxwell, at Christmas, or drive his bays, or – oh, a hundred things! I can *always* get Giles to let me have my own way, in the end!'

Nell could not help smiling at the naïveté with which Letty classed these trivialities with her marriage, but before she could make any attempt to show her sister-in-law how the very fondness which led Cardross to indulge her in small matters would stiffen his resolve not to permit her (as he thought) to throw herself away in a marriage doomed to failure, Farley, her butler, had entered the room, bearing on a salver a sealed billet, and on his countenance the expression of one who not only brought evil tidings but had foreseen from the outset that this was precisely how it would be.

'My Lord Dysart's groom, my lady, has desired me to give this instantly into your ladyship's hands,' he announced, proffering the salver.

'Only *wait* until I next see Dysart!' uttered Letty direfully.

Feeling as conscience-stricken as though she and not Dysart had been the culprit, Nell broke the wafer that sealed his note, and hastily unfolded the scrawled message. A sigh of relief escaped her, for although the news the message contained was bad, it was not as bad as it might have been. Dysart must certainly have lingered overlong at Epsom, but he had not forgotten that he was engaged to escort his sister to a masquerade. He begged her pardon for being unable to dine with her, but promised faithfully to pick her and Letty up in Grosvenor Square not a moment later than ten o'clock, unless (in a postscript) he should be unavoidably detained, in which case they were to set forward for Chiswick, and might be sure that he would meet them there, his mask in his hand.

'Ten o'clock! And we are invited for half-past nine!' said Letty wrathfully, when this was read to her.

A gleam of mischief shone in Nell's angelic eyes. 'My dear, *surely* you would not be so *gothic* as to arrive at the very start of the party?'

'I daresay he won't come here at all!' said Letty crossly.

This seemed more than likely to Dysart's experienced sister, but loyalty as much as disinclination to drive out to Chiswick without male escort hardened her resolution not to order her landau to come round to the house a moment earlier than ten o'clock. The hour was by this time so far advanced that they had not very long to wait after dinner before Farley announced that the carriage waited for their ladyships. Dysart had put in no appearance, and although a loving sister would have given him a few more moments' grace she dared not, in face of Letty's kindling glance, suggest this. The dominoes, one rose-pink and the other sapphire-blue, were assumed; long gloves of French kid drawn on; loo-masks tucked into reticules; and evening mantles carefully donned over the silken dominoes. A final prinking, on tiptoe before the gilded looking-glass over the mantelpiece, and the ladies were ready to be escorted down the staircase, and handed up into the waiting carriage. Their respective women were in attendance, jealously arranging their delicate skirts, and laying shawls across their knees, Letty's Martha presuming on long service to warn her young mistress against adding any more Bloom of Ninon to an already perfect complexion; and Nell's lofty dresser reminding her to take care that her train of ivory satin did not brush the steps of the landau when she alighted from it.

Those steps were at last let up, and the door shut; the footmen nimbly mounted up behind; the coachman set his horses in motion; and the landau swayed forward over the cobbles.

It had not occurred to Nell, or, indeed, to any of her servants, that a drive to Chiswick could be attended by danger, so no one had thought it necessary to provide the equipage with outriders to protect her from possible highwaymen. But no one had foreseen that the Cardross carriage, instead of joining a procession of vehicles bound for Brent House, would be the last to arrive there by more than half an hour. There was hardly any traffic beyond the first pike off the stones. Kensington village seemed to be sleeping in the bright moonlight; only a post-chaise and an Accommodation coach were met in Hammersmith, coming in from the west; no other vehicle was seen except one of the mails, which swept past the Cardross carriage, its four fresh horses going along at a spanking pace, and its guard blowing a very loud blast of warning on his yard of tin. Shortly after this, the carriage turned off the high road towards Chiswick Mall; and then, just as Letty was saying: 'Well, at all events it hasn't been nearly as tedious a drive as if we had been obliged to dawdle behind some rumbling coach!' both ladies were unpleasantly startled by a sudden pistol-shot, followed by a medley of alarming noises, in which the equal of a frightened horse mingled with various rough voices upraised either in command or expostulation, and the trampling of hooves.

Letty uttered a whimper of fright, and clutched her sister-in-law, saying on a rising note of panic: 'What must we do? What will happen to us? Oh, Nell, we are being *held up*! Why don't those *cowards* of footmen do something? This is all Dysart's fault! Will they murder us? Oh, I wish we hadn't come!'

Nell was not feeling very brave herself, but she was made of sterner stuff than this, and managed to reply with very creditable command over her voice: 'Nonsense! Of course they will not murder us, though I am afraid they will take our jewels. Thank God I am not wearing the Cardross necklace, or my precious sapphires!'

'Give them *everything*!' begged Letty, her teeth chattering. 'I feel sick with apprehension, and I am sure I shall faint! What is the use of taking footmen, when they do *nothing* to protect us? I shall tell Giles, and he will turn them off directly! He ought to be here: he had no *right* to go off to Merion, when he might have known –'

'Oh, do, pray, hold your tongue, Letty!' interrupted Nell, exasperated. 'I wonder you should not have more pride than to let the wretches see you are afraid! And as for the footmen, what could the poor men do against armed ruffians? *They* are not carrying pistols! I don't suppose they ever dreamed we should be held up on the road to Chiswick, of all places! Oh, dear, it sounds as if there were several of them! I do hope they will be satisfied with our jewels, and not wish to ransack the carriage for a strong-box!'

This horrid thought made Letty shake with terror. Then she screamed, for a hideous figure, enveloped in a dark cloak, and with a mask covering his face, loomed up, and wrenched open the door of the carriage, presenting the barrel of a large horse-pistol, and growling in ferocious accents: 'Hand over the gewgaws, and be quick about it!'

The moonlight glinted on the pistol, and the hand that held it. Letty cried: 'Don't, don't!' and tried with feverish haste to unclasp the single row of pearls from round her throat.

'Not you!' said the highwayman, even more ferociously. '*You!*'

The pistol was now pointing straight at Nell, but instead of shrinking away, or making haste (as Letty quaveringly implored her to do) to strip off her bracelets and rings and the large pendant that flashed on her breast, she was sitting bolt upright, her incredulous gaze fixed at first on the hand that grasped the pistol, and then lifting to the masked face.

'Quick!' commanded the highwayman harshly. 'If you don't want me to put a bullet through you!'

'*Dysart!*'

'Hell and the devil confound it!' ejaculated his lordship, adding, however, in a hasty attempt to cover this lapse: 'None o' that! Hand over the gewgaws!'

'Take that pistol away!' ordered Nell. 'How dare you try to frighten me like this? Of all the outrageous things to do – ! It is a great deal too bad of you! What in the world possessed you?'

'Well, if you can't tell that you must be a bigger sapskull than I knew!' said his lordship disgustedly. He pulled off his mask, and called over his shoulder: 'Bubbled, Corny!'

'There, what did I tell you?' said Mr Fancot, putting up the weapon with which he had been covering the coachman, and riding up to bow politely to the occupants of the carriage. 'You ought to have let me do the trick, dear boy: I *said* her ladyship would recognize you!'

'Well, I don't know how the devil she should!' said the Viscount, considerably put-out.

'Oh, Dy, how absurd you are!' Nell exclaimed, trying not to laugh. 'The moonlight was shining on the ring Mama gave you when you came of age! And then you said, *Not you!* to Letty! Of course I recognized you!'

'Then you might have had the wit to pretend you didn't!' said the Viscount, with asperity. 'Totty-headed, that's what you are, my girl! Hi, Joe! No need to keep those fellows covered any longer! I've lost the bet.'

'Dysart, how abominable of you!' Nell said indignantly. 'To bring your groom into this is utterly beyond the line!'

'Fiddle!' said the Viscount. 'You might as well say it was beyond the line to bring Corny in! I've known Joe all my life! Besides, I told him it was for a wager.'

'I *do* say it was beyond the line to bring Mr Fancot in. And I should have supposed he would have thought so too!' added Nell, with some severity.

'No, no! Assure you, ma'am! Always happy to be of service,' said Mr Fancot gallantly. 'Pleasure!'

Letty, to whom relief had brought its inevitable sequel, said in a furious undervoice: '*Idiot!*'

'Nothing of the sort!' said the Viscount, overhearing. 'In fact, if we're to talk of idiots –'

'I think you are detestable! You broke your engagement with Nell in the rudest way, just that you might play this odious trick on her, and frightened us to death for sport! *Sport!*'

'What a hen-hearted girl you are!' remarked his lordship scornfully. 'Frightened you to death, indeed! Lord, Nell's worth a dozen of you! Not but what *she's* got more hair than wit! Of course I didn't do it for sport! I had a devilish good reason, but one might as well try to milk a pigeon as set about helping a female out of a fix!'

Letty was so much intrigued by this cryptic utterance that her wrath gave place to the liveliest curiosity. 'What can you mean? Who is in a fix? Is it Nell? But how – Oh, do tell me! I'm sorry I was cross, but how could I guess it was a plot, when no one told me?'

'Ask Nell!' recommended Dysart. 'You'd best be on your way, if you don't wish to be late. I'll follow you presently.'

'Dysart!' said Nell despairingly. 'It must be nearly eleven o'clock already! How can you possibly follow us? You cannot attend a masquerade in your riding-dress, and by the time you have returned to town, and –'

'Now, don't fly into a fidget!' begged Dysart. 'I'm not going all the way back to London! You must think I'm a gudgeon!'

'Oh, I *do*!' she interpolated, on a quiver of laughter.

'Well, that's where you're fair and far off,' he told her severely. 'I've got all my toggery waiting for me at the Golden Lion here, and a chaise hired to bring me on to Brent House. Yes, and when I think that I never planned anything so carefully in my life, only to have it overset because nothing would do for you but to show how clever you are by screeching that you knew me, I have a dashed good mind to wash my hands of the whole business!'

'Good God, dear boy, mustn't say things like that!' intervened Mr Fancot, considerably shocked. '*I* know you don't mean it, but if anyone else heard you –'

'Well, there isn't anyone else to hear me,' said the Viscount snappishly, walking away to where his groom was holding his horse.

Mr Fancot, feeling that it behoved him to make his excuses for him, pressed up to the carriage, and bowed again to its dimly seen occupants, saying confidentially: 'He don't mean what he says when he gets in a miff – no need to tell you so! *I* know Dy, *you* know Dy! *He* won't buckle!'

'Mr Fancot,' said Nell, almost overcome by mortification, 'I am persuaded *I* have no need to beg you not to tell anyone why Dysart tried to hold me up tonight!'

'I shouldn't dream of it!' Mr Fancot assured her earnestly. 'Wild horses couldn't drag it out of me! Well, it stands to reason they couldn't, because, now I come to think of it, I don't know.'

'You don't know?' she repeated incredulously.

'Forgot to ask him,' he explained. 'Well, I mean to say – no business of mine! Dy said, Come and help me to hold up m'sister's carriage! and I said, Done! or some such thing. Nothing else I could say. Dashed inquisitive to be asking him why, you know!'

At this moment Dysart called impatiently to him, so he made his bow, and went off. Nell sank back into her corner of the carriage, exclaiming: 'Thank heavens! I was ready to sink!' She became aware of her footman awaiting orders, and said hastily: 'Tell James to drive on, if you please! His lordship was – was just funning!'

'I should think he must believe his lordship to be out of his mind,' observed Letty, as the carriage moved forward. 'Why did he do it, Nell?'

'Oh, for a nonsensical reason!'

'Very likely! But what nonsensical reason?'

'I wish you will take a leaf out of that absurd Fancot's book, and not ask inquisitive questions!'

'I daresay you do, but I shan't! Come, now, you sly thing!'

'No, pray don't tease me!' Nell begged.

'Oh, very well! I wonder what Giles will say to it?' said Letty, all sprightly innocence.

'Letty! You wouldn't – !'

'Not if I were in your confidence, of course!' replied Letty piously.

'Really, you are the most unscrupulous girl!' declared Nell.

Letty giggled. 'No, I am not, for I never betray secrets! I shan't rest till I know this one, I warn you, for I cannot conceive what was in Dysart's head, unless he was just knocking up a lark, and that I know he was not.'

'Well, pray don't think too badly of him!' Nell said, capitulating.

But Letty, listening entranced to Nell's story, did not think at all badly of Dysart. She said handsomely that he had far more wit than she had ever guessed, and was much inclined to join him in blaming Nell for not having held her peace. 'For if only you had pretended not to recognize him everything would now be in a fair way to being settled. And you can't deny that if you had truly not known him you wouldn't have cared a button for your jewels. I suppose you might have guessed how it was, when he brought you the money, but that wouldn't have signified!'

'How can you say so? My peace would have been utterly cut up! I *must* have told Cardross – yet how might I have done so, when already he thinks Dy too – too rackety? Oh, it would have been worse than anything!'

'I declare you are the oddest creature!' Letty exclaimed. 'For my part, I think you should have sold some of your jewels, and I don't wonder at it that Dysart is out of all patience with you! I suppose you may do what you choose with what is your own!'

She continued arguing in this strain until Brent House was reached; and when Dysart presently joined his sister, in something very like a fit of the sullens, did much to restore him to good-humour by heartily applauding his ingenuity, commiserating him on the mischance which had brought his scheme to nothing, and abusing Nell for having such stupid crotchets. For once they found themselves much in sympathy, but when the Viscount said that if Nell made such a piece of work over a little necessary deception she had better screw up her courage and tell Cardross she was under the hatches again, agreement was at an end between them. Letty strongly opposed this suggestion. In her experience, Cardross, in general so indulgent, was abominably severe if he considered one had been extravagant; and if confronted by debts (however inescapable) he became positively brutal. She spoke with feeling, her last encounter with her exasperated brother still vivid in her mind. 'Only because I purchased a dressing-case, which *every* lady must have, and desired him in the *civillest* way to pay for it, for how could I do so myself on the paltry sum he allows me for pin-money – he *sent it back to the shop*! I was never so mortified! And, would you credit it, Dysart? – he promised me that if I again ran into debt he would send me down to Merion in charge of a strict governess! A *governess* – !'

The Viscount was not much impressed – and, indeed, he would have been still less impressed had he been privileged to set eyes on the necessary adjunct to a lady's comfort in question. A handsome piece of baggage, that dressing-case, with every one of its numerous cut-glass bottles fitted with gold caps, embellished with a tasteful design in diamond-chips. It had made the second footman, a stout youth, sweat only to carry it up one pair of stairs; and when it was flung open it had quite dazzled the eyes of all beholders. It had dazzled Cardross's eyes so much that he had closed them, an expression on his face of real anguish.

'That has nothing to say to anything. I daresay he thought it not the thing for you,' said the Viscount, with unconscious shrewdness. 'But everyone knows court dresses cost the deuce of a lot of money, and I shouldn't wonder at it if –'

'When Giles discovered that Nell was so monstrously in the wind he said such things as cast her into the greatest affliction!'

'Were you there?' demanded the Viscount suspiciously.

'No, I was not there, but I saw her directly afterwards, and she was quite overset! She cried in the most affecting way, and ever since she has been subject to fits of sad dejection. If you abandon her, it will the most abominable thing I ever heard of!'

'Who said I meant to do so?' retorted his lordship. 'All I said was – But it ain't to the purpose! It's a pity tonight's affair came to nothing, but I shall come about. And I'll thank you not to start meddling!' he added, in a very ungallant way.

'I have not the remotest intention of *meddling*!' said Letty, rigid with wrath.

'Well, see you don't!' recommended Dysart. 'And don't go blabbing either!'

These ungentlemanly words brought to an abrupt end the excellent understanding which had seemed to be flourishing between them. Letty, in freezing accents, requested his lordship to restore her to her chaperon, and his lordship did so with unflattering alacrity. Finding that Nell was attended by a great many of her friends he did not feel that it behoved him to remain at her side, but went off to amuse himself in his own way. Since he was, regrettably, one of those dashing blades who could not be trusted to keep the line at a masquerade he managed to do

77

this tolerably well by flirting outrageously with any lady obliging enough to encourage him. By the time that had palled he had been so fortunate as to have rubbed against a crony, in whose company, and that of several other bucks of the first head, he spent the remainder of the evening, rejoining his sister finally in very merry pin. He was not precisely castaway (as he would himself have phrased it), and only a high stickler could have found anything to object to in the affable, not to say rollicking, mood engendered by champagne punch; but it was evident that he had temporarily banished care, and could not be expected to bend his mind to the solving of Nell's difficulties. Instead, he entertained the ladies during the drive back to town with snatches of song, delivered in a fine, forceful baritone.

Five

*I*n spite of the absence from it of Mr Allandale Letty had much enjoyed the masquerade. Like the Viscount, she had indulged in a good deal of flirtation, allowing her vivacity to carry her to lengths only possible under the disguise of a mask and domino; she had received a great many audacious compliments; and her spangled gown had been much admired. Her giddiness added nothing to Nell's comfort, but she was powerless to check the liveliness that several times put her to the blush. A gentle admonition was met merely with a laugh, and a toss of the head; and when she ventured to say: 'Letty, if you won't keep a proper distance for your own sake, do so for mine, I beg of you!' her wilful sister-in-law replied: 'Oh, fudge! You place yourself on too high a form! There's no harm in romping a trifle at a masquerade: everyone does so! It is all just fun and gig!'

'It is unbecoming,' Nell said. 'Bath miss manners! You wouldn't behave with so little particularity if Mr Allandale were here!'

'*Dear* Jeremy! No, indeed! I should flirt with him instead. But he is not here, and I've no notion of being moped and die-away at *such* an agreeable party, I can tell you. I think we are having a splendid night's raking, don't you?'

It was useless to persist; useless too to hope that Letty would not be recognized. At midnight there would be a general unmasking, when disapproving eyes would see that the fast girl in the shimmering domino and the spangled gown was none other than Cardross's little half-sister. Youth and a naturally volatile disposition led Letty, carried away by excitement, into behaviour that was beyond the line of being pleasing. The evils of her former situation in her aunt's house were never more clearly shown: she had neither precept nor example to guide her, her aunt being both indolent and shatterbrained, and her cousins over-bold young women with nothing in their heads but finery and dalliance.

Having perceived Lady Chudleigh amongst the gathering of unmasked chaperons, Nell braced herself to meet the inevitable strictures which she did not doubt her husband's most formidable aunt would feel it her duty to address to her. In the event, however, Lady Chudleigh was surprisingly gracious. She certainly condemned the spangled dress, and was thankful that she had no cause to blush for her own daughter, but she said that she did not blame Nell for Letty's want of conduct. 'It is much to be regretted that Letitia does not take a lesson from you, my dear Helen,' she said majestically. 'I shall not deny that I have been used to think that Cardross made a great mistake when he chose to offer for you. I always speak my mind, and I told him at the time that he would do better to ally himself to a female nearer in age to himself. But I must own, and do not hesitate to do so, that I have been agreeably surprised in you. It is a sad pity that Letitia has neither your discretion nor your good taste.'

With these measured words of approval she moved on, which was just as well, since Nell could think of nothing whatsoever to say in reply to them. Her daughter, a rather angular girl, unkindly described by her cousin Felix as an antidote, lingered to exclaim: 'Only fancy Mama's saying *that* to you! She does not often praise people, I can tell you, Cousin Helen!'

The congratulatory tone in which this was uttered was a little too much for Nell. She said tartly: 'I am sure I ought to be very much obliged to her!'

'I knew you must feel it so. Do you know, she said to me yesterday that you were a very pretty-behaved young woman? There!'

'Did she indeed? Well, don't repeat any more of her compliments, for they might puff me up too much in my own conceit!'

Miss Chudleigh tittered. 'That is precisely what Mama said! At least, I mean she said that it was a wonder your head was not turned by all the compliments you receive. But I quite expected her to censure you for permitting Letty to wear such an improper gown. I can't think how she can do so without blushing. *I* could not!'

'No, and I must own that I think you would be very unwise to attempt anything in the same style,' instantly retorted the pretty-behaved Lady Cardross. 'But Letty, you know, has so perfect a figure that she can carry off anything! For my part, I never saw her in greater beauty!'

'And I hope she told her detestable mother!' Nell said, when later recounting this exchange to Letty.

'Well!' said Letty, giggling. 'What a bouncer! When you took one look at my dress, and said you had never seen anything so improper!'

'Yes, but I didn't say it was not *becoming*! And in any event it was a great piece of impertinence for Miriam to criticize you. Or for Lady Chudleigh to do so either, for now I come to think of it she is not your aunt, but only Giles's!'

'*Dear* Nell!' gurgled Letty.

Nell submitted to an enthusiastic embrace, but said, in rather a conscience-stricken tone: 'But I must tell you, Letty, that I agreed with every word they said! It is a *shocking* dress, and don't say you didn't damp your petticoat, for I know you did! Nothing else could have made it cling so! What Cardross must have said, had he seen it –'

'You sound *just* like a governess!'

'So I do!' Nell said, much struck, and looking quite aghast. 'Oh, what an odious girl you are, Letty, to put me to that necessity! You make me *feel* like a governess!'

'*I* did not purchase a lace gown for more than three hundred guineas,' said Letty, folding her hands, and gazing piously at the ceiling. '*I* am not in a quake lest my husband should discover it!'

Quite confounded, poor Nell remained speechless for several moments. She made a gallant recovery. 'No, *you* bought a dressing-case for five hundred pounds, didn't you? And you are not in debt because Cardross sent it back! And least *that* has not happened to me!'

'I hoped you wouldn't remember that,' said Letty candidly. 'Oh, Nell, it *has* put a famous notion into my head! Send the gown back to Lavalle! You may say that it is not in the least what you wanted, and doesn't become you!'

'Well, if that is your famous notion I never heard anything so unscrupulous in my life!' gasped Nell. 'Besides, I tore it a little at Carlton House that night, and Lavalle would instantly see where Sutton darned it!'

'What a pity! There is nothing for it, then, but to order another dress from the horrid creature,' said Letty, unconsciously echoing Dysart. 'That is what my aunt does when her dressmaker duns her. And if you keep on sending it back, saying it does not fit, or that you prefer a floss trimming instead of lace, or some such thing, it won't be finished until the quarter, and then you may pay for both the gowns! Why, in less than two months it *will* be quarter-day, and you will find yourself in funds again! I see no difficulty.'

The suggestion found no favour with Nell, but since Madame Lavalle had followed up her bill with a polite letter, drawing my lady's attention to it, and trusting that my lady would find it convenient to defray it within the immediate future, she felt her case to be desperate, and resolved on a course which, disagreeable though it might be, seemed to hold out more promise of success than any scheme Dysart was likely to evolve. She would pay Madame Lavalle a visit, not to bespeak another expensive dress, but to explain with what dignity she could muster that although it was not at all convenient to her to pay the account in the immediate future she would faithfully do so at the end of the following month. That this would dig an uncomfortably large hole in her next quarter's allowance Nell realized, but decided, with the optimism of youth, that with a little economy she would contrive to scrape through the summer months.

She had been startled to receive Madame's letter, and shrewd enough to perceive, underlying its smooth civility, a threat; but she was as yet too inexperienced to know that some unusual circumstance must lurk behind it, or that no *modiste* of high fashion would dream, for the paltry sum of three hundred and thirty guineas, of alienating a patroness of such rich promise as the young Countess of Cardross. But after a very few minutes in Madame Lavalle's company she learned that the circumstances governing Madame's action were very unusual indeed. Madame, after a long and lucrative career in Bruton Street, was about to retire from business. She was, in fact, returning to her native land, but this she naturally did not disclose to Lady Cardross, preferring to say with a vagueness at odd variance with her sharp-featured face, with its calculating sloe-eyes and inflexible mouth, that she would henceforward be out of the way of collecting debts. Lady Cardross was certainly an *innocente*, but even a bride from the schoolroom might wonder how it would be possible for Madame to return to France in time of war. It was possible, if one had money and time to spend on the journey, influential connections to assist one over the obstacles in the path, and, above all, relations well-placed in Paris. From England one might still travel to Denmark, and after that – *eh bien*, the matter arranged itself!

On the whole Madame had done very well out of her last London Season, but this was now in full swing, her most valued clients had purchased quite as many gowns as they were likely to need, and it was time to close her accounts. She had several bad debts: that went without saying; it was not worth the pain of attempting to recover those losses; but she knew well that although Lady Cardross might be at a temporary standstill her lord was as wealthy a man as might be found, and would certainly pay his wife's debts. The sense of this she managed to convey to Nell in the most urbane manner conceivable, not an ungenteel word spoken, the sugared smile never deserting her lips.

'Oh, if it is the case that you are retiring from business – !' said Nell, shrugging her shoulders with splendid indifference. 'I had not perfectly understood: naturally you will wish to be paid immediately! Rest assured that I will attend to the matter!'

She then sailed away, her head high, and her heart cowering in her little kid shoes. Madame, having curtseyed her off the premises with the greatest deference, rubbed her hands together, and said: 'She will contrive, that one!'

That she must somehow contrive, and without Cardross's knowledge, was by this time a fixed determination in Nell's mind. Every day that had passed since the first appearance of Madame's account had added to her dread that he would discover the debt; reason was lost sight of; the debt, and Cardross's sentiments, if he should be called upon to pay it, assumed grotesque proportions, until it seemed to her as though it might wreck her life. No sobering counsel was at hand to cast a damper on lurid imagination, and give her thoughts a saner direction. Letty, exaggerating her own experiences, recommended her at all costs to settle the matter before Cardross got wind of it; and Dysart, knowing how much his own depredations on her purse were responsible for her present predicament, was apparently prepared to go to extraordinary lengths for the furtherance of this end. By Dysart had shaken her faith in him. Letty might applaud his scheme for her relief: she could not. It seemed to her a shocking thing to have attempted; and the thought of what next his wild humour might prompt him to do put her in a quake of apprehension. There must be no depending on Dysart; and there was no one else to whom she could turn.

Such a reflection as this was scarcely soothing to nerves already irritated. The conviction that she was friendless, and hunted into the bargain, began to take strong possession of Nell's mind. She sank into a slough of self-pity, seeing her debt as a sum large enough to have ruined a Nabob, and her husband as a miser with a heart of flint.

It was in this mood that she presently stepped down from her barouche, and it was her coachman who rescued her from it, by desiring to know whether she would be requiring the carriage again that day. The very mention of it dispelled that unjust vision of Cardross. Just because she had once admired a friend's barouche he had given her one for her very own, and with a pair of horses that took the shine out of every other pair to be seen in town. She had not liked the famous Cardross necklace, an awe-inspiring collection of emeralds and diamonds heavily set in gold, and instead of being offended he had told her to keep it for state occasions, and had given her the most charming pendant to wear in its stead. 'For everyday use!' he had said, with the smile that had won her heart in his eyes.

Self-pity turned in an instant to self-blame. From being a tyrannical miser Cardross became the most generous man alive, and quite the most ill-used; and she the embodiment of selfishness, extravagance, and ingratitude. And, if Dysart were to be believed, she had added blindness and stupidity to these vices. It now seemed to her wonderful that Cardross should have remained patient for so long. Perhaps he was regretting the impulse that had made him offer for her; perhaps, even, disgust at her coldness and depravity had already driven him back to Lady Orsett.

A year earlier Nell, instructed by Mama, had steeled herself to accept the fact of Lady Orsett as one of the inescapable crosses a wife must bear with complaisance; but between the girl who had supposed herself to be making a marriage of convenience and the bride who had been brought to realize that hers was a love-match there was a vast difference. Mama would scarcely have recognized her docile, beautifully mannered daughter in the bright-eyed young woman who uttered between clenched teeth: 'She shan't have him!'

This determination, excellent though it might be, only strengthened her resolve to settle Madame Lavalle's account without applying to Cardross. In her view nothing could more surely jeopardize her whole future than to cast out lures to her husband while presenting him with yet another debt. He must certainly believe her to be hoaxing him, playing off a detestable cajolery that could only disgust a man of sensibility.

Her thoughts flickered to the second of Dysart's suggestions, that she should sell some of her jewellery. Not, of course, Cardross's gifts, but perhaps the row of pearls Mama had given her? But every feeling revolted. They were Mama's own pearls, jealously preserved by her for her eldest daughter, and bestowed upon her with such affecting tenderness. Stress of circumstances had obliged poor Mama to sell nearly all her jewellery, but her pearls she had clung to through the direst of her straits, and for her daughter to sell them only to pay for an extravagant gown must sink her forever below reproach.

A very little reflection convinced Nell that there was only one way in which she could raise three hundred pounds. It must be borrowed. Dysart had rather unexpectedly condemned this expedient, but Nell knew that even Mama had had dealings with a moneylender, so that borrowing upon interest, though it might be an expensive practice, could not be a crime. Papa, of course, had carried it to unwise lengths: Nell perfectly understood how ruinous continued borrowings could be, but it was surely absurd to suppose that anything very dreadful would happen if one borrowed three hundred pounds only for a few weeks. It would be paid back at the end of June, and no one need ever know anything about it.

The more she considered it, the more Nell liked the scheme, and the more she was inclined to attribute Dysart's severe attitude to some antiquated notion of propriety. Even the most careless of brothers could be amazingly stuffy on any question of conduct affecting the ladies of his family: that was one of the incomprehensible things about men. To hear Papa, in the bosom of his family, one would suppose that modesty and discretion were the two virtues he considered most indispensable in a female. But there had been nothing in Papa's career to suggest this: indeed far otherwise! Dysart, warmly approving the generously displayed charms of a certain actress, almost in the same breath could speak censoriously of his sister's gown, if it were cut rather lower than usual, or clung too closely to her form for his suddenly austere taste. Even Cardross suffered from this peculiarity. He had not criticized her raiment, but he made no secret of the fact that he expected from his wife and sister a degree of decorum which he did not practise himself. 'I will have no scandal in *my* household,' said Cardross inflexibly, just as though he had not been creating scandal in Lord Orsett's household for years. Nell didn't doubt that he would disapprove strongly of his wife's patronizing a moneylender, but she didn't allow it to worry her very much. Imprudent it might be, but what Mama had done could not be a crime.

Nell gave Dysart a day's grace, and when he neither came to see her nor wrote to tell her what next he meant to do, set forth, not without some inward trepidation, on a visit to Mr King, in Clarges Street. It had been Mr King who had enjoyed Mama's custom.

There were certain difficulties in the way of setting forth from Grosvenor Square alone and on foot, but she overcame these by ordering her carriage round to take her to the Green Park, where (she said) she was going to walk with some friends. At the last moment Letty nearly spoilt this careful plan by going with her, but she had the happy thought of saying that she had arranged to meet in the park two ladies whom Letty violently disliked, so Letty decided instead to go with her maid on a shopping expedition. Nell might tell herself that there was no harm in her projected errand, but she could not tell herself that it would be proper to take Letty into her confidence, for, oddly enough, although it might be allowable for herself to seek relief from her difficulties with Mr King, for Letty to do the same thing would be quite shocking. And she could not help feeling that that was just what Letty would do, once the idea had been put into her head, for she was never out of debt, and had lately been warned by Cardross that he was not going to encourage her extravagant habits by continuing to defray all the totally unnecessary expenses she incurred.

Nell dressed herself with great care for her expedition, choosing from the formidable collection of walking dresses in her wardrobe one of cambric, made high to the neck, and with long sleeves, and only a border of cable trimming to relieve its austerity. For some reason which she could not have explained she felt that when one visited a moneylender one's habit should be as modest as possible, so she added a sarsnet pelisse of dark blue to her ensemble. This lent her an undeniable note of sobriety, but when it came to the selection of a hat the only one she possessed that approached sobriety was made of olive brown silk. No exigency could induce her to wear this with a blue pelisse, so she was obliged to choose instead a frivolous bonnet that matched the pelisse but was trimmed with lace and flowers. A thick veil served the double purpose of providing a disguise and a touch of rather dowdy respectability. It also staggered her dresser, and certainly made her suspicious; but Nell said glibly that the dust from the streets had slightly roughened her cheeks, an explanation which seemed to satisfy Miss Sutton.

Set down at the Bath Gate, Nell entered the Green Park, and strolled for a little while beside the Basin, trying to recruit her ebbing courage. Two unwelcome thoughts had occurred to her: Mama, when she had turned in desperation to Mr King, had employed a go-between; and would not Mr King wish to know her identity? She had not previously considered this possibility, but as she rehearsed, during the drive from Grosvenor Square, what she must say at the coming interview she realized that not the most obliging moneylender was in the least likely to advance a large sum of money to an unknown and heavily veiled lady. Not only would he wish to know what were the circumstances of his client, but no doubt he would demand a note of hand from her. One might, of course, sign this with a fictitious name, but that would hardly satisfy Mr King. Nell was quite shrewd enough to know that an obscure Mrs Smith of no address would find it very much harder to borrow money upon interest than would the wife of an extremely wealthy peer.

A good deal daunted, it was with lagging steps that she left the

Park, and crossed the ruts and cobbles of Piccadilly. Her errand no longer seemed so innocuous, for while it would be a simple matter, and surely quite unembarrassing, to arrange a loan under a cloak of anonymity, it was another matter altogether to be obliged to announce: 'I am Lady Cardross.'

She turned into Clarges Street, and was soon abreast of the discreet-looking house in which Mr King carried on his business. She hesitated, saw that a man on the opposite side of the street was looking at her, and walked on, blushing under her veil. When she ventured to look round, he had disappeared from her view, so she turned, and began to walk back. By this time she was wishing herself a hundred miles away, dreading what lay before her, no longer sustained by the comforting reflection that it was not so very wrong after all. A small but insistent inner voice told her that on this occasion Mama would not wish her example to be copied; and again she walked past Mr King's house.

From a window in a house on the other side of the street Mr Hethersett had for several minutes been observing these vacillations through his quizzing-glass. The particular crony whom he had come to visit, having addressed several remarks to him without receiving any other answer than an absentminded grunt, at last demanded if anything was amiss, and came to see what was claiming his attention. Mr Hethersett, letting his glass fall on the end of its ribbon, ejaculated: 'Good God!' and hastily picked up his hat and gloves. 'Can't stay!' he said. 'Remembered something important!'

His astonished friend protested, but Mr Hethersett, in general polite to a point, did not stay to listen. He was out of the house in a matter of seconds, and crossing the street with long strides.

Nell, drawing a resolute breath, had mounted the first of the steps leading to Mr King's front door when she heard herself accosted in slightly breathless accents.

'Cousin!' said Mr Hethersett.

She jumped, and looked round. Mr Hethersett raised the hat from his head and executed the bow for which he was famous.

'Very happy to have met you!' he said. 'Beg you will allow me to escort you home!'

'Sir!' uttered Nell, in what she hoped was the outraged voice of a stranger.

Apparently it was not. 'Can't hope to deceive me in that bonnet,' explained Mr Hethersett apologetically. 'Wore it the day I drove you to the Botanic Gardens.' Acutely aware of the goggling gaze fixed on him from a window across the street, he added: 'Take my arm! George Burnley has his eye on us, and it won't do for him to recognize you. Not that I think he will, but no sense in running the risk.'

'I am very much obliged to you, but pray don't stay for me!' Nell said, trying to speak in a careless way. 'I – I have some business to transact!'

'Yes, I know. That's why I came across the road.'

'You *know*?' she repeated, rather scared. 'But you cannot know, Felix! Besides –'

'What I mean is, know whose house this is,' he explained. 'It ain't any concern of mine, but it won't do for you to be doing business with Jew King, cousin. What's more, if Cardross knew –'

'You won't tell Cardross?' she cried involuntarily.

He was just about to refute with considerable indignation the suggestion that he was a tale-bearer when prudence intervened. He temporized. 'I won't tell him if you let me escort you home. If you don't, nothing else for me to do.'

'Felix, I never thought you could be so ungentlemanly!'

'No,' he agreed. 'To tell you the truth, I didn't either. But the thing is it would be a dashed sight more ungentlemanly to go off and leave you to get into a pickle. Jew King! Lord, cousin, do you know the fellow owns an ornamental villa on the river? Slap up to the nines – never saw such a place in your life!'

'No, and I don't see what that has to say to anything!' retorted Nell crossly.

'Point is, where did he fund the blunt to pay for it? From people like you, cousin! Take my word for it!'

'Yes, yes, but I only wish for a loan for a particular reason, just – just a very temporary one!'

He drew her hand through his arm, and obliged her to walk with him up the street. 'Believe me, fatal!' he said earnestly.

She sighed, but attempted no further argument. After a pause, Mr Hethersett coughed, and said delicately: 'Very reluctant to offend you – awkward sort of a business! Thing is, might be able to be of service. Tolerably plump in the pocket, you know.'

She was a good deal touched, but said at once: 'No, indeed! I am sure there was never anyone half as kind as you, Felix, but *that* would be the outside of enough! And you mustn't suppose that I am in the habit of borrowing money: this – there are reasons – why I don't wish to apply to Cardross for this particular sum! Don't let us talk about it! It is of no moment, after all.'

'Certainly not: shouldn't dream of prying into your affairs, cousin!' he replied. 'Only wish to say – at least, I don't, but must! – feel myself obliged to ask you to give me your word you won't come running back here as soon as my back's turned!'

She sighed, but said submissively; 'No, I won't do that, if you think it so very bad.'

'Worst thing in the world!' he assured her.

'I don't see why it should be. After all –'

'You may not see why, but it ain't a bit of use telling me you didn't know it, because I've been watching you,' said Mr Hethersett severely. 'Going backwards and forwards like a cat on a hot bake-stone!'

'Oh, how can you say such an uncivil thing?' she protested. 'I did *not*!'

'That's what it looked like to me,' he said, with great firmness. 'Not the moment for civility, either. Got great regard for you, cousin. Dashed fond of Giles, too. Wouldn't wish to see either of you in a tangle. Thing is – nothing he wouldn't give you! Officious thing to do – giving you advice – but if you're in a fix you tell him, not Jew King!'

She said unhappily: 'There are circumstances which – Oh, I can't explain it to you, but he mustn't know of this!'

To her relief he forbore to press her. She would have been dismayed, however, had she known the construction he had put on her words.

Mr Hethersett, who had so strongly disapproved of his cousin's alliance with any member of Lord Pevensey's family, had now the doubtful felicity of realizing how just had been his objections to the marriage. If Nell had incurred a debt she dared not disclose to Cardross, it was as plain as a pikestaff that she had embroiled herself in her brother's chaotic affairs. In Mr Hethersett's view that was almost the only form of expenditure Cardross would not tolerate in his wife. Probably he would not take gaming debts in good part either, but Mr Hethersett did not think that Nell was a gamester. He had once struggled to support her through several rubbers of whist, an experience which had left him in doubt of her ability to distinguish spades from clubs.

He had made his offer to rescue her from her embarrassments in good faith, but he was considerably relieved by her instant refusal of it. He enjoyed a considerable independence, but the last settling-day at Tattersall's had not been happy, and to have advanced what he feared must be a very large sum of money to Nell must have left him in uncomfortably straitened circumstances. It might also, if the truth leaked out, have involved him in a quarrel with Cardross, who would certainly feel that he had behaved in a very improper way. Cardross was a man of calm judgement, so it was perhaps unlikely that he would suspect his cousin of having formed a warmer attachment for Nell than was seemly. At the same time, there was no predicting what crackbrained notion a man deeply in love might take into his head; and Mr Hethersett was uneasily aware that by assuming the rôle of Nell's cicisbeo-in-chief he had certainly laid himself open to attack. Nor had he the smallest desire to contribute towards Dysart's relief. Mr Hethersett, a gentleman of the first respectability, and a high stickler in all matters of taste and conduct, disapproved unequivocally of such dashing blades as Dysart. Such feats as jumping one's horse over a loaded dinner-table awoke no admiration in his breast, for anything that set people in an uproar was bad ton, and to be in bad ton was to be beyond pardon. The world of fashion might embrace all manner of men: the Out-and-Outers, the Tulips, the Dashes, Tippies, and Bloods: but the first style of elegance could only be achieved by those whose dress and deportment were characterized by an exquisite moderation. Dysart was never moderate. In the saddle he was a hard-goer; on the road his ambition was to give the go-by to every other vehicle; in the gaming-room, not content, like Mr Hethersett, to sport a little blunt on the table, he played deep. He engaged in hare-brained pranks; and the chances were that if you met him any time after noon you would find him ripe already. None but the very strait-laced objected, of course, to a man's becoming foxed during the course of a convivial evening; but either Dysart had an uncommonly weak head, or he was carrying his drinking propensity beyond the line of what was acceptable. As for his debts, he had been monstrously in the wind at the time of his sister's marriage, and he had had ample time, since being relieved by Cardross of his more pressing obligations, to run himself to a standstill again. It would be typical of him, Mr Hethersett considered, to apply to his sister for succour; and ridiculous to suppose that she could bring herself to deny him. He did not blame her in the least, but he was strongly of the opinion that such reckless generosity ought to be checked before it had run to such lengths as must put her as well as Dysart heavily in debt. A hazy recollection of the appalling load of debt under which Devonshire's mother had died flitted through his mind. Astronomical figures had been whispered: probably false, for no one knew the exact truth, but it must have been a monstrous sum. It was said she had lost a huge fortune at play: queer sort of fellow the old Duke must have been, not to have known what his wife was about, thought Mr Hethersett. Things would never get to that pitch of disaster in Cardross's household, of course; still, they might become pretty bad before he discovered what was happening. He was rich enough to be able to stand the nonsense, but Mr Hethersett had a very fair idea of what his feelings would be if he found Nell out in such deception.

Someone, he decided, ought to drop him a hint now, before any serious mischief had been done, and while he was still so much in love with Nell that he would find it easy to excuse her folly. He was inclined for a moment to regret having promised Nell he would not betray her to Cardross; but as soon as he played with the notion of making such a disclosure to his cousin his imagination boggled at it. Under no circumstances could he have done it. The proper person to intervene was Lady Pevensey, and had she been in town he might, he thought, have contrived to hint her on to the trouble. Only she was miles away, tied to that ramshackle husband of hers, and there was no saying, after all, that she would see the matter as she ought: she had never seemed to Mr Hethersett to have much more wit than a pea-goose; besides, she doted on Dysart so fondly that she might possibly think his interests of more importance than Nell's.

Nell's voice, would-be cheerful, but decidedly nervous, intruded on these ruminations. 'You are very silent!' she said.

'I beg pardon!' he said. 'I was thinking.'

'About – about *this*?' she asked anxiously.

'No,' he said unblushingly. 'Thinking we should take a look-in at Gunter's. You'd like an ice, I daresay. Just the thing!'

She thanked him, but declined the treat. She would have declined the offer of a chair to carry her home, too, but on this point Mr Hethersett was firm, knowing well what was due to her consequence. To be strolling through the streets of London with only himself as escort would not do for Lady Cardross. So he beckoned to a couple of chairmen before suggesting to her that he should do so, handed her into the chair, and completed his politeness by walking beside it to Grosvenor Square, and engaging her in a commonplace conversation that gave her to understand that he had dismissed the episode in Clarges Street from his mind.

Six

Rescued from the perils of Clarges Street, and restored to the shelter of her own house, Nell hardly knew whether to be grateful to Mr Hethersett for having thrust a spoke in her wheel, or resentful. When the moment had come for knocking on Mr King's door she had certainly been extremely reluctant to do so, and had suffered very much the same sensations as if she had been about to have a tooth drawn; but her dependence now was all on Dysart, whom she had not seen since the night of the masquerade, and who might, for anything she knew, have taken a pet at having his ingenious plot frustrated, or (which was even more likely) have forgotten all about her troubles. She and Letty were going to the Opera that evening, where it was extremely improbable that she would meet him; so she wrote a letter to him, telling him how urgent her need had become, and begging him he would call in Grosvenor Square.

She had hardly dispatched this missive, by the hand of her footman, when Letty came in. In general, when Letty went shopping, she returned laden with parcels, and eager to display to her sister-in-law a collection of expensive frivolities which had happened to catch her eye; but on this occasion she had nothing to show but a disconsolate face. She said she had had a stupid morning, but when Nell asked if she had been able to find a muslin she liked, she replied: 'Oh, yes! Martha has it. I met my cousins, and went with them to Grafton House, all amongst the quizzy people. Selina *would* have me go, because she said there were amazing bargains to be had there. I must say, they had a great many muslins. I chose a checked one, but I daresay I shan't like it above half when it is made up. It cost seven shillings the yard, too, and I don't consider *that* a bargain, do you?'

'No, but checked muslin is always dearer than the plain colours. I hope the Miss Thornes are quite well?' Nell said politely.

'Yes – at least, I didn't enquire. Selina seemed pretty stout. Fanny was gone with my aunt to Mrs Mee, to arrange to have her likeness taken. They are persuaded Humby means to come to the point, and Selina says my aunt and uncle are in transports, though I can't think why they should be, for he presents a very off appearance, don't you think? besides having some odd humours.'

'I don't know that. I believe he is very respectable,' Nell responded, wondering whether her cousin's approaching betrothal was accountable for the clouded look on Letty's vivid little face. 'I collect it was Mrs Thistleton, then, who was with Miss Selina Thorne?'

'Yes, and I can tell you I was soon wishing her at the deuce!' said Letty, with a disgusted pout. 'She is increasing, and bent on telling the whole of London! You would suppose no one had ever before been in her situation, for she can talk of nothing else! And then what must we do but walk into Lady Eastwell! *She* expects to be confined next month, and nothing could be like her simperings and sighings and affectations! Sir Godfrey is *aux anges* over the *petit paquet* she means to present to him. *Petit paquet! Un très grand paquet,* I should think, for I never saw anyone so large! I was vexed to death, dawdling along in her company, and being obliged to listen to such insipid stuff! And Maria at least was used to be the most entertaining creature! I do hope *you* won't turn into a bothersome bore when you start increasing, Nell!'

The colour rushed up into Nell's cheeks; she said: 'I hope not, indeed!' but in a constricted voice, for Letty's careless words had touched her on the raw. It was some months since Lady Pevensey, tearing herself away from her stricken lord to visit her daughter, had soothed an anxiety which was even then teasing Nell. 'Think nothing of it, dearest!' she had said, adding, with simple pride: 'You are like me, and you know I had been married for three years before dear Dysart was born.'

Nell had been comforted; and although the prospect of being obliged to wait for three years before she gave Cardross an heir was dismal, it was permissible to indulge the hope that she might find herself in an interesting situation considerably earlier than had Mama. And since Cardross, neither by word nor by look, gave the least sign of disappointment, and her mind was pleasantly occupied with the manifold gaieties of fashionable life, she had not thought very much about it. But Letty's petulant remark was ill-timed: her quite uninteresting situation now seemed to Nell of a piece with all the rest of her iniquities. She was proving herself to be in every way a deplorable wife: foolish, deceitful, spendthrift, and barren!

Fortunately, since her deep blush betrayed her, Letty had picked up the latest number of the *Ladies' Magazine*, and was contemptuously flicking over the pages, and commenting disparagingly on the fashions depicted in this valuable periodical, so that Nell had time in which to recover her countenance.

'Good heavens, I never saw anything so dowdy! . . . Slate-coloured twilled sarsnet, lined with white – *what* a figure to make of oneself! . . . Do these new Bishop-sleeves hit your fancy? I don't think them pretty at all, and as for this evening gown, with French braces over the bodice – !'

'I liked the picture of the pelisse, with the round cape,' Nell said, trying to infuse her voice with interest.

'For my part, I think it no more than tolerable. Unless one is a regular Long Meg, those capes make one appear positively *squat*! Hair-brown merino, too! Horridly drab!' Letty cast the *Ladies' Magazine* aside, and, after hesitating for a moment, said, in a voice whose carelessness was a little studied: 'By the by, I shall have to cry off going with you to Somerset House tomorrow, Nell. Selina has been telling me that my aunt is hipped because

I have not been to visit her quite lately, and is saying she had not thought I could show such a want of affection, or have my head turned so utterly that I don't any longer care to be with her. You know how it is with her! She is cast into raptures, or down in a minute. So, if you do not very particularly wish to look at pictures tomorrow – I daresay they will be a dead bore, too! – I think I should go to my aunt's, and make her comfortable again.'

Nell agreed to it, though she might, had she been less preoccupied, have wondered at Letty's sudden concern for Mrs Thorne's comfort. That Mrs Thorne might be piqued by a lack of proper observance could surprise no one who knew Letty, for without having the least ill-nature, or want of disposition to render attention where it was due, she had never been taught to consider the feelings of others, or to consult any convenience but her own. Having so easily won Nell's acquiescence, she took herself off to her own bedchamber, there to peruse for the third time the very disturbing letter she had received from Mr Allandale.

Nell waited in vain for Dysart to put in an appearance that afternoon. Her footman brought back no answer to her note, his lordship having gone out. No, his lordship's man had not been able to say when he expected him to return.

His lordship did not return to his rooms, in fact, until an advanced hour of the day; and since he was engaged to dine at Watier's, with a select company of his intimates, and afterwards to try his luck at that most exclusive of gaming-clubs, it was rather too much to expect him to keep the best dinner in town waiting while he danced attendance in Grosvenor Square. A fortunate bet had (as he phrased it) brought the dibs into tune again, and encouraged him to think that a long run of bad luck had come to an end. With a little ready to sport on the table there was no saying but what he might by the end of the evening be in a position to settle any number of damned dressmakers' bills, and through no more exertion than was required to cast, instead of the worst chances in the game, a few winning nicks. Inured by custom to all the stratagems known to creditors, he considered that Madame Lavalle's story of being about to put herself out of the way of collecting the monies due to her was a piece of gammon. In his experience, no creditor ever put himself out of the way of collecting money. Having pursued a precarious course for some years, he was not at all alarmed by duns, and thought that Nell was being more than commonly gooseish. However, he was fond of her, and if she was as sick with apprehension as her letter seemed to indicate he would not, on the following morning, grudge an hour spent in soothing her alarms. Moreover, the morning might find him out of ebb-water, and hosed and shod again, for it was nothing for a man enjoying a run of luck to win three or four thousand pounds in one night's sitting at the Great Go.

It might have been thought that a club where the minimum stake was double the sum fixed at any other gaming establishment, and the play was known to be tremendous, was scarcely the place for a young blood, living on an inadequate allowance and a grossly encumbered expectation. The Viscount's well-wishers shook their head over it, but they could scarcely blame him for playing there, since he had become a member of the club under the auspices of his own father. In general an indifferent parent, Lord Pevensey every now and then awoke to a sense of his responsibilities. Finding that his heir, after an adventurous period at Oxford, had established himself in London and was about to make his début in fashionable circles, he had felt that it behoved him to do what lay within his power to launch him into society. He introduced him to White's and to Watier's; franked him into the subscription-room at Tattersall's; pointed out to him certain individuals whose business in life it was to diddle the dupes; recommended him to let none but Weston make his coats; advised him to purchase his hats at Baxter's, and to have his boots made by Hoby; and warned him of the dangers of offering a carte blanche to too high-flying an Incognita. He was obliging enough to instruct his son in some of the signs by which he might recognize, amongst the muslin company, those prime articles who might be depended on to ease a protector of all his available blunt; and to counsel him strongly not to visit any but the highest class Academies. After that, and feeling that he had left nothing undone to ensure for the Viscount a prosperous career, he cast off his parental responsibilities, which had by that time begun to bore him very much, and left his son to his own devices.

Watier's, which was situated on the corner of Bolton Street and Piccadilly, in an unpretentious house which had once been a gaming establishment of quite a different order, was generally supposed to owe its existence to the Prince Regent. Watier had been one of his cooks, but the Prince, upon learning from some of his friends that a good dinner was not to be had at any of the London clubs, had conceived the benevolent notion of providing gentlemen of high ton with a dining-club not just in the common style, and had suggested to Watier that he was the very man to carry out this pleasing design. The idea took; in partnership with two other of the royal servants Mr Watier embarked on the venture, and prospered so well that within a very few years he was able to retire from active participation in the business of running the club. By that time what had begun as a dining-club, with excellent cooking, carefully chosen wines, and harmonic assemblies as its attractions, had blossomed into the most exclusive as well as the most ruinous of all London's gaming clubs. The dinners, under the surveillance of Mr Augustus Labourie, continued to be the best that could be had in town; it had a bank of ten thousand pounds; Mr Brummell was its perpetual president; and to be admitted to membership was the object of every aspirant to fashion. Play began at nine o'clock, and continued all night, the principal games being hazard, and macao: a form of vingt-un introduced into England by the emigrés from France, and still enjoying a considerable vogue.

The Viscount, after an evening devoted to faro, had not found that this alteration in his habits answered as well as he had hoped it might; and when he rose from a very convivial dinner he resisted all attempts to lure him into the macao-room. He would give the bones another chance, he said, for he had a strong presentiment that fortune was at last about to favour him. So, indeed, it seemed. Being set twenty pounds, and naming seven as the main, he threw eleven, nicking it, which promised well for the night's session. Even Mr Fancot, who had been trying to lose money to him for months and had begun to despair of achieving his ambition, felt hopeful.

From the circumstance of the Prince Regent's holding one of his bachelor parties at Carlton House that evening, the club was rather thin of company. Mr Hethersett, strolling in at midnight, found the macao-room deserted by all but a collection of persons who figured in his estimation either as prosy old stagers or tippies on the strut. He took a look-in at those intent on hazard, but here again the company failed to attract him, and he was just about to leave the premises when he was suddenly smitten by an idea. It was not a very welcome idea, nor did he look forward with the least degree of pleasure to the putting of it into action, but it was the best that had occurred to him during the course of a day largely devoted to wrestling with the problem of Lady Cardross's financial difficulties.

The more he considered this matter the greater had grown his uneasiness, for the mild *tendre* he felt for Nell did not lead him to place any very firm trust in her promise to keep away from usurers. A just man, he was obliged to own that if she dared not confess her debts to Cardross no other solution than to borrow upon interest suggested itself. In his opinion, she was magnifying Cardross's wrath rather absurdly. It was unlikely that he would hear the confession with complaisance, but he was not only a man very much in love; he was also a man of generous temper, and a good deal more than common sense. No one would be quicker to make allowance for youth and inexperience; and although there could be little doubt that he had forbidden Nell to keep her brother in funds Mr Hethersett had still less doubt that he would understand, and even sympathize with, the very natural feelings which had led her to disobey him. He would know how to put a stop to such practices, too; and that was something that ought to be done immediately, if Nell was not to founder at the last in a morass of debt and deception. Cardross would pardon her now with no loss of tenderness, but if he discovered in the future that she had been playing an undergame with him, perhaps for years, the very openness of his disposition would cause him to regard her with revulsion.

Mr Hethersett, gloomily pondering, had reached the conclusion that although it would be of some advantage if his cousin were to be put in possession of the facts by almost any agency, the only happy outcome to the affair would be for Nell herself to make the disclosure. But when he had urged her to do so she had recoiled from the suggestion, and had begged him in considerable agitation not to betray her to Cardross. The suspicion had crossed his mind that all might not be so well with that marriage as appeared on the surface. Thinking it over, it occurred to him that the couple were not as often in company together as might have been expected. It was not, of course, in good *ton* for a man to live in his wife's pocket; but the cynicism which had prompted the higher ranks of the previous generation to regard marriage as a means of advancement or convenience was going out of fashion. Amongst his father's contemporaries, Mr Hethersett knew of more than one man who could never be sure how many of his lady's offspring had been fathered by himself; while the number of middle-aged couples of the first stare who never willingly spent as much as half an hour together was past counting. But that sort of thing was going out of fashion. Lovematches were being indulged in by persons of consequence; and public signs of affection, instead of being thought intolerably bourgeois, were even smiled on. Mr Hethersett, whose fastidiousness had lately been offended by the sight of a newly-married pair seated side by side on a small sofa with their heads together at an evening party, was inclined to think that the pendulum was swinging too far, and he certainly did not expect Cardross to behave with such a want of breeding. At the same time, he did sometimes wonder that Nell, married to a man who had not only chosen her, for love, from amongst a dozen more eligible ladies, but was also possessed of a charm which made him generally fascinating to females, should so frequently appear in public either unescorted, or with some quite inferior gallant at her side. There was nothing to take exception to in that, of course; and never anything in her manner towards her admirers to encourage the most inveterate seekers after crim. cons to suspect her of having formed a guilty attachment. Mr Hethersett was pretty well persuaded that she had no eyes for any man but Cardross: he had seen them light up when his cousin had unexpectedly entered a room where she was sitting. No: he did not think that if anything had gone amiss with the marriage it arose from any lack of affection. He recollected having heard it said that in love-matches even more than marriages of convenience the first year was often one of tiffs and misunderstandings, and decided that so much profound cogitation was leading him to refine too much upon the couple's public conduct. But if there had been disagreements, Mr Hethersett, knowing just how formidable his cousin could be when he was angered, could readily understand the reluctance of his very young bride to confide her sins to him. It would be useless to press her to do so, he thought; but having reached this conclusion he found himself at a stand, for there was no one other than herself who could tell Cardross of the fix she was in without setting up his back.

But just as he was about to leave the hazard-room, Dysart, who had been too deeply concerned with the fall of the dice to notice his entrance, happened to look up, and to see him. He called a careless greeting, and on the instant Mr Hethersett was smitten by his idea.

If he could be persuaded to do it, Dysart was the one person who could tell Cardross, unexceptionably, even, perhaps, with advantage, the truth. Mr Hethersett had no doubt at all that Nell's debts had been incurred on his behalf, and very little that a frank confession made by him of the whole would win plenary absolution for Nell, and in all probability pecuniary assistance for himself. It would be an easy matter for him to convince Cardross that Nell had yielded only to his urgent entreaties; and

Cardross would be swift to recognize and to appreciate the courage that enabled him to perform so unpleasant a duty. Only, did he possess that courage? Mr Hethersett, joining the scattering of lookers-on gathered round the table, glanced speculatively at him, considering the matter. Physical courage he certainly possessed to a pronounced degree; but in spite of taking a perverse pride in being thought a Care-for-Nobody he had not as yet given anyone reason to suppose that he had any strength of moral character. Mr Hethersett, several years his senior and a man of a different kidney, was not one of his friends, and even less one of his admirers, but he did him the justice to acknowledge that although he was a resty young blade, decidedly loose in the haft, incorrigibly spendthrift, and ready at any moment to plunge into whatever extravagant folly was suggested to him by his impish fancy, he had never been known, even in his most reckless mood, to step over the line that lay between the venial peccadilloes of a wild youth and such questionable exploits as must bring his name into dishonour. He was both generous and goodnatured, and Mr Hethersett rather thought that he held his sister in considerable affection. He knew, too, that Cardross, better acquainted with him, and increasingly exasperated by his starts, by no means despaired of him. Without going to the length of forecasting for him a future distinguished by sobriety or solvency, he said that if a cornetcy could but be provided for him he would find an outlet for his restless energy, and might do tolerably well.

'He may be a scamp,' said Cardross, 'but there's no sham in him – nothing of the dry-boots! It would give me great pleasure to go sharply to work with him – but he's pluck to the backbone, and I own I like that.'

Mr Hethersett had a great respect for his cousin's judgement, and, remembering these words, he made up his mind to have at least a touch at Dysart. Since the task was not one he looked forward to with relish, he thought that the sooner it was accomplished the better it would be, and decided that unless Dysart arose from the table a loser he would broach the matter that very day. From the flush in the Viscount's cheeks, and the over-brightness of his eyes, he had at first glance supposed him to be a trifle foxed; but he soon realized that for once he had wronged him. The Viscount, whose exuberance could lead him to become top-heavy at almost any hour of the day, was by far too keen a gamester to join a gaming-table when in his altitudes. There was certainly a glass at his elbow, but the brandy it held sank hardly at all during the time Mr Hethersett stood watching the play, and from time to time making his bet on the odds monotonously declared by the groom-porter.

The table broke up at a comparatively early hour, even the Viscount agreeing, after a series of throw-outs, that the game had become languid and boring. He did not rise a loser, but his winnings were not large. However, when one of the company joked him about his uncertain luck, saying that he would be obliged to go back to faro after all, he replied cheerfully that only a muttonhead could have been blind to the signs of reviving fortune that night. 'Not a vowel of mine on the table!' he said.

'And upwards of forty guineas in your purse!' added Mr Fancot encouragingly. 'To my mind, that clinches it, Dy: stick to the bones!'

'Yes, I think I shall,' agreed Dysart. 'Dashed if I won't try my luck at this new house Jack was talking to me about! I remember my father's telling me once that he often found it answered to shift one's ground.'

Lord Pevensey's notorious unsuccess as a gamester notwithstanding, everyone, except Mr Hethersett, thought that the Viscount could hardly do better than follow his advice, only one slightly muddled gentleman demurring that no one should play at a hell who was not up to the sharps. But as he became hopelessly incoherent in his subsequent attempt to illustrate this remark by recounting the sad history of a flat who went from a nibble at a club to a dead hit at a hell, no one paid any heed to him.

The morning light was faintly illuminating the scene when the party dispersed on the steps of the club. Mr Hethersett, who knew that it might be days before he again found the opportunity to approach Dysart, considerably surprised him by suggesting that they should bear one another company on the way to their respective lodgings. 'Duke Street, isn't it?' he said. 'Take a look in at my place, and play off your dust! All on our way, and the night's young yet.'

Dysart looked at him, suspecting him of being slightly mellow. He showed no sign of it, but Dysart, perfectly well aware of his disapprobation, could think of no other reason to account for his sudden friendliness. Before he had had time to answer him, Mr Fancot, who lived in St James's Square, and had sent the porter out to procure a hackney, generously offered to take both him and Mr Hethersett up, and to set them down again at their lodgings.

'Very much obliged to you,' responded Mr Hethersett, a shade of annoyance in his face. 'Think I'll walk, however. Devilish stuffy in the club tonight: need a breath of air!' He met the Viscount's alert, speculative gaze, and said curtly: 'Got something to tell you!'

'Have you though?' said Dysart, considerably intrigued. 'I'll go along with you, then!'

They left the club together, but were overtaken almost immediately by a gregarious gentleman, who fell into step with them, saying chattily that since his destination was in King Street he would walk with them. His company was accepted cheerfully by Dysart, and by Mr Hethersett, who foresaw that he would be difficult to shake off, with resignation. It would be a hard task to avoid the necessity of including him in his invitation to Dysart, but he was determined to do it, however much it went against the grain with him to appear inhospitable.

He managed to perform this feat at the cost of standing patiently at the corner of Ryder Street and St James's, while the Viscount and Mr Wittering maintained for twenty minutes an argument which had been started before the party had crossed over to the south side of Piccadilly. It was pursued with considerable animation, and it afforded Mr Hethersett, mildly contributing his mite whenever he was granted the opportunity, with a novel view of the Viscount. The victory of Bonaparte at Lützen over General Wittgenstein, commanding the combined forces of Russia and Prussia, had not long been known in London, and was still being much discussed. Shaking his head over the disaster, Mr Wittering expressed the opinion that there was no doing anything against Boney, and never would be. Since this pessimism was shared by many, such remarks having been heard for years past at any social gathering, Mr Hethersett did not think it worth while to reply. It was otherwise with the Viscount. He was ready to agree that none of the foreign generals could have the smallest hope of defeating Boney, but he recommended Mr Wittering to wait and see how quickly Wellington would knock him into flinders. Mr Wittering said disparagingly that a victory or two in Spain made no odds; the Viscount instantly offered to bet a monkey that the English army would be over the Pyrenees before the year was out; and the argument rapidly became heated. Mr Wittering, no supporter of the Wellesleys, was unwise enough to say that Wellington's victories had been exaggerated; and within a very few minutes was not only being dragged relentlessly through the previous year's campaigns, but was being given a lesson in strategy into the bargain. To Mr Hethersett's surprise, the Viscount, whom he had always supposed to be perfectly feather-headed, not only appeared to be passionately interested in the subject, but had very obviously studied it with some thoroughness. Mr Wittering, on the retreat, acknowledged that Wellington was a good defensive general, but added that he was too cautious, and had no brilliance in attack.

'No brilliance in attack?' demanded the Viscount. '*After Salamanca?*'

'Well, I don't know about Salamanca,' said Mr Wittering unguardedly. 'All I say is –'

But the Viscount cut him short. Mr Hethersett, standing in patient boredom while armies manœuvred about him, and the Viscount drew invisible lines on the flagway with the point of his cane, reflected that it would henceforward be impossible for Mr Wittering to say (if there was any truth in him) that he didn't know about Salamanca. When Dysart, passing from the general to the particular, spoke of Le Marchant's charge, he did so with so much enthusiasm that Mr Hethersett was moved to say that he seemed to know as much about it as if he had taken part in it.

'By Jove, don't I wish I had!' Dysart said impulsively.

'Well,' said Mr Wittering, preparing to take his leave, 'what you ought to do, Dy, is to join! I shouldn't wonder at it if you got to be a general. You go and tell old Hook-nose what you want him to do! There's no saying but what it *might* make him break up from cantonments before the summer's over!'

With this Parthian shot, he went off down the street, leaving the Viscount to explain to Mr Hethersett that the lack of news from Wellington's headquarters undoubtedly presaged some brilliant move, probably in an unexpected direction. 'Everyone thinks he means to march on Madrid again, but you mark my words if he don't strike north! He's kept his plans mighty dark this time, but I've been talking to a cousin of mine. You know my cousin Lionel?' Mr Hethersett believed he had not that pleasure. 'Been serving on one of our frigates,' said the Viscount. 'Sent home a month ago, on sick-furlough. Plain as a pikestaff all those fellows have been warned to keep their mummers dubbed, but one thing he did let slip: we've been landing stores along the northern coast. You can say they're for that guerrilla-fellow, Longa, if you choose, but it don't look like it to me. No need to keep the thing so dark if that's all it is.'

Mr Hethersett did not avail himself of this permission, but said instead, glancing curiously up at his tall companion's profile: 'Why *don't* you join?'

'Oh, I don't know!' replied Dysart, with a return to his customary insouciance. 'I rather thought I should like to at one time, but I daresay I shouldn't. Anyway, my father won't hear of it.'

Mr Hethersett did not pursue the matter. He could only be

thankful that his question seemed to have cast a damper over the Viscount's desire to fight past battles again. They had by this time reached his lodging. He ushered his guest into the comfortable parlour he rented on the entrance floor of the house, begged him to take a chair, and produced from a large sideboard a bottle of smuggled French cognac. 'Eye-water?' he enquired. 'Mix you a Fuller's Earth, if you like it better; or I've got a pretty tolerable madeira here.'

The Viscount said he would take a drop of eye-water. He watched Mr Hethersett pour some of the cognac into two heavy glasses, and remarked with engaging frankness that he was damned if he knew what Mr Hethersett wanted with him. 'Thought at first you must be a bit on the go, but you don't seem to be,' he said.

Mr Hethersett handed him one of the glasses. 'Got something to tell you,' he replied briefly.

'You haven't had a tip for the Chester races, have you?' asked Dysart hopefully.

'No: nothing like that.' Mr Hethersett took a fortifying sip of brandy. 'Awkward sort of business. Been teasing me all day.'

'It sounds to me like a dashed havey-cavey business!' said Dysart, eyeing him in astonishment.

'No, it ain't exactly that, though I don't mind telling you I'd as lief not break it to you,' said Mr Hethersett, who was finding his self-imposed task even more difficult to accomplish than he had foreseen.

'Good God, you ain't going to tell me you've been set on to tell me my father's slipped his wind?' exclaimed Dysart, sitting up with a jerk.

'No, of course I haven't!' said Mr Hethersett, irritated. 'Is it likely that I'd be the man to break that sort of news to you?'

'No, but if it comes to that you ain't the man to invite me at half-past four in the morning either!' retorted Dysart. 'It's no use bamming me you've got a sudden fancy for my company, for I know dashed well you haven't.'

'Never said anything of the sort. No objection to your

company, mind, but it wasn't that I wanted. The thing is, it's a deuced delicate matter!'

'Well, I can't guess what the devil it can be, but there's no need to skirt around it!' said Dysart encouragingly. 'In fact, I'd lief you cut line: I can stand a knock or two!'

Mr Hethersett tossed off the rest of the brandy in his glass. 'Concerns your sister,' he said.

The Viscount stared at him. 'Concerns my sister?' he repeated. 'What the devil – ?'

'Didn't think you'd like it,' said Mr Hethersett, with a gloomy satisfaction in the accuracy of his prognostication. 'Don't like it myself. You know George Burnley?'

'*What?*' thundered the Viscount, setting his own glass down with such violence that he nearly broke it.

Mr Hethersett winced, and protested. 'No need to bellow at me!'

'No need to – What has that ginger-hackled court-card to do with my sister?' demanded the Viscount, a very dangerous light in his eyes.

'Hasn't anything to do with her,' replied Mr Hethersett, faintly surprised. 'What's more, though I don't say he ain't ginger-hackled, he ain't a court-card. Friend of mine. Dashed if I know why you should get into a miff just because you're asked if you're acquainted with him!'

'You said it concerned my sister Cardross!'

'Didn't say anything of the kind. At least, not about poor George. And if you weren't the biggest gudgeon on the town you'd know I wouldn't have said a word about it, if he *had* been concerned with her!' he added severely.

'Well, what has Burnley to do with it?' asked the Viscount, mollified, but impatient.

'Gave him a look-in this morning. He lives in Clarges Street.'

'Yes, I know he does, and if that's all you wanted to tell me –'

'Got a house opposite Jew King's,' said Mr Hethersett, contemplating his elegant snuff-box with rapt attention.

There was a momentary silence. 'Go on!' said Dysart grimly.

Mr Hethersett glanced up at him. 'Well, that's it,' he said apologetically. 'Saw Lady Cardross. Recognized her bonnet. Heavily veiled – no need to fear George knew her!'

'Are you saying she went into Jew King's place?'

'No. Meant to, but I stopped her.'

'I'm much obliged to you, then! Bird-witted little fool!' said Dysart savagely.

'Don't have to be obliged to me: got a great regard for her! Besides, related to Cardross, you know! Dashed well had to stop her. Seemed to be all in a pucker. Very anxious I shouldn't blab to Cardross. Well, stands to reason I shouldn't!'

'No, my God! What did she tell you?'

'Just said she wanted a temporary loan. Something she was devilish anxious Cardross shouldn't discover. Told her I wouldn't say a word to Giles if she promised to give up the notion of borrowing from a cent-per-cent. So she did, but I ain't easy. Made up my mind the best thing to do was to tell you, Dysart.'

The Viscount nodded, and got up. 'Much obliged to you!' he said again. 'I'll give her pepper for this. I told her that was no way to raise the recruits – damme, I forbade her to, now I come to think of it! Promised her I'd see all tidy. I might have done it, too, if she hadn't taken a distempered freak into her head. And why she should be cast into high fidgets only because she's a trifle scorched I'm damned if I know. Anyone would think Cardross was going to discover it tomorrow! Unless I miss my tip, there's no reason why he should ever know a thing about it, but it's no use expecting me to raise the wind in the twinkling of an eye. But that's women all over!'

He turned to pick up his great-coat. Mr Hethersett watched him shrug himself into it. He was strongly tempted to let him go, but although he was not very hopeful of being able to prevail upon him to approach Cardross, he felt that it behoved him to make the attempt.

'Been thinking about it all day,' he said. 'Seems to me Cardross ought to know of it.'

'Well, he ain't going to,' replied Dysart shortly.

'Wouldn't do if he were to get wind of it,' insisted Mr Hethersett. 'Wouldn't like it, if he found her ladyship had been hoaxing him.'

'Now, don't you start fretting and fuming!' begged Dysart. 'I told my sister I'd settle it, and so I will!'

'No business of mine, of course, but how?' asked Mr Hethersett.

'By hedge or by stile,' replied Dysart flippantly.

'It won't fadge. All to pieces yourself. Daresay you're thinking of a run of luck, but it ain't when one's run off one's legs that one gets the luck: more likely to be physicked! Ever noticed that it's pretty near always the best-breeched coves who win? Seems to me there's only one way you can help Lady Cardross.'

Dysart looked at him with a slight frown creasing his brow. 'Well, what is it?'

Mr Hethersett took snuff with deliberation. 'Best way out of the fix is for her to tell Cardross the whole. Tried to get her to do it, but she wouldn't hear of it. Seemed to be in the deuce of a quake. No use telling her not the slightest need. Got the notion fixed in her head. *I* can't tell him. The thing is for you to do it.'

'*I* tell Cardross my sister's swallowed a spider, and is trying to break shins with Jew King?' gasped the Viscount. 'Well, I thought you must be a trifle disguised when you asked me to come home with you, but I can see now that you're either ape-drunk, or touched in your upper works!'

'No, I ain't,' replied Mr Hethersett stolidly. 'I know it's a dashed difficult thing to do: in fact, it needs a devilish good bottom, but they say you've got that.'

'Bottom! A damned whiddling disposition is all I'd need, and I'll have you know that's something I've *not* got!' Dysart shot at him. 'Cry rope on my own sister? By God, if I hadn't been drinking your brandy, damned if I wouldn't tip you a settler, Hethersett!'

Mr Hethersett was thrown into disorder. It was not that he particularly feared the Viscount's fists, both of which were suggestively clenched; but that, in face of that fiery young man's quick wrath, the horrid suspicion assailed him that he had been doing him an injustice. This was a breach of *ton* the very thought of which made him turn pale. He hastened to make amends. 'Beg you won't give the brandy a thought!' he said. 'Not that I wish to sport a painted peeper, but shouldn't like you to feel yourself at a disadvantage. Boot might be on the other leg, too. What I mean is, not a thing I'm partial to, but I can mill my way out of a row.'

'I should like to know what the devil you mean by thinking I'm the sort of rum touch who –'

'Spoke under a misapprehension!' said Mr Hethersett. 'Took a notion into my head! Stupid thing to do!'

'What notion?' demanded the Viscount.

Mr Hethersett, much embarrassed, coughed. Upon the question's being repeated, with a good deal of emphasis, he said: 'Couldn't think why Lady Cardross should be afraid to tell my cousin she was in debt. Very well acquainted with Cardross, you know. Boys together. Ready to swear he'd give her anything she wanted. Might be in a tweak if she'd taken to gaming but can't be that. I mean, she don't know one card from another! Occurred to me that perhaps it was something Cardross wouldn't allow.' He once more studied the design on his snuff-box. 'Might even have forbidden it. Mind you, very understandable thing for her to do! Persuaded my cousin would think it so, too. Natural affection, I mean.'

'Are you saying you thought she was under the hatches because she'd lent her blunt to me?' demanded the Viscount.

'Only thing I could hit on!' pleaded Mr Hethersett. 'See I was mistaken, of course.'

The Viscount was just about to tell him extremely forcefully that so far from being responsible for Nell's difficulties he had had nothing whatsoever to do with them when he suddenly remembered his own obligation to her. It was true that this had not put her in debt at the time; but it was equally true that it had made it impossible for her to pay, later, for a Chantilly lace court dress. For a moment he felt abominably ill-used. She had assured him that she was flush in the pocket; and it was rather too bad of her subsequently to run into debt, instead of exercising a little economy.

He eyed Mr Hethersett smoulderingly. He had never liked the fellow above half, and to be unable to refute his ignoble suspicions made him seethe with rage. He wanted more than anything to plant him a facer, but since that also, under the circumstances, was impossible, he had to content himself with saying in a voice of ice: 'Accept my thanks for your kind offices! And rest assured that you have no need to tease yourself further in the matter! I wish you good-night!'

With these dignified words he picked up his hat and cane, bowed stiffly to his host, and departed. Mr Hethersett, closing the front door behind him, was left to mop his brow, and to wonder what would now be the outcome of the affair. Convinced of Dysart's innocence, he was still profoundly sceptical of his ability to rescue his sister from the River Tick.

Seven

Not very many hours later Nell was surprised and gratified to receive a visit from her brother. She had been hopeful that he would call that day, but since his habits were by no means matutinal she had had no expectation of seeing him until after noon. She and Letty had returned to Grosvenor Square at eleven o'clock, after spending more than an hour walking in Hyde Park, and the Viscount reached the house just as they were rising from the breakfast-table. He declined an offer of breakfast, saying that all he wanted was a word with his sister. From his tone Nell was not encouraged to hope that he had hit upon a solution to her problem; and the look on his face warned her that something had happened to put him out of humour. Letty, with deplorable want of tact, informed him that he looked to be as cross as a cat, and demanded to know the reason. He replied that he was not at all cross, but wished to be private with his sister. Since this could only be regarded as a heavy set-down, Letty instantly took umbrage, and a very spirited dialogue ensued, during the course of which several personalities of an uncomplimentary nature were exchanged. The Viscount emerged victorious from the engagement, taking unhandsome advantage of his greater years, and informing Letty, with all the air of a sexagenarian, that pertness was neither proper nor pleasing in chits of her age. Unable to think of anything crushing enough to say in reply, Letty flounced out of the room, slamming the door behind her.

'How could you, Dy?' exclaimed Nell reproachfully. 'I never

heard anything so uncivil! And if we are to talk of impropriety, you know it is quite improper for you to be scolding Letty! *You* are not her brother.'

'No, and thank God for it!' he returned. 'If she don't take care she'll grow into one of those hurly-burly women there's no bearing.'

'But, Dy, why are you so out of reason cross?'

'I'll tell you!' he said awfully. 'And don't put on any innocent airs, my girl, because you can't gammon me, or turn me up sweet by making sheep's eyes at me! You've been playing an undergame, and well you know it! What the devil did you mean by going off to Jew King after I'd told you I wouldn't have you dealing with a cent-per-cent?'

She looked a little conscience-stricken, but demanded hotly, 'Did Felix tell you that? I had not thought he could use me so shabbily!'

The Viscount was incensed with Mr Hethersett, but he informed his erring sister, in a few pithy words, that she might think herself much obliged to him. He then drew a picture of the horrifying fates that overtook persons so cork-brained as to walk into the clutches of usurers; moralized in a very edifying way on the evils of improvidence; and demanded from Nell a solemn promise that she would never again try to visit Jew King, or any other moneylender. 'And if you think jauntering to ruin is something to go into whoops over,' he added wrathfully, 'let me tell you that you much mistake the matter!'

'Oh, no, indeed I don't!' Nell said, trying to speak soberly. 'It – it was just that I c-can't help laughing when you talk like that about being improvident, and careless, and – and all the things you are yourself, Dy!' She saw that this remark had had anything but a softening effect, and said contritely: 'I will never do so again! Of course it would be very bad if I were to *continue* borrowing, but *that* I had not the least intention of doing. I should have paid the money back after quarter-day, I promise you!'

'I daresay! And have found yourself in the basket again before the cat had time to lick her ear! Don't I know it!' returned the

Viscount, with feeling. 'And why the devil you had to meddle, when you knew I had the business in hand, the lord alone knows!'

'Yes, but I thought perhaps it would be better if I did the thing myself,' said Nell frankly. 'In case you did anything dreadful!'

'Oh, you did, did you? Coming it too strong, Nell! What the deuce should I do, pray?'

'Well, to own the truth,' she confessed, 'I was afraid you might hold someone up!'

'Afraid I might hold someone up?' gasped Dysart. 'Well, upon my soul! A pretty notion you have of me, by God!'

'You held me up!' Nell pointed out. 'And if I hadn't recognized you you would have robbed me – you know you would!'

'If that doesn't beat all hollow!' ejaculated Dysart. 'When all I meant to do was to have sold your curst jewellery *for* you! If you think I should have kept a groat of the ready for myself, you're fair and far off, my girl!'

'No, but it *was* a desperate thing to do, Dy, and it quite cut up my peace. I can't but wonder what next you may do, which puts me in high fidgets. Because –'

'Gammon!' interrupted Dysart. 'Why, I wasn't even going to take Letty's trinkets! What's more, this is all humdudgeon! You wouldn't have cared a button for losing your jewels – now, would you?'

'N-no, but –'

'And you'd have been devilish thankful *not* to have recognized me, if I'd handed over the dibs to you next day. And it's my belief,' pursued the Viscount relentlessly, 'that you'd have taken good care not to have asked me how I'd come by them!'

Stricken, she said: 'Oh, Dy, I am sadly afraid that that is true! It is the most mortifying reflection, too!'

'Stuff!' said the Viscount contemptuously. 'Now, there's no need for you to sit there looking as blue as a razor, Nell! I don't mean to leave you in the lurch, I promise you. I've got one or two capital notions in my head, but I can't raise the wind all in a trice, so it ain't a bit of use fretting like a fly in a tar-box, and wanting to know every time you see me what I've been doing! Give me a week, and see if I don't have the business blocked at both ends!'

She regarded him in some apprehension. '*What* notions have you in your head, Dy?'

'Never you mind!' he replied crushingly. '*One* notion I've got is that the less you know about it the better!'

Her apprehension grew; she said: 'I won't tease you, but I think I would *rather* know!'

'Yes, I daresay, but you can't expect me to pull you out from under the hatches if you turn maggotty every time I hit on a scheme,' said the Viscount. 'And that's just what you would do, for you seem to me to be regularly betwattled!'

'I am very sorry!' she said humbly. 'I do try to take it with composure, but it is excessively hard to do so when one is in such affliction, Dy! Every time I hear the door-knocker I think it may perhaps be Lavalle, coming to demand her money from Cardross, and alarm suspends all my faculties!'

'Now, don't be such a goosecap, Nell!' recommended the Viscount, putting his arm round her shoulders and giving her a slight hug. 'She won't do that. Not for a week or two, at all events. You may depend upon it she knows, if you don't, that it must take you a little while to raise the ready. Ay, and unless she's as big a greenhead as you are yourself, which it stands to reason she can't be, she knows you will pay her,' he added shrewdly. 'All she meant to do was to frighten you into paying down the dust as soon as possible. She'll give you a week's grace at the least, and very likely longer. When does Cardross come back to town?'

'On Monday, I think. I am not perfectly sure, but he said that he would be away for a se'ennight.' Nell was silent for a moment, and then said, turning her face away: 'I quite dread his coming, and *that* is more lowering than all the rest!'

He was spared the necessity of answering her by Letty's coming back into the room at that moment. She was wearing her hat, and a light shawl, draped gracefully across her elbows; and she had come merely to take leave of Nell, and to inform her that she should send the carriage back immediately from her aunt's house, in case her sister should be needing the services of the coachman. She pointedly ignored the Viscount, but kissed Nell's cheek very affectionately, and told her not to dream of sending the carriage to fetch her away from Bryanston Square, since her aunt would undoubtedly provide for her safe return.

'All that finery just for an aunt?' said Dysart, critically surveying her. 'I must say, that's a deuced fetching bonnet!'

Becoming aware of his existence, Letty raised her brows as haughtily as she could, and said in freezing accents: 'You are too kind, sir!'

'Silly chit!' said Dysart indulgently.

Her eyes flashed, but Nell intervened hastily, before she could again cross swords with her incorrigible tormentor. 'You look charmingly,' she assured her, edging her towards the door. 'I will come and see you into the carriage. Will you be warm enough, do you think, with only that shawl?'

'No, I daresay I shan't be,' Letty replied candidly, 'but it is so dowdy to wear a pelisse!' She paused in the hall to draw on her gloves, and said in a brooding tone: 'I don't wish to distress you, Nell, but I think Dysart is the most odious, uncivil person I ever met!'

Nell laughed. 'Yes, indeed! I am sure you must. The thing is, you see, that because you are my sister he treats you as though you were his as well.'

'*My* brother has a great many faults, but he doesn't use me in *that* fashion!'

'No, for he is so much older than you. If you had had one of your own age you wouldn't be such a goose as to let Dy put you in a miff,' Nell said, smiling.

'I am excessively thankful that I have *not* one, and I assure you, Nell, I *feel* for you!'

'Thank you! Mine is a hard case indeed,' Nell said, her eyes brimful of amusement. 'You nonsensical creature! There, don't take me in aversion as well! Good-bye: you will say everything from me to your aunt that is proper, if you please. I fear she may hold me to blame for your neglect of her, but I hope she may give me credit for sparing you to her today.'

She spoke lightly, but she was very sensible of Mrs Thorne's claims on Letty. Cardross, believing that Letty's faults were to be laid at the poor lady's door, might wish to detach her from that household, but Nell could never bring herself to promote this object. Indeed, she had more than once suggested to Letty that she should pay her aunt a morning visit. It did not surprise her to learn that Mrs Thorne thought herself ill-used, for she too thought that Letty showed sadly little observance to one who had stood to her in place of her mother. She would, in fact, have been very much surprised had she known that so far from begging her niece to visit her that morning Mrs Thorne had not the smallest notion that she was to receive this treat, and had gone out with her daughter Fanny on a tour of the silk warehouses.

It was Miss Selina Thorne who awaited Letty; and as soon as she saw the carriage draw up outside the house she came running down from the drawing-room to greet her, which she did with every manifestation of surprise and delight, whispering, however, in a very dramatic way, as she kissed her: 'Have no fear! All is safe!'

She then said, for the benefit of the servant who had admitted Letty into the house: 'How glad I am I didn't go with Mama and Fanny! Come upstairs, love: I have a hundred things to tell you!'

She was a fine-looking girl, a little younger than Letty, but very much larger. Beside her exquisite cousin she appeared over-buxom, a little clumsy, but she did not resent this in the least. She was as goodnatured as her mother, liked to think that she had a great deal of sensibility, and had so romantic a disposition that she was inclined to think real life wretchedly flat, and to fancy that she would have found herself very much more at home in one of Mrs Radclyffe's famous novels. Having swept Letty up to the drawing-room, she shut the door, and said, lowering her voice conspiratorially: 'My sweetest life, such a morning as I have had! I thought we must be wholly undone, for Mama almost commanded me to go with her! I was obliged to prevaricate a little: I said that I had a headache, and so it passed off at last, though I was frightened almost out of my senses by her dawdling so much that it seemed she and Fanny would not be gone before you reached the house! How delightfully you look! Mr Allandale will be in raptures!'

'If he doesn't fail!' Letty said. 'I begged him most particularly to meet me here today, but it might not be possible, perhaps. If there is a press of business, you know, he might be detained all day at the Foreign Office. Only would he not have contrived to send me word?'

Miss Thorne was strongly of the opinion that the violence of Mr Allandale's feelings would outweigh all other considerations. She drew Letty to the window, to watch for his arrival, for she had formed the intention of running down to admit him into the house before he could advertize his presence to the servants by knocking on the door. 'For it would be *fatal* if Mama were to discover that he had been here! If her suspicions were aroused, depend upon it, she would instantly go to your brother, for she likes the connection as little as he does. She was talking about it only yesterday, calling it a shockingly bad match, and wondering that Mr Allandale should be so *encroaching*! I kept my eyes lowered, and my thoughts *locked* in my bosom, but you may guess how I *felt*, on hearing such words from one whom I have believed to be all sensibility! Oh, my dearest Letty, I vowed to myself that if any exertion on my part could save you from the misery of being sacrificed to pride and consequence it should not be lacking!'

Letty thanked her, but said in a more practical spirit that since it was very unlikely that Cardross would listen to her advice there was really nothing that she could do to achieve this noble end. Miss Thorne, who had embraced with enthusiasm the rôle of go-between so suddenly thrust upon her, was daunted. Upon reflection, she was obliged to own that the ways in which a young lady in her seventeenth year could aid a pair of star-crossed lovers were few. In the fastness of her bedchamber it was possible to weave agreeable romances in which she played a leading and often heroic rôle. 'Noblest of girls! We owe it all to you!' declared

Mr Allandale, having been joined in wedlock to Letty upon the eve of her marriage to a nobleman of dissolute habits (chosen for her by her brother), by a clergyman smuggled into the house at dead of night through the agency of her devoted cousin. In these romances, Selina overcame all difficulties by ignoring them, but in the cold light of day she was not so lost in dreams as to be unable to perceive that in a world depressingly humdrum certain insurmountable obstacles stood in the way of her ambition, not the least of·which was Mr Allandale himself. Though Letty would perceive in a flash the beauty of that marriage-scene in a dim room lit by a single branch of candles held up by her cousin, it would probably take a great deal of persuasion to induce the ardent lover to lend himself to such an improper proceeding. As for the indispensable cleric, not the wildest optimist could suppose that the Reverend William Tuxted, who happened to be the only clergyman with whom Selina was well acquainted, could be suborned by any means whatsoever into performing his part in this affair.

Melancholy though they were, these considerations had not the power to depress Selina for long. Letty's love affair might not attain the heights of drama, but it was still a very romantic story; and there was comfort in the thought that without her cousin's assistance she would have been hard put to it to have contrived a clandestine meeting with her suitor. Selina's good offices had not been required to promote her elder sisters' espousals; and nothing, in her opinion, could have been more insipid than Maria's marriage to Mr Thistleton unless it were Fanny's betrothal to Mr Humby: an event which had taken place on the previous evening. Neither lady had encountered the least opposition, each gentleman being possessed of a genteel fortune, and a situation in life which made him a very eligible suitor. Fanny's betrothal was perhaps more tolerable than Maria's, Mr Humby having been unknown to the Thornes until he began to dangle after her. This, it must be allowed, was less deplorable than Maria's marriage to John Thistleton, whom she had known all her life; but Miss Selina Thorne was going to think herself pretty hardly used if Fate did not provide for her a dashing lover of such hopeless ineligibility as must assure for her the most determined parental opposition, accompanied by persecution, which she would bear with the greatest heroism, and culminating in an elopement. Pending the appearance on the horizon of this gentleman, she was prepared to throw herself heart and soul into Letty's cause. She found no difficulty in crediting Cardross with all the attributes of a tyrant; and if Mr Allandale's propriety seemed at first to indicate that there was little hope of his engaging on any desperate action she soon decided that this was the expression not of an innate respectability, but of interesting reserve.

She was giving Letty an account of the degrading congratulations which had greeted the news of Fanny's betrothal when she caught sight of Mr Allandale approaching the house. She at once put her plan into execution, flying with such swift feet down the stairs that she reached the front door considerably in advance of him, and found herself inviting only the ambient air to come in and fear nothing. However, Mr Allandale soon arrived; and from having rehearsed (though involuntarily) her speech of welcome she was able to improve on it. 'I knew you would not fail!' she uttered. 'I will lead you to her immediately. Do not fear that you will be interrupted! Not a soul knows of your coming! Hush!'

Mr Allandale, already surprised to find the front door being held open by one of the daughters of the house, blinked at her. 'I beg your pardon?' he said.

'Do not speak so loud!' she admonished him. 'The servants must not suspect your presence.'

'But how is this?' he demanded. 'Is not Mrs Thorne at home?'

'No, no, you have nothing to fear!' she assured him. 'She and my sister are gone into the City. If they should return, you may depend on me to warn you of their approach!'

'I should not be here,' he said, looking vexed. 'It is quite improper for me to be visiting the house in Mrs Thorne's absence.'

She was somewhat daunted by this prosaic attitude, but she made a gallant recover. 'This is no time to be considering the proprieties!' she said earnestly. 'Your case is now desperate, and strive though she may to support her spirits under this crushing blow, my cousin is in the greatest affliction! You must come to her immediately!'

The thought of his Letty's agony made Mr Allandale turn pale; but still he hung back. 'I had not supposed that the assignation was of a clandestine nature,' he said. 'I cannot think it right! I assured Lord Cardross that such conduct was repugnant to me, and to be visiting your cousin behind his back, and in such a way, cannot be thought to be the part of a man of honour!'

None of Selina's romantic schemes had included a lover who had to be urged into the presence of his inamorata, and could she but have found a substitute to take his place in the drama she would then and there have thrust Mr Allandale out of the house. But since she knew of no substitute, and was rather doubtful of Letty's willingness to accept one, she was obliged to make the best of the unpromising material to her hand. 'I am persuaded you will not permit such trifling scruples to keep you from Letty's side!' she said. 'Only consider her agitation! She is quite worn down by despair, and I should not wonder at it if her mind were to become wholly overset!'

Mr Allandale was but human. The dreadful picture conjured up by these words took from him all power of resistance, and without further argument he followed Selina up the stairs.

'I have brought him to you, dearest!' announced Selina, throwing open the door into the drawing-room.

Mr Allandale's afflicted love, who had been trying the effect of a slightly different tilt to her fetching new hat, turned away from the looking-glass, and showed him a countenance glowing with health and beauty. 'Thank goodness you are come!' she said. 'I have been quite in a worry, thinking that perhaps you might not be able to. To be sure, I should have known that you would contrive it by some means or other. *Dear* Jeremy!'

Selina could have improved upon this speech, but she had no

fault to find with the way in which Letty cast herself upon Mr Allandale's broad bosom, and flung both arms about his neck. This was a spectacle which might well have impelled Cardross to have consigned his ward to a strict seminary for the young ladies of quality but it afforded Selina intense, if vicarious, gratification. Lingering for long enough to see that Mr Allandale, his propriety notwithstanding, was returning this artless embrace with a fervour that made Letty squeak, and protest that he was crushing her ribs, she withdrew reluctantly, to take up a post of vantage on the half-landing.

Mr Allandale, casting an uneasy glance over his shoulder, was relieved to see that she had left the room. Relaxing his hold on Letty, he said seriously: 'You know, my love, this is not at all the thing! That cousin of yours – !'

'Oh, do not mind her!' Letty said. 'She will never betray us!'

'No, but for a girl of her age – why, she is not yet out, I believe! It is very shocking.'

'Fiddle!' said Letty, drawing him to the sofa, and sitting down beside him there. 'We have so much to discuss, Jeremy! This dreadful news which you sent me! Six weeks! Oh, dearest, *pray* tell them you won't go!'

Mr Allandale was by this time pretty well acquainted with his love, but this ingenuous plea startled him. 'Not go! But, my sweetest life – !'

'It is too soon!' she urged. 'If you are to sail in six weeks' time, only consider the difficulties that confront us! I have the most melancholy persuasion that I can never, in so short a time, prevail upon Giles to consent to our marriage.'

He possessed himself of her hands, and sat holding them in a close grasp. 'Letty, you will never prevail upon him to do so,' he said heavily.

She stared at him, her eyes round in astonishment. '*Never?* Oh, how absurd! Of course I shall! It is merely that this comes so suddenly, before he has grown *accustomed* to the notion, you know!'

He shook his head. 'He will do everything that lies within his power to prevent our marriage. I have been as sure as a man may be of that ever since the day I called in Grosvenor Square. Nor can I blame him. From the worldly standpoint –'

'Well, I *can* blame him!' Letty interrupted, her eyes flashing, and her colour considerably heightened. 'If I do not care a fig for worldly considerations I am sure he need not! And if my happiness means so little to him I shall think myself perfectly justified in marrying you in despite of anything he may say!'

He got up, and began to pace about the room, kneading one fist into the palm of his other hand. 'If it were only possible! I do not know but what, with this appointment and my prospects, which I do not scruple to say are excellent, I too should think myself justified – But it is to no purpose! Circumstances have placed us wholly in his power.'

'What?' cried Letty. 'No such thing! I am not in *anyone's* power, and I hope you are not either!'

'You are under age,' he said gloomily.

'Oh, well, yes!' she conceded. 'But if we were to be married he would be obliged to countenance it, because he would dislike excessively to make a scandal.'

He was silent for a moment. When he did speak it was in a voice of deep mortification, and as though the words were forced from him. 'In his power – because I am unable to support a wife. *That* is what renders my position so hopeless!'

'I would *try* not to be expensive,' offered Letty.

He threw her a warm look, but said: 'You are used to enjoy the elegancies of life. As my affairs now stand I cannot even offer you its comforts. To remove you from the protection of your brother only to place you in a situation where you would be obliged to practise the most stringent economy would be the action of a scoundrel! I must not – indeed, I *will* not do it!'

'No, for I don't think I could practise *stringent* economies,' agreed Letty, considering the matter in an impartial spirit. 'But we could live upon my expectations, couldn't we?'

'*Borrow* on your expectations? No! – a thousand times no!' declared Mr Allandale, with every evidence of repulsion.

'Well, it is what Nell's brother does,' argued Letty. 'I don't know precisely how he contrives to do it, but if *he* can I am persuaded I could too, for mine are much better than his, you know.'

'Put it out of your mind!' begged Mr Allandale, blanching visibly at the appalling vision of debt conjured up by her artless suggestion. 'Nothing shall prevail upon me to take Lord Dysart for my model!'

'No, very true!' she replied, recalling his lordship's unamiable behaviour. 'I am sure he is the most ramshackle person – besides being excessively disagreeable! Only what is to be done, if you don't think my allowance sufficient? I have five hundred pounds a year, you know, and I need spend very little of it on my dresses, because I have a great many already.' She stopped, and her eyes brightened. 'Yes, and besides that I have suddenly had an excellent notion! I can very well buy *hundreds* of ells of silk, and muslin, and cambric – enough to set me up for *years*, I daresay – and tell all the mercers to send their bills to Giles!'

'Good God!' ejaculated Mr Allandale, pausing in his perambulations to gaze upon her with starting eyes.

She perceived that her suggestion had not found favour. 'You don't think that is what I should do? But consider, Jeremy! Even if he refused to pay – and I don't think that in the least likely – they couldn't dun me, because I should be in South America, and so all would be well.'

It spoke volumes for the depth of Mr Allandale's love that after the first stunned moment he recovered from an involuntary recoil, and realized that this ingenious solution to their difficulties arose not from depravity but from a vast and touching innocence. 'That,' he said gently, 'would be dishonest, my dearest.'

'Oh!' said Letty.

It was plain that she was unconvinced. Mr Allandale was aware that it behoved him to bring her to a more proper frame of mind, but he felt, at this present, unequal to the task, and merely said: 'Besides, if I were to marry you out of hand there can be little doubt that Cardross would discontinue your allowance.'

She was quite incredulous. 'No! He would not be so shabby!'

'He warned me that your fortune remains in his hands until you remain the age of twenty-five. How much of its income you may enjoy is at his discretion. I could not mistake his meaning.'

'Twenty-five?' gasped Letty. 'Oh, of all the *infamous* things! Why, I shall be quite old! I declare I am excessively thankful that I can't remember my papa, for if he served me such a trick as that he must have been a most detestable man! You would think he *meant* Giles to chouse me out of my inheritance!'

'No, there is no question of such a thing as that,' said Mr Allandale painstakingly. 'It is only –'

'Well, I don't mean to be worsted by either of them, and so I promise you!' Letty said briskly. 'Depend upon it, I shall hit upon a way of bringing Giles about. But I must own, love, that it makes it very hard if you must sail so soon. Jeremy, pray do not!'

'You don't understand,' he said. 'I could not refuse such an adventitious appointment! You would not have me do so.'

'Oh, no! Not refuse it, but could you not tell them that it is not perfectly convenient to you to go to Brazil so soon? Tell them that you will go in three months! I am persuaded we shall have come about by then.'

This drew a slight, melancholy smile from him, but he shook his head. 'No, indeed I could not do such a thing! Consider, dearest, how unwise in me it would be to offend my kind patron! I owe this advancement to Lord Roxwell, you know, and to give the least appearance of ingratitude –'

'I have been thinking about that,' she interrupted. 'I daresay he was anxious to oblige you, only the thing is that he has quite mistaken the matter.'

'How so?' he demanded, looking bewildered. 'He was good enough to say that he had my advancement very much to heart, certainly. I believe I told you that he held my father in great affection.'

'Yes, you did, and it has given me a very good notion. You

must go to him instantly, and tell him that you would prefer to be made ambassador!'

'Tell him that I would prefer to be made ambassador?' repeated Mr Allandale, in a bemused voice.

'In a very civil way, of course,' she urged, seeing that her notion was not having that success with him which it deserved. 'You could say that now you have had time to consider the matter you feel that it would be better if you became an ambassador; or – But you will know just how to say it in an exceptionable way!'

'No!' said Mr Allandale, with a good deal of conviction. 'I do not know! My dearest life, you don't know – you have not the least conception – ! It will be many years before I can hope to be so elevated. As for asking Lord Roxwell – Good God!'

'Should you prefer it if I were to ask him?' enquired Letty. 'I am not particularly acquainted with him, but Giles knows him, and we meet him for ever at parties.'

Mr Allandale sat down again beside her, and grasped both her hands. 'Letty, promise me you will do no such thing!' he begged. 'It is not to be thought of! Believe me, it would be quite disastrous!'

'Would it? Then I won't, of course, and I expect it will answer best for you to approach him, after all,' said Letty sunnily. 'The only thing is that perhaps you might not like to tell him that you would make an excellent ambassador, while for me there could be nothing easier.'

Much moved, Mr Allandale pressed several kisses on to her hands, ejaculating in a thickened voice: 'So sweet! so innocent! Alas, no, my love! it cannot be! I must be content with what is offered to me – and, indeed, it is more than ever I expected!'

'Well, I am sure it is not more than you deserve,' said Letty warmly. 'However, if you believe it would be useless to apply to Lord Roxwell, I won't tease you. We must think of some other scheme.'

She spoke with optimism, but Mr Allandale sighed. 'I wish we might! But my thoughts lead me only to the melancholy necessity of waiting. If your present allowance were secured to you I should be *tempted* indeed, though I trust I should find the strength to withstand the impulse of my heart. Situated as we both are – you dependent upon your brother's caprice, I with such charges upon my purse as I cannot but consider sacred – our case is hopeless. *One* of my sisters is on the point (I hope) of contracting an eligible marriage; my uncle has always promised to present Philip to a living, as soon as he shall have been inducted into Holy Orders, which, I trust, will be this year; but Edward is still at school, and Tom must be sent to join him in September. I could not reconcile it with my conscience, love, to leave my widowed parent to bear, without assistance, these heavy charges.'

Letty agreed to this, but without enthusiasm. She ventured to say: 'You don't feel that perhaps Tom would as lief not go to school?'

Mr Allandale dismissed unhesitatingly a tentative suggestion which would have won for Letty her future brother-in-law's esteem and approval.

'Perhaps your uncle would pay for Tom?'

He shook his head. 'I fear – You must know that he has himself a numerous progeny, and has, besides, been responsible for a part of Philip's education. Philip is his godson, but it would not be right to expect him to provide for Edward or Tom.'

A depressed silence fell. Mr Allandale broke it, saying with a praiseworthy attempt to speak cheerfully: 'We must be patient. It will be very hard, but we shall have the future to look forward to. Cardross has said that if we are of the same two minds when I return from Brazil he will not then withhold his consent. I believe him to be a man of his word; and that thought, that hope, will help us to bear with fortitude our separation. I do not consider him unfeeling, and I trust he will not forbid us to correspond with each other.'

'He may forbid it if he chooses, but I shall pay not the least heed!' declared Letty, her voice trembling. 'Only I am not a good hand at letter-writing, and I don't *wish* to correspond with you! I wish to be with you! Oh, don't talk of our being separated, Jeremy! I can't bear it, and I won't bear it! Cardross must and *shall* continue to pay my allowance!'

He could not feel hopeful; nor did he think well of a scheme for Cardross's subjection which depended for its success on her ability to bring herself to the brink of a decline by refusing to let a morsel of food pass her lips. Letty then broke into a passion of weeping, and by the time he had soothed and petted her into a calmer state he was obliged to tear himself from her side. His haggard countenance, when he emerged from the drawing-room, did much to restore Selina's good opinion of him; and when she found her cousin still hiccuping on convulsive sobs she felt that matters were progressing just as they should. It now only remained for Letty to suffer abominable persecution at the hands of her cruel guardian.

'Well, I had as lief not be persecuted, I thank you!' said Letty crossly. 'Besides, he *is* persecuting me!'

'Not enough!' declared Selina positively. 'Do you think, if you threatened to run away, that he would lock you in an attic at the top of the house?'

'No, of course he wouldn't, you silly creature!'

'They do in general,' argued Selina. 'If only you could prevail upon him to, you could throw a note down from the window to me, and I would instantly deliver it to Mr Allandale. He would feel himself bound to rescue you, and then you could fly to the border.'

'That only happens in novels,' said Letty scornfully. 'I should like to know how Jeremy could possibly rescue me! Why, he could not even enter the house without knocking on the door, and what, pray, would you have him say to the porter?'

'I suppose there isn't a secret way into the house?' asked Selina, rather daunted.

'Of course not! You only find them in castles!'

'No, that is not true at all!' Selina cried triumphantly. 'Because I have seen a secret way into quite a commonplace house! I don't precisely remember where it was, but I drove there when Mama took Fanny and me to stay with my uncle, in Somerset!'

'It's of no consequence *where* it is, because there are no secret doors in Grosvenor Square.'

'No,' agreed Selina regretfully. Another idea presented itself to her, but although her eyes brightened momentarily they clouded at the thought of Mr Allandale gaining an entrance to Cardross House in the disguise of a sweep.

'And now I come to think of it,' said Letty, clinching the matter, 'the attics are all as full as they can hold with servants. I wish you will stop talking nonsense, like a goose!'

'It is not nonsense! *You* did not think it so, when we read that capital story about the girl who was imprisoned by her uncle, so that she should consent to wed his son – the one that had a villainous aspect, and two savage mastiffs, and –'

'Books!' cried Letty impatiently. 'But this is *real*!'

Eight

*L*etty remained in Bryanston Square all day; and
great was Mrs Thorne's delight to find her there
when she returned from a protracted shopping
expedition with Fanny. Silks and muslins for the making of
Fanny's bride-clothes had been their object; and while the tour
of the warehouses had been in the nature of a preliminary
skirmish so much had been bought, and so many patterns had
been brought home to be studied at leisure that little else was
talked of during the remainder of Letty's visit. Mrs Thorne did
indeed notice that she was rather languid in spirit, but this
circumstance she ascribed to pique, and paid no heed to it,
beyond remarking, not very felicitously, that in spite of her three
years' seniority she had never expected Fanny to go off before
her cousin.

Nell, meanwhile, spent an unexceptionable if rather dull day,
and since such sedentary occupations as netting, tatting, knotting
a fringe, or trying to bring to a successful conclusion a game of
Patience, a new form of recreation which the Prince Regent had
been so condescending as to explain to her, left her mind rather
too much at liberty to fret over her troubles, she soon began to
be sorry she had refused even so mild a form of entertainment as
an invitation to practise French country-dances at a select
morning-ball. In general, there never seemed to be enough time
into which to fit her various engagements, for once the season
was in full swing every sort of amusement offered, from Venetian
breakfasts to Grand Balloon Ascensions; and in brief respites

from these she was either submitting to the ministrations of Mr Blake, who combined a laughable coxcombry with a positive genius for cutting ladies' hair; or sitting for her portrait to Mr Lawrence. Cardross had commissioned this full-length likeness of his lovely bride, and since Lawrence had become, since Hoppner's death, the most fashionable portrait painter in England it was going to cost him not a penny less than four hundred guineas. But Mr Blake had given her a smart new crop only a week earlier; Mr Lawrence's work on the portrait had had to be suspended until he had recovered from an indisposition. She did not care to visit the Royal Academy's exhibition at Somerset House alone, for that would not only be dull work, but might render her an easy prey to some other unaccompanied lady: probably Miss Berry, whom one ought to admire, but could not contrive to like. London was overfull of elderly ladies who were Mama's dear friends, and Somerset House was just the place where one might be sure of meeting them. So after knotting a few inches of fringe, reading three pages of *Corinne*, rather wistfully watching some children playing at battledore and shuttlecock in the Square-garden, and trying to make up her mind to write an overdue letter to Miss Wilby, she decided that the day was too fine for such sedentary pursuits, and determined, in default of livelier amusements, to drive to Chelsea, on a visit to Tubbs' Nursery Garden, in the King's Road, and to select there such plants as would transform the ballroom at Cardross House into a fairyland of flowers.

This lavish scheme had its birth in Letty's desire to hang the ballroom with pink calico. She had seen this novel form of decoration at one of the first balls of the season, and it had instantly hit her fancy. Hundreds of ells of calico had been gathered to form the likeness of a huge tent: everyone had exclaimed at it, and had complimented the hostess on such a charming notion; and Letty, convinced that it would shortly become all the crack, had been alternately hectoring and cajoling Cardross for weeks past to have his own ballroom turned into a pink tent for the grand dress-party to be held there at the end of the month. Unfortunately Cardross had not admired the effect of pink calico; and upon Letty's agreeing that to be sure calico was shabby, and it would be far more elegant (besides going one better than Lady Weldon) to use silk, he had expressed himself so unequivocally on the subject as to confirm her in her belief that his taste was as old-fashioned as his disposition was mean. She had not scrupled to tell him so, and his way of receiving this terrible indictment did him no honour at all. 'I know it,' he had said sympathetically. 'I assure you, Letty, it astonishes even *me* that I could be such a hog-grubber as to grudge the expenditure of I daresay not much above a few hundred pounds on the suitable decoration of the ballroom to set off your charms.' He had cast a laughing glance towards Nell, and had added provocatively: 'Now, had you asked me for *blue* hangings – !'

Letty had been perfectly willing to compound for blue, but had met with no support from Nell. Nell, quite as desirous as she to cut a dash, had no notion (she thanked Letty) of imitating Lady Weldon, or any other fashionable hostess. If Cardross approved, she would make the ton exclaim much more loudly by creating a flower-garden in her ballroom. It had often astonished her that hostesses made such meagre use of flowers: they should be made to gnash their teeth with envy at the result to be achieved by taste, ingenuity, and the services of a first-rate florist. Cardross promptly gave her carte blanche; and Letty, having rather reluctantly listened to her scheme, was obliged to own that it would be at once pretty, and quite out of the ordinary way.

So off Nell went to Chelsea. No sooner did Mr Tubbs, greeting her ladyship with flattering deference, grasp the purpose of her visit than he became an enthusiastic supporter of it, summoning up his chief minions, and rapidly devising several alternative plans for the tasteful decoration of her ballroom. They differed in many respects, but in one they were alike: they were all extremely costly. But since Cardross had said Nell might do anything she chose, provided she didn't drape his ballroom in pink calico, this consideration was of no moment.

In choosing the flowers and the ferns, and discussing with Mr Tubbs the rival merits of garlands, hanging-baskets, and a trellis-work set against the walls and covered with greenery, out of which flowers could be made to appear as if growing, she passed an agreeable hour, her cares for the time being forgotten. She parted from Mr Tubbs on the most cordial terms, that excellent horticulturist begging her to do him the honour of accepting a bouquet composed of all the choice blooms she had particularly admired during her tour of the garden. It was such a large bouquet that it had to be laid on the floor of the barouche, but Mr Tubbs did not grudge a single bloom in it: it was not every day of the week that he received so magnificent an order as Lady Cardross had given him. He assured her ladyship that she might repose the fullest confidence in his ability to achieve a result that would hold her guests spellbound with admiration; and no sooner had her barouche driven away than he took his foreman apart, and exhorted him to put forth his best endeavours. 'For mark my words, Andy,' he said earnestly, 'if this does not set a fashion! I shouldn't wonder at it if we were soon turning orders away!'

Nell was rather hopeful, too, that she might be starting a new mode. There had been a number of parties at Cardross House since her marriage, but this would be the first grand ball she had held, and she wanted people to say something more of it than that it had been a dreadful squeeze.

Letty had not returned from Bryanston Square when she reached home again, so after putting off her hat and her gloves she occupied herself with the arrangement of her bouquet in several bowls and vases. She was trying the effect of one of these on a pie-crust table in a corner of the drawing-room when a voice said behind her: 'Charming!'

It was fortunate that she was not holding the bowl, for she must certainly have dropped it, so convulsive was the start she gave. She gasped sharply, and turned, to find that Cardross had come quietly into the room, and was standing by the door, quizzically regarding her. He had shed his driving-coat, but he had plainly but that instant arrived in town, for he was still wearing a country habit of frock-coat, buckskins, and top-boots.

The shock of hearing his voice when she had believed him to be a hundred miles away was severe, and her first sensation was of consternation. She made a quick recovery, but not before he had seen the fright in her eyes. The quizzical look faded, to be replaced by one of searching enquiry. She exclaimed a little faintly: 'Cardross! Oh, how much you startled me!'

'I appear, rather, to have dismayed you,' he said, making no movement to approach her, but continuing to watch her face with hard, narrowed eyes.

'No, no! How can you say so?' she protested, with a nervous laugh, and reddening cheeks. 'I am so glad – I did not expect to see you until Monday, and hearing you speak suddenly – made me jump out of my skin!'

'I beg your pardon,' he replied, unsmilingly. 'I should, of course, have warned you of my arrival. You must try to forgive my want of tact.'

'Giles, how absurd!' she said, holding out her hand.

He strolled forward, and took it, bowing formally, and just touching it with his lips. He released it immediately, saying: 'Yes, in the manner of the farce we saw at Covent Garden, and thought so stupid. I shall stop short of searching behind the curtains and under the furniture for the hidden lover.'

The chilly salute he had bestowed on her hand had both alarmed and distressed her, but this speech fell so wide of the mark that she laughed. 'In the expectation of finding your cousin Felix? It is a *most* improper notion, but how very funny it would be to discover him in such a situation!'

He smiled slightly, and some of the suspicion left his eyes. He still kept them on her face, and she found it hard to meet them. 'What is it, Nell?' he asked, after a moment.

'But indeed it is nothing! I – I don't understand what you can mean! Are you offended with me for having jumped so? But that was quite your own fault, you know!'

He did not answer for a moment, and when he did at last speak it was in a colourless voice. 'As you say. Which of your many admirers bestowed that handsome bouquet on you? You have arranged it delightfully.'

'None of them! At least, I don't flatter myself that he admires me precisely!' she replied, thankful for the change of subject. 'I had it – but this is only a part of it! – from Tubbs, the nurseryman! I have been there today, to order the flowers for our dress-ball, and at parting he begged me to accept the most enormous bouquet imaginable!'

'Did he indeed? Then it seems safe to assume that you've lodged a very handsome order with him.'

She looked a little anxious. 'Well, yes,' she admitted. 'But it will be the prettiest ball of the season, and – and you *did* tell me I might spend as much as I wished on it!'

'Certainly. I wasn't criticizing you, my love.'

She felt impelled to justify herself, for in spite of this assurance there was an alarming want of cordiality in his voice. 'It is the first ball we have held here – the first *grand* ball,' she reminded him apologetically. 'You wouldn't wish it to be talked of as just another jam – nothing out of the common style!'

'My dear Nell, you have no need to excuse yourself! By all means let it be of the first stare. Shall we give our guests pink champagne?'

'Are you joking me?' she asked cautiously. 'It *sounds* excessively elegant, but I think I never heard of it before.'

'Oh, no, I'm not joking you! I assure you it will lend a great *cachet* to the party.'

'More than pink calico?' she ventured, a gleam of fun in the glance she cast at him.

That did draw a laugh from him. 'Yes – or even pink silk! Where is Letty, by the by?'

'She has gone to visit Mrs Thorne. She will be back directly, I daresay.' She fancied there was a frown in his eyes, and added: 'You don't like that, but indeed, Giles, it would not be right to encourage her to neglect Mrs Thorne.'

'Very true. Tell me, Nell, what does my aunt Chudleigh mean by writing to inform me that Letty's conduct at that masquerade you took her to set everyone in a bustle?'

'If your aunt Chudleigh would be a little less busy we should go on very well!' cried Nell, flushing with wrath. 'She is never happy but when she is making mischief! Pray, has she any animadversions to pass on me?'

'No, she exonerates you from all blame.'

'Obliging of her! I hope with all my heart that you will give her a sharp set-down, Cardross!'

'I probably shall. What, in fact, did Letty do to bring this scold down upon me?'

'Nothing at all! That is to say, nothing to make a piece of work about! You know how it is with her, when she is in high gig! She allows her vivacity to carry her beyond the line of what is pleasing, but she is so young that it is only people like Lady Chudleigh who don't know that it is all done in innocence.'

'And want of upbringing,' he said, with a sigh. 'I can blame no one but myself for that. You didn't, in sober truth, let her wear an improper gown, did you?'

'No – oh, no!' she replied guiltily. 'Not – not *improper* precisely! I own it was not just the thing for a girl of her age, but – well, she won't wear it again, so pray don't mention it to her, Cardross!'

'If it made her look like a class of female which my aunt prefers not to particularize, she most assuredly won't wear it again!' he returned.

'Nothing of the sort! Lady Chudleigh knows very well that such gowns are worn by women of the first consequence. Do, pray, let the matter rest! To scold Letty will only set up her back – and it was my fault, after all.'

'I don't mean to scold either of you, but I must own, Nell, that I could wish you had put your foot down,' he said, looking displeased.

'Perhaps I should have done so,' she replied, in a mortified tone. 'I am very sorry!'

'Yes – well, never mind! I don't doubt that it is very hard for you to check Letty's starts. And while we are speaking of the masquerade, what, in heaven's name, is this extraordinary story I have been hearing about Dysart's holding you up on the road to Chiswick?'

'Oh, good God, Lady Chudleigh knows nothing of *that*, surely?' she exclaimed, rather aghast.

'No, I had it from your coachman. According to him, your carriage was stopped by Dysart and two companions, all of them disguised as highwaymen. It seems quite incredible, even in Dysart, but I can hardly suppose that Jeffrey would entertain me with a Canterbury story. Do you mind explaining the matter to me?'

She had forgotten that her servants would be very likely to tell him of Dysart's strange exploit, and for an ignoble moment wished that she had had the forethought to have bought their silence. She was instantly ashamed of herself, and said, her colour rising: 'Oh, it was one of Dy's mad-brained hoaxes, and a great deal too bad of him! I must own that I hoped it wouldn't come to your ears.'

'That, Nell, is patent!' he said.

'Yes – I mean, I knew you would be vexed! There was no harm in it – it all arose out of a – a stupid wager – but of course it was a most improper thing to do, and so I told him.'

'All arose out of a *wager*?' he repeated incredulously. 'With which of his associates did Dysart see fit to make you the subject of a wager?'

'N-not with any of them!' she stammered, frightened by the look on his face.

'Then what the devil do you mean?' he demanded.

'It was with me!' she said, improvising desperately. 'We – we were talking about masquerades, and I said it was nonsense to suppose that one wouldn't recognize somebody one knew well just because they wore a mask. Dy – Dy said that he would prove me wrong, and – and that was how it was! Only I did recognize him, so I won the wager.'

'Gratifying! Did you also recognize his companions?'

'No – that is, it was only Mr Fancot!' she said imploringly. 'Oh, and Joe, of course – Dy's groom! But he doesn't signify, because he has always been with us, ever since I can remember! *Pray*, Cardross, don't be vexed with Dy!'

'Vexed with him! I am very much more than vexed with him! To be giving you such a fright for the sake of a prank I should find it hard to pardon in a schoolboy goes beyond anything of which I believed him to be capable!' he said wrathfully.

'I wasn't frightened!' she assured him. 'Only a very little, at all events!'

'Oh?' he said grimly. 'What, then, made you scream?'

Her eyes sparkled with indignation. 'I did not scream! I would *scorn* to do anything so paltry! It was Letty who screamed.'

'How chicken-hearted of her, to be sure!' he said sardonically.

'Well, that's what I thought,' she said candidly.

'Are you quite blinded by your doting fondness for Dysart?' he demanded. 'He is fortunate to possess a sister who can find excuses for his every folly, his every extravagance, and for such *larks* as this latest exploit! I am aware – I have for long been aware! – that he holds a place in your affections that is second to none, but take care what you are about! Encourage him to think he may turn to you in any extremity! smile upon kick-ups unworthy of a freshman! You will not smile when the *high spirits* you now regard with such indulgence carry him beyond the line of what even his cronies will pardon!'

She shrank a little from the harshness in his voice, but she was quick to recognize the note of jealousy in it. She heard it with a leap of the heart, and it took from his words all power of wounding. Instead of flying to Dysart's defence, she said merely: 'Indeed I didn't smile upon such a prank! It was very bad – quite unbecoming! But it is unjust in you, Cardross, to say that his wildness will lead him into doing anything *wicked*! You dislike him very much, but that is going too far!'

'No, I don't dislike him,' he replied, in a more moderate tone.

'On the contrary! I like him well enough to wish to be of real service to him. You think me unjust, but you may believe that I know what I am saying when I tell you that his present way of life is ruinous.'

She said, in swift alarm: 'Oh, pray, pray don't thrust him into the army!'

'I have no power to thrust him into the army. I own I have offered to buy him a commission, and I have not the smallest doubt that there is nothing I might do for him which he would like better, or which would be of more benefit to him. If the only bar in the way of his accepting it is your father's dislike of the project I will engage to make all right in *that* quarter.'

'No, it is not that. I should not say such a thing, but I am afraid Dy doesn't care much for what poor Papa wishes. But Mama made him promise he wouldn't do it, and however ramshackle you may think him Dy doesn't break his promises!'

'If that is how the case stands,' he said, 'I recommend you, my dear, to use your best endeavours to persuade your mother to release him from a promise which I don't scruple to tell you should never have been extracted from him!'

'I could not! Oh, she would sink under the very thought of his exposing himself to all the dangers of war!' She hesitated and then said, with a little difficulty: 'Mama has had so many trials to bear. Poor Papa, you know . . .'

'Yes, I know,' he replied. 'For that very reason I am persuaded that if she was aware of the truth she would think the hazards of war less perilous than those of the metropolis. Living, as she now must, so far from London, I fancy she cannot know how closely Dysart is following an example she must dread.'

She looked a little frightened, but said: 'I know he is sadly wild, and – and expensive, but surely – no worse than that?'

'Well, that is bad enough,' he replied. He saw that she was inclined to question him more closely, but he was already vexed that he had allowed his irritation to betray him into saying so much. Before she could speak again he had turned the subject;

and very soon after he left her, saying that he must change his habit. Whatever bitter feelings he might cherish he could not shock her by disclosing the full sum of Dysart's folly. She probably did not even know of that little narrow pink room behind the stage at the Opera House, where the dancers practised their steps in front of long pier-glasses, and any buck in search of amatory adventures could have his pick of the west-end comets. Dysart was a familiar figure in that saloon, and so was his latest chère amie. Nell had certainly seen him driving with this article of virtue – a dasher of the first water, too! reflected Cardross – but what she had made of her one couldn't tell. She had asked no questions, so perhaps she had guessed. But she didn't guess that Dysart frequently sallied forth with the Peep o' Day boys, starting the evening with a rump and dozen at Long's, and gravitating thence to a less respectable world of which she was wholly ignorant. It diverted the wilder blades to mix on equal terms with the roughest elements of society; buttoning up, they would plunge into the back-slums of Tothill Fields, rubbing shoulders (and often falling into a mill) with all-sorts, from honest coal-porters to petermen. They saw badger-baiting in the reeking squalor of Charles's, where a man must be a very fly-cove to avoid having his pockets picked; they rubbed shoulders with bing-boys and their mollishers in the sluiceries; became half-sprung on blue ruin in these gin shops, and wandering eastward, deepcut at the Field of Blood. The night music of the watchmen's rattles marked their progress through the sleeping town; often a drowsing Charley was overturned in his box, and sent sprawling into the kennel; many were the respectable householders brought down to their doors on false alarms of fire, or thieves. Sometimes these larks ended in a roundhouse, with its sequel of Bow Street, a false name, and a fine; sometimes a blade, fortunate enough to be numbered amongst Mother Butler's favourites, sought refuge at the Finish, and spent what was left of the night snoring on a settle beside the dying embers of the fire in the tap. No, Nell knew nothing of such exploits as these, and no prompting of jealousy was going to seduce her husband into

143

enlightening her. The shock would be severe, and her innocence as much as her affection for Dysart would lead her to regard his excesses in a far more serious light than that in which they appeared to her husband. He was vexed by them, and he viewed their continuance with grim foreboding; but he believed that they sprang from the boredom of idleness rather than from any ingrained depravity. What disturbed him far more was the suspicion he had formed that Dysart, in his restless quest for novelty and excitement, had lately become enrolled as a member of the Beggars' Club.

This decidedly unsavoury institution had its locality in a cellar at the back of Broad Street, and was generally presided over by the Earl of Barrymore, with Colonel George Hanger as his Vice. It was patronized by all the raff of town, and such persons as those who thought it amusing to eat their suppers out of holes carved in the long table, and with knives and forks that were chained to their places. There was no particular harm in this, but the evils that could accrue from a young man's getting into Barrymore's set were grave enough, Cardross knew, to alarm even so casual a parent as Lord Pevensey. Old Georgie Hanger, for all his eccentricities, exercised little influence over the younger men. He was over sixty; and after a varied career, which began at Eton, rose to a commission in the 1st Footguards, reached its nadir in the King's Bench prison, and included an excursion into trade (when, upon his discharge from the Abbot's Priory, he set up as a coal-merchant), he had contrived to get himself restored to full-pay, and was now living rather more moderately. His age and his oddities caused him to be tolerated by society, but his manners were too coarse to render him an attractive figure; and, to do him justice, he had not the smallest desire either to figure as the leader of a set or to corrupt the morals of its members.

The noble Earl of Barrymore was a bird of another feather. Neither his rank nor his achievements on the box or in the saddle sufficed to make him acceptable to the ton. He had been one of the founders of the Whip Club; he had introduced the fashionable practice of driving with a small Tiger perched up beside him; his colours were to be seen on any race-course; but society, with the exception of the Prince Regent, who too often appeared to have a strong predilection for disreputable company, was obstinate in avoiding him. An Irish peer, he had inherited the title from his brother, who had earned for himself the unenviable nickname of Hellgate. This circumstance, coupled with the possession of a club-foot, naturally led to his being dubbed Cripplegate. A younger brother, in orders, was known as Newgate, from having (according to his boast) been imprisoned in every gaol in the country; and an excessively foul-mouthed sister became, inevitably, Billingsgate. Cripplegate, with his fame as a Nonesuch, his cool daring in the saddle, and his dark reputation, constituted a real danger to such reckless young bloods as Dysart; and if the hint dropped in Cardross's ear held so much as a grain of truth neither Lady Pevensey's maternal fears nor Nell's distress at being separated from her brother was going to prevent his putting a summary end to that troublesome young man's career as a town buck of the first cut. The demon of jealousy apart, he liked Dysart well enough to make a push to save him from the consequences of his own folly; for Nell's sake he was prepared even to undertake the disagreeable task of disclosing to Lord Pevensey the exact nature of the course his heir was treading. He could only hope that the news would not prove fatal to his lordship's shattered constitution, but he thought it extremely probable that a second stroke might result from it, and could only trust that it would not prove necessary for him to approach his father-in-law. Lord Pevensey might shrug up his shoulders at a tale of fashionable dissipations, but in his day not the most dissolute rake amongst the Upper Ten Thousand sought diversion in the back-slums. Unless the stroke he had already suffered had rendered him very much more incapable than Cardross had reason to suppose, he could be trusted to overbear his lady's opposition the instant he received the intelligence that Dysart was not only associating on the friendliest terms with scamps, pads, and drivers, but was also in a fair way to becoming a boon companion of one whom his lordship had been amongst the first to ostracize.

Nine

*C*ardross feared that his unguarded words would lead
Nell to enquire more particularly into her brother's
mode of life, but in point of fact she was less disturbed
by them than by the possible consequences of the story she had
fabricated to account for his holding up her carriage. She had
certainly been startled by what he had said, but a few minutes'
reflection led her to think that the jealousy she had so clearly
perceived in him had led him to exaggerate. That he had so
abruptly turned the subject seemed to her to lend colour to this
belief; and since her own troubles were looming large she
thought very little more about the matter.

Her encounter with him had quite overset her; it was a
struggle to support her spirits, for never before had he treated her
with such cool reserve of manner, or looked at her with such
hard, searching eyes. The fault was her own: that frightening
expression had not been in his face when first he had entered the
room. She had been terrified that he might demand an
explanation of the dismay she had betrayed, but when he had
refrained, as though in disdain or indifference, she had found his
cold forbearance more alarming than any display of wrath. She
felt herself to have been set at a distance, and although his voice
had been kinder when he had asked her what was the matter she
had not been conscious of any impulse to confide in him. In her
view no moment could have been more unpropitious for
confession. Rendered suspicious by her reception of him, vexed
with her for not having taken better care of his sister, and his

temper dangerously exasperated by Dysart's conduct, the disclosure that his wife was again badly in debt, and had been putting forth her best endeavours to deceive him, could only be expected to act on him like a match to gunpowder. Nor did it seem at all probable that the knowledge of Dysart's motive in holding her up would lead him to regard him with more lenient eyes. In fact, far otherwise, she thought: for if she had been shocked by the scheme it seemed safe to suppose that Cardross would utterly condemn it. Once the truth was out Dysart would be more than likely to tell him that he had had three hundred pounds from her, and then, surely, the miserable tangle would be past unravelling.

This melancholy conviction at once put her in mind of the immediate necessity of conveying a warning to Dysart. Cardross plainly meant to call him to book, and it would never do for him to tell a different story from hers. She sat down to dash off a note to him then and there, but she was obliged to pause several times to wipe the blinding tears from her eyes. Try as she would to compose herself, they would keep welling up, because it was so very dreadful to be plotting with Dysart against Cardross.

She had just given the sealed billet to her footman when Letty came in, and at once it occurred to her that she too must be warned to say, if Cardross should question her, that Dysart had held them up for a wager. She could feel herself blushing as she told Letty what she had said to Cardross, but Letty was not at all shocked. 'Oh, certainly!' she said, taking it as a matter of course. Nell hardly knew whether to be glad or sorry.

'So Giles is come home!' Letty remarked, slowly pulling off her gloves. 'Well! I am positively *glad* of it!'

'Oh, yes!' Nell murmured. 'Of course! I mean –'

'Because,' pursued Letty, a martial light in her eye, 'my affairs have now reached a Crisis!'

'Good God!' exclaimed Nell, quite alarmed. 'What in the world, love – ?'

'In six weeks – in *less* than six weeks! – Jeremy sails for South America!' announced Letty, in a voice of doom.

'Oh, dear!' said Nell. 'As soon as that! I am so very sorry!'

'Well, you need not be,' said Letty. 'Though I own I had rather not be married in such a scrambling way. However, I don't mean to repine, for that is a small thing, after all.'

Nell regarded her uneasily. 'But, dearest, there is no question – You cannot suppose that Cardross will permit it!'

'And neither he nor you,' flashed Letty, 'can suppose that *I* will permit my adored Jeremy to leave England without me! Unless he has a heart of stone, Giles cannot now refuse his consent.'

Nell was unable to perceive why the imminent departure of Mr Allandale should be supposed to melt Cardross's heart, and ventured to say as much. It was ill-received. Letty broke into an impassioned diatribe. This was not very coherent, but one plain fact emerged from it: Cardross was to be given a last chance to rehabilitate his character.

As far as Nell was concerned, this supplied all that was needed to set the crown on a singularly disastrous day. She begged Letty with great earnestness not to attempt to argue her case that evening; and when Letty, with a toss of her head, declared that *she* was not afraid of Cardross, warned her that his back had already been set up by Lady Chudleigh's letter.

A thoughtful silence descended upon Letty. After a few moments she said, with a nonchalance that would have deceived no one: 'It is not of the least consequence. I shan't regard it if he does give me one of his scolds. Is he very angry, Nell?'

'No, but – oh, a good deal displeased, I fear! I believe he won't speak of it to you, if only you won't vex him!'

'Well, I won't say anything to him tonight,' Letty decided. 'What a fortunate thing it is that we are going to the play! I had meant to ask you if we need, because I haven't any inclination for it. Still, it won't do to fall into a lethargy, even though Cardross is determined to break my heart. He will be very well served if I go into a decline, for although I daresay he doesn't care a button what becomes of me I shall leave a letter to be opened after my death, saying that it was all his doing, and he won't like *that*!'

Slightly heartened by this reflection, she then went off to change her dress. With rare tact she selected from her wardrobe a very demure half-dress of French muslin, and further heightened its modesty by arranging round her shoulders a lace fichu. This led her adoring abigail to look upon her with anxious concern, but upon the matter's being explained to her Martha entered at once into the spirit of the thing, and contributed her mite by substituting a pair of silk mittens for the elegant kid gloves she had previously laid out. Letty eyed them with disfavour, but consented to wear them; and presently burst upon her half-brother's sight as the embodiment of virtuous maidenhood. The effect of this modest ensemble, though not what she had expected, was good. When she entered the drawing-room Cardross was looking stern, but after one glance at his pious little sister his countenance relaxed. He put up his glass, the better to study her appearance, and said dryly, but with a quivering lip: 'Doing it rather too brown, Letty!'

Her saintly expression melted into one of engaging mischief. She twinkled roguishly, and stood on tiptoe to kiss his cheek. '*Dear* Giles! What an agreeable surprise, to be sure!'

'Turning me up sweet, my pet?'

She giggled. 'No, no, it is the luckiest chance that you have come home, because the case is that we mean to go to the play tonight, and have no one to escort us!'

'What an abominable girl you are!' he remarked.

'Yes, but don't be cross!' she begged.

'It would be a waste of time. I entertain serious thoughts, however, of sending you to stay with Aunt Honoria. She *may* take you to the Assemblies at the Upper Rooms now and then – by the by, they end punctually at eleven! – but only if you are excessively well-behaved.'

'Oh, what a horrid notion!' cried Letty, shuddering. '*Aunt Honoria!* Bath, too, of all places! But of course I should run away – to become an actress, I daresay, just to serve you out!'

'Nonsense! She will have you in subjection within a week! She frightens *me* to death!' he retorted.

'Very likely! There is more steel to *my* nerves, I promise you!'

He laughed, and upon dinner's being just then announced bowed both ladies out of the door, and followed them downstairs to the dining-room. Bent on charming him into an acquiescent mood, Letty kept him amused by a good deal of nonsensical raillery, in which Nell took little part, merely smiling mechanically at Letty's more outrageous absurdities. Her spirits were oppressed; and she was on tenterhooks lest Letty, encouraged by her brother's indulgent mood, should think the time opportune to broach the subject of her marriage. Dinner seemed interminable, though it was, in fact, shorter than usual, his lordship not having been expected. The artist belowstairs had had time only to fling together the merest travesty of a second course, supplementing the soup, the pigeons, the poulard à la Duchesse, and the morels of the first course with a grilled breast of lamb with cucumber, prawns in a wax basket, and some cheese-cakes. This very commonplace repast had not escaped censure from the steward; and Farley, who maintained a guerrilla warfare with the Gallic ruler of the kitchens, prophesied that his lordship would send a pretty sharp message downstairs. His lordship, however, made no comment; and as for her ladyship, although she rejected most of the dishes, and ate very sparingly of the others, this abstinence seemed to arise from loss of appetite rather than from any particular distaste of what was offered her.

When they rose from the table the Earl, who had glanced rather narrowly at his wife several times during the course of the meal, asked her quietly if she was feeling quite the thing.

She said hurriedly: 'Yes – oh, yes! A little tired, but nothing to signify!'

Letty, interposing in a helpful spirit, said that they were both of them quite fagged with balls and routs; and when Cardross suggested that they should remain at home, instead of going to Drury Lane, she at once lent her support to the scheme, reminding Nell that there had been no play put on for months that had been worth seeing. For her part, she said, she would as lief stay at home, and enjoy a comfortable coze. But as Nell was well aware that her comfortable coze would speedily develop into an extremely uncomfortable altercation with her brother, she said that she wanted very much to see the play. Cardross at once bowed his acquiescence, but gone was the gentler note in his voice when he replied, with civil indifference: 'As you wish, my love.'

The play was neither better nor worse than any other that had been performed at Drury Lane that year, and even Letty, who was young enough to think herself hardly used if brought away from a theatre before the final curtain, greeted with approval Cardross's suggestion that they should not stay to see the farce. London was passing through a dramatic doldrums, and with the exception of an occasional appearance of Mrs Siddons, in charity performances, and the promise of a new melodrama by Charles Kemble, to be produced at the end of the month, under the intriguing title of *The Brazen Bust*, there was really nothing in prospect to lure the most inveterate playgoer into any of the theatres. The Haymarket Theatre being closed, owing to the preoccupation of the management in the Court of Chancery, the Surrey, on the south bank of the river devoting itself to *burlettas* that were not at all the thing for ladies, the Regency fast sinking into decay, and both the Lyceum and the Olympic staging displays that resembled Astley's circuses, lovers of the drama were obliged either to stay at home, or to attend a succession of indifferent plays put on at Drury Lane, or at the Sans Pareil.

'I can't think what made you wish so particularly to see such a stupid piece!' said Letty frankly, when Cardross, having conveyed his ladies back to Grosvenor Square, had gone off to spend an hour or two at White's Club. 'I did my best to save you from it, too, for I could see you were not in spirits.'

'I didn't wish to see it,' replied Nell, rather wearily. 'I said so only because I was in such dread that you would begin to tease Giles about your marriage, and I thought that anything would be better than that!'

'How can you be so nonsensical?' demanded Letty, quite

astonished. 'Why should you care if I did tease him? He would not blame *you* for that!'

'No, very likely he would not – until you had dragged me into the quarrel, which you would have, if I know you! And in any event I can't bear to be obliged to listen to you driving Cardross into losing his temper, which no one can wonder at his doing, for you must own, Letty, that as soon as you are cross you express yourself in the most improper way to him!'

'Pooh! why shouldn't I say what I choose to him?' said Letty scornfully. 'He is not my father, after all! I don't wish to distress you, Nell, but I warn you I mean to speak to him tomorrow morning, before he goes out. And, what's more, I shall continue to press the matter every time I see him, until he yields, which I don't doubt he will, because I have frequently observed that gentlemen dislike excessively to be continually teased, and will do almost anything only to win peace again!'

Upon hearing this pleasing programme, Nell expressed the fervent hope that providence might see fit to strike her down with influenza during the night, so that she would be obliged to keep to her room for several days, and went off to bed, a prey to what her sister-in-law was uncivil enough to call the blue devils.

There was no intervention by providence, but Nell very prudently put in no appearance at the breakfast-table. Since it was Sunday, and she liked to breakfast before attending Morning Service, this was served earlier than on weekdays: early enough to afford Letty ample time to launch her preliminary skirmish.

That she availed herself of the opportunity Nell soon knew. She was seated before her dressing-table, while Sutton arranged her shining ringlets in a fashionable mode known as the Sappho, when Letty erupted into the room, out of breath from having rushed upstairs in pelting haste, and with her eyes and cheeks blazing. '*Nell!*' she uttered explosively.

Well aware that she would not be deterred from pouring forth the tale of her wrongs by Sutton's presence, Nell at once dismissed her stately dresser. She would probably learn the whole from Martha presently, since that devoted and uncritical abigail was deeply in her mistress's confidence, but that couldn't be helped, and at least Nell would be spared the embarrassment of her presence while Letty gave rein to her first fury of indignation.

Hardly had the door closed behind Miss Sutton than the storm broke. Pacing about the room in a fine rage Letty favoured her sister-in-law with a graphic and embittered account of what had taken place in the breakfast-parlour. The preliminary skirmish had clearly developed rapidly into a full-scale attack. Equally clearly Letty had been beaten at all points. Her recital was freely interspersed with animadversions on Cardross's character, cruel, callous, tyrannical, and odious being the mildest epithets she used to describe it. After one quite unavailing attempt to check her, Nell resigned herself, listening with half an ear to the various measures (most of them, happily, impossible) Letty was prepared to resort to if Cardross should persist in his uncompromising attitude; and wondering whether either of them would be in time for Morning Service. Not surprisingly, considering the overwrought state of her nerves, Letty's diatribe ended in a flood of tears, violent enough to make Nell entertain serious fears that she was about to fly into a hysterical fit. This danger was averted by a mixture of hartshorn and common sense, and the sufferer from fraternal persecution presently subsided into milder weeping. Nell had just succeeded in soothing her, and was bathing her temples with Hungary water, when Cardross, after the curtest of knocks on the door, walked into the room. At sight of Letty, languishing upon the sofa, he stopped short on the threshold, and said cuttingly: 'An affecting spectacle!'

'Oh, Giles, pray hush!' begged Nell.

The stricken maiden on the sofa bounced up, and in a husky voice of loathing promised to go into strong convulsions if Cardross did not instantly leave the room.

'By all means do so if you have a fancy to be well slapped!' retorted Cardross, looking as though it would give him considerable satisfaction to carry out his threat. 'If you have not, stop enacting Cheltenham tragedies, and go to your own room!'

'Do you imagine,' gasped Letty, 'that you can order me to my room, as though I were a child?'

'Yes, and carry you there, if you don't instantly obey me!' he said, pulling the door open again. 'Out!'

'For heaven's sake, Cardross!' expostulated Nell, in the liveliest dread that Letty would relapse into hysterics. 'Do, pray, go away, and leave her to me! This is *my* room, and really you have no right to order Letty out of it!'

'You have an odd notion of my rights,' he said grimly. 'I don't question that she is more welcome in your room than I am, but you will own that I at least have the right to be private with you when I choose!'

She whitened, but said quietly: 'Most certainly, and if it is the case that you wish to speak to me, shall we go into my dressing-room?'

'You need not put yourself to so much trouble!' declared Letty, trembling with anger. 'I would not for the world, love, expose *you* to the sort of ill-usage *I* am compelled to suffer, and to spare you I will go!'

This very noble speech wiped the thunderous look from Cardross's face, and made him burst out laughing: an unlooked-for event which exacerbated Letty, but considerably relieved Nell. Letty, pausing only to inform her brother that his manners were as disgusting as his disposition was malevolent, swept out of the room, sped on her way by a recommendation to go and take a damper. Cardross then shut the door, saying: 'Little termagant! I shall be sorry for Allandale, if ever she does marry him.'

'She is very much overset by this news that he must leave England so soon,' Nell replied excusingly. 'One cannot but feel for her, and for my part – But I don't wish to tease you any more.'

'Thank God for that! I have had as much as I can support in one day, I assure you. At breakfast, too!'

'I must say, I think that was a very foolish time to choose,' admitted Nell.

'Very! But she would not have found me more persuadable at

any other hour.' He added, as she sighed: 'Yes, I am aware of what your sentiments are, but I didn't come to enter into argument with you over this lamentable affair. What I did come for was to discuss with you what will be the wisest course to pursue now. We may be sure of one thing: until that regrettable young man is out of the country there will be no peace for either of us. I shall no doubt be subjected to endless repetitions of today's scene; and you, I suppose, will be obliged to sustain the exhausting rôle of confidante. Well, I know of no reason why you should be called upon to endure Letty's tantrums, so tell me frankly, if you please, if you would wish me to pack her off to Bath?'

'Upon no account in the world!' she said quickly. 'Surely you were only funning when you made that threat?'

'I was, but I didn't then know that Allandale was to leave England so soon.'

'No, no, don't think of it! It would be so dreadfully unkind to send her out of town when she has so little time left before Mr Allandale sails! I am persuaded, too, that she would run away – perhaps to Mrs Thorne, and you would very much dislike that. Only think how it would look!'

'If I know my Aunt Honoria, she would be given no chance to run away,' he said, with a wry smile. 'Don't imagine, however, that I wish to send her there! She's a tiresome little wretch, and when she starts brangling and brawling I could willingly wring her neck, but so much must be laid at the door of her upbringing that I can't feel she deserves quite such a fate as to be delivered up to that dragon of a female. But I don't wish you to be worn to a bone by her nonsense.'

'Indeed I shan't be, and I beg you won't dream of sending her to Lady Honoria! *One* thing you may be sure of: you have no need to fear an elopement.'

'No, very true!' he agreed. 'Allandale's inability to support a wife must put that disaster beyond the range of possibility!'

'Yes, but that is not quite just, Cardross!' she said reproachfully. 'He may be an ineligible match for poor Letty, but you cannot doubt that his principles are high, and his sense of propriety too great to allow of his entertaining the thought of an elopement, whatever might be his fortune!'

'His principles and his propriety may be as high as the moon, but I have no great opinion of his resolution!' Cardross replied. 'Had that been on the same level he would never, as his affairs stand, have allowed his fancy for Letty to carry him to the length of applying to me for her hand! She can be an engaging little devil when she chooses, and I will own myself astonished if he is not being led about with a ring through his nose, like a performing bear. My dependence is all upon his straitened circumstances. We will keep Letty in London, then – and you won't blame me if she drives you to distraction!'

He left the room on these words, and after a discreet interval Miss Sutton returned to it, to complete, with lofty dignity, her task of presenting her mistress suitably coiffed and gowned for an appearance in the Chapel Royal.

In the event, Nell decided that the hour was too far advanced to admit of her making anything but an undesirably spectacular arrival at the Chapel Royal; and she presently dismissed her carriage, setting out on foot for the Grosvenor Chapel, which place of worship, though frequented by persons of ton, was hardly worthy of Miss Sutton's best efforts. She was accompanied by Letty, having coaxed that injured damsel to go with her in the hope that religious exercise would bring her to a more proper frame of mind. Unfortunately, the officiating cleric announced as the text for his sermon a verse from the Epistle to the Philippians. '*Let nothing be done through strife or vainglory,*' he pronounced sonorously, '*but in lowliness of mind let each esteem others better than themselves.*' Nell felt Letty stiffen.

Nor was there anything in the discourse that followed to produce in either lady any thoughts suitable to the Sabbath. So apposite to the events of the morning was the sermon that Nell, far from being edified, was hard put to it to stifle a shocking fit of giggles; while Letty, swelling with wrath, could not afterwards be persuaded that Cardross had not suborned the blameless cleric into choosing a text aimed directly at herself.

Upon their return to Grosvenor Square Nell found a note from Dysart awaiting her. No, the porter informed her: his lordship had not called in person, but had sent it by the hand of his groom. Nell bore it upstairs to her dressing-room to peruse it in private, but its contents were disappointing. The Viscount had scrawled no more than a couple of lines to say that he had received her warning, and would take care to keep out of Cardross's way. He remained her affectionate brother, Dysart. It was only by the exercise of all the resolution at her command that she was able to refrain from dispatching another letter to him then and there, reminding him of the urgency of her need. Lady Sefton called during the course of the afternoon, and stayed for an hour, uttering cryptic remarks, and peeping at Letty through her fingers as she did so in a roguish manner that caused that young lady to apostrophize her later as a nasty creature, which was unjust, since beneath her tiresome affectations she was the kindest of creatures. From having been acquainted with Mrs Allandale for many years she was pretty well aware of the state of affairs in Grosvenor Square, but even Nell, who liked her, could not acquit her of having come to discover, if she could, any interesting circumstances which had not reached Mrs Allandale's ears. Hardly had she departed than a much more unwelcome visitor arrived, in the person of Lady Cowper, who came with the ostensible object of begging dear Lady Cardross to lend her support to a charitable organization of which she herself was a leading patroness, but lost little time in trying to ferret out, in the most caressing way possible, all the details of Letty's romance. Nell was mortified indeed to realize that her lord's little sister had become one of the on-dits of London, and glancing towards her, thought that she too looked to be rather struck. Lady Cowper, like all the Lambs, was possessed of a degree of charm that too often lured the unwary into reposing confidences in her which would later provide her with matter for her witty tongue; but her insinuating manners won her nothing from the two Merion ladies but a stony stare from Letty, and from Nell a gentle civility that rebuffed all hints and enquiries, and caused her later to tell her numerous acquaintances that it was a sad pity that so beautiful a creature should be so insufferably insipid. As for her hostesses, no sooner had she taken herself off than they spent an agreeable half-hour abusing her, and in trying to decide whether her worst fault was cutting at people behind their backs, or paying visits in dresses trimmed with positively dirty lace.

The evening was enlivened by a spirited attempt made by Letty to convince her brother that in withholding her fortune from her he was guilty of embezzlement. He refused to be drawn into altercation, and even listened to her with great patience when, abandoning this unpromising line of attack, she expatiated on the manifold, if somewhat nebulous, advantages of life in Brazil, and the miseries she would undergo if separated by thousands of miles and an æon of time from Mr Allandale. He even tried to coax her into viewing her circumstances with rather more moderation, representing to her in a little amusement, but with a good deal of kindness, that two, or even three, years could hardly be thought an æon of time; and that the possibility of Mr Allandale's being snatched into marriage by a designing female of Portuguese extraction was too remote to be worthy of consideration. 'Don't put yourself in this passion, my dear little sister!' he said, taking her hand, and giving it a squeeze. 'You might be so very much worse off, you know! If I were the unfeeling tyrant you believe me to be, I should have told Allandale never to think of you again – and that is certainly what the world will say I should have done! I haven't said it, and I shall not. But you must not expect me to allow you, at seventeen, to throw yourself away on a young man who has neither birth nor position, and stands as yet only on the threshold of his career. I shan't do it, so stop coming to cuffs with me, like a good girl, and try to be a little wiser!'

She stared bleakly up into his face, her own very set. 'You wouldn't talk so if you had ever loved anyone as I love Jeremy. You cannot know what it is to form a lasting passion!'

He dropped her hand. 'You are mistaken,' he said, in an even tone, and turned away from her to address some light common-place to his wife.

Letty flushed vividly, and said: 'I am not mistaken! You may think you have a heart, but you haven't! You don't like to be told that, but it's true!'

He said, over his shoulder: 'Letty, you are not only becoming a dead bore, but you want manner as well as sense! Let me tell you that until you learn to behave with propriety you will make the worst wife imaginable for a diplomat!'

'Jeremy,' said Letty, her bosom heaving, 'thinks me *perfect!*'

'Which,' remarked Cardross, as she slammed herself out of the room, 'gives me no very high idea of his understanding.'

Nell smiled, but said only, as she rose from her chair: 'I think I should follow her. She has been very low and oppressed all day, and you know how it is with her! When she is happy I never knew anyone whose spirits mounted so high, but they can be all dashed down in a minute, and then she knocks herself up with one of her fits of crying.'

'I have very little patience to waste on such distempered freaks,' he replied. 'The truth is that she has been spoilt to death, and cannot endure to have her will crossed!'

'Oh, yes!' she agreed. 'But you would not wish her to cry herself into a fever.'

'Nonsense!' he said irritably, adding, however, after a frowning moment: 'I don't wish her to wear *your* spirits down, at all events! I suppose she will make us endure weeks of sulks. There's no doing anything until Allandale has sailed, but how would it be if I took a house in Brighton, after all, instead of going home to Merion at the end of the season? Do you remember how cross she was when I refused to take her there? I had nothing but scowls from her for a full week! Well! Prinney's parties are not what I would choose for her, but if it would divert her to go there – ?'

'Perhaps it would divert her a little,' she answered. She raised her eyes, and added, after a moment's hesitation: 'Not very much, however. I don't mean to vex you, Cardross, but I think you don't perfectly understand. You hope that Letty will forget Mr Allandale, but she won't. You see, she *loves* him!'

'A child of her age! What does she know of the matter?'

She coloured faintly, and managed to say, though not easily: 'I was not very much older – when you offered for me.'

His eyes turned towards her, an arrested expression in them. He did not answer her immediately, and when he did speak it was with a certain deliberation. 'No. You were not, were you?' he said.

Ten

The following day was one of gloom, relieved only at nightfall, when the guests began to arrive for a loo-party. It began inauspiciously, with a further reminder from Madame Lavalle, which threw Nell into such a fever of apprehension that she could no longer forbear to plague Dysart, but sent round a letter to his lodgings immediately, imploring him either to tell her what she must do, or to negotiate a loan for her 'with a respectable usurer'. Hardly had this been dispatched than Martha came to her with a message from her mistress. Letty, it appeared, had awakened with a toothache, after a troubled night, and begged to be excused from accompanying her sister to North Audley Street, on a morning visit to the Misses Berry.

Nell found the sufferer still abed, a trifle heavy-eyed, but looking remarkably pretty, and without the vestige of a swollen jaw. This seemed to indicate that at least there was no abscess; but when Letty announced in the voice of one dwindling to decay that she thought perhaps the pain would go off if she remained quietly in bed, Nell was resolute in insisting that she should visit the dentist. She was not surprised by Letty's reluctance to do so, for the prospect of having a tooth drawn was not one which she herself could have faced with equanimity; but when Letty said at last that she would go, and that Martha should accompany her, so that Nell need not postpone her duty-call in North Audley Street, she began to suspect that the toothache was not unconnected with this call. The late Lady

Cardross had been a close friend of both the Berry sisters, but her daughter, ungrateful for the kindly interest they took in her, could be depended on to find ingenious excuses for not visiting them. She said that Miss Berry was quizzy, and Miss Agnes cross, and nothing bored her more than to be obliged to drive down to Little Strawberry to spend the day with them. Indeed, she had brightened so perceptibly when Miss Berry, on the occasion of her last visit to the Merion ladies, had confided, with a sigh, that she was compelled to find a tenant for Little Strawberry, that Nell had been positively ashamed of her, and had later taken her severely to task for heartlessness and incivility. So she now eyed the spoiled beauty measuringly, and said that she would herself take her to visit Mr Tilton. Had she been feeling less oppressed she must have laughed at the smouldering look of resentment cast at her from beneath Letty's curling eyelashes.

Happily for Letty, who, by the time she was handed into the sinister chair in Mr Tilton's room, was in a quake of fright, that worthy practitioner could find nothing amiss with her teeth. In his opinion, the passion she was enduring so bravely was due to a nervous tic. He recommended bed, and a few drops of laudanum as a composer: a prescription which Nell inexorably forced her unwilling sister to carry out, with the result that by four o'clock Letty announced herself to be perfectly cured, and got up to array herself for the evening's party. She was not in spirits, but somewhat to Nell's surprise, and greatly to her relief, she had made no further reference, after a bitter outburst on the previous evening, to Cardross's cruelty. She seemed to have realized that there could be no moving him; and while the droop to her mouth, and the brooding look in her eyes, held out every promise of a fit of the sullens, Nell could not but feel she could bear this better than the exhausting and quite fruitless discussions she had lately been compelled to enter into.

Dysart did not come, but as the retired gentleman's gentleman, in whose establishment he resided, rather thought that he had gone out of town to see a prize-fight, this was not wonderful. Nell could only hope that he would find the time to send a written answer to her letter, since, if he were to call in person in Grosvenor Square on the following day, he would not find her at home. She was engaged to take Letty to an al fresco party at Osterley.

There was no letter from him in the morning; and had her hostess been any other than Lady Jersey, whom it would be very dangerous to offend, she would have been much inclined to have cried off from the party. It was impossible to do so, however, without giving grave offence, for Lady Jersey had been one of the guests at her loo-party, and would certainly not believe any tale of sudden indisposition.

'Oh, no!' Letty agreed. 'It would be quite shocking if you did not go! But I am sure I need not, for I have not the least heart for it, besides being teased by this horrid tic. I mean to stay at home, with a shawl round my head.'

'And Paley's *Sermons* in your hand, I daresay!' exclaimed Nell. 'For shame, Letty! You have no more tic than I have!'

'Even if I have not I won't be forced to go to parties when I am in the deepest affliction!' said Letty, flushing. 'I don't doubt it would suit Cardross very well to be able to say that if I continue to do so it is plain he has not done his best to break my heart, but he shan't have *that* satisfaction, and so you may tell him! I won't go!'

'Indeed, Letty, you must go!' Nell said earnestly. 'You cannot, surely, wish to have your affairs made the subject of gossip! Think how vexed you were when Lady Sefton and Lady Cowper came here on Sunday to try if they could discover what truth there is in the rumours that are going about! Pray do not wear your heart on your sleeve, my dear! It is so very unbecoming!'

'I won't go!' Letty reiterated mulishly.

'Won't go where?' asked Cardross, coming into the room in time to hear this declaration.

'I won't go to Osterley with Nell! And I don't care if people do gossip!'

'Of course you will go to Osterley!' he said calmly. 'What excuse could you possibly offer for crying off?'

'I have already told Nell I have the tic, and if she doesn't choose to believe me she need not, but you can neither of you force me to go!'

'Doesn't Nell believe you? How unfeeling of her! *I* believe you, my pet, and I will send a message round to Dr Baillie, desiring him to call.' He added, the glimmer of a smile at the back of his eyes: 'My own engagements are of no particular moment, and I will promise to remain at home with you.'

'Rather than endure *your* company I will go to Osterley!' said Letty, quivering with suppressed fury.

'Yes, I thought you would,' he observed, holding the door for her to pass out of the room. He raised an eyebrow at Nell, and said, as he shut the door again: 'What mischief is she plotting? A clandestine meeting with Allandale?'

'I don't know,' Nell said worriedly. 'I *hope* not, but I own I can't feel easy about her: I do most sincerely sympathize with her, but it will not *do* for her to be meeting him in such a way. You won't mention this to her, but I fear she has let her partiality for him be too clearly seen, and there is already a little gossip about her, in a certain set.'

'The devil there is! Take care, then, she doesn't give you the slip! Secret meetings I will not endure!'

'No, indeed! But I have been wondering, Cardross, if you would permit me to invite Mr Allandale to dine with us before he leaves England. Poor Letty! It is very hard if she is not even to be granted the opportunity of taking leave of him.'

'Lending my countenance to an engagement of which I disapprove?' he said quizzically.

'Not more than you have done already, in saying that they may be married when he returns from Brazil!' she urged. 'I am persuaded she would be very sensible of your kindness in granting her that indulgence; and then, you know, there would be no need for her to meet him without our knowledge.'

He looked sceptical, but shrugged, and said: 'Very well: you may do as seems best to you.'

'Thank you! I will tell her, and I do hope it may comfort her a little.'

But Letty, informed of the treat in store, betrayed no enthusiasm for it; nor, when Nell represented to her the impropriety of her meeting Mr Allandale in secret, did she return any very satisfactory answer. She sat beside Nell in the carriage looking the embodiment of discontent, but grew rather more cheerful at Osterley. She was always susceptible to admiration, and she received so many compliments on her appearance in a new and dashing dress of pale lemon-coloured crape worn over a slip of white sarsnet, that Nell soon saw, to her relief, that she had abandoned her die-away air, and was prepared to enjoy herself.

Shortly after noon the porter at Cardross House opened the door to the Viscount Dysart. His lordship, who was dressed for travel, in breeches and top-boots, trod briskly into the hall, and demanded his sister. Upon learning that she had gone off on an expedition of pleasure with the Lady Letitia, he looked first thunderstruck, and then wrathful, and exclaimed: 'Gone to Osterley? Well, hell and the devil confound it! Did she leave any message for me?'

No, the porter said apologetically, he did not think her ladyship had left a message, unless, perhaps, with Farley.

The Viscount turned an impatient and an enquiring look upon Farley, who had appeared from the nether regions, and was bowing to him with stately civility. 'Did her ladyship say when she would be back?' he demanded.

'No, my lord – merely that she had no expectation of being late. I understand it is an al fresco party: something, doubtless, in the nature of a pic-nic.'

'Well, if that don't beat all hollow!' said the Viscount involuntarily, and in accents of disgust.

'I fancy that his lordship has not yet gone out, my lord, if you would care to see him? Mr Kent *was* with him, but –'

'No, no, I won't disturb him, if he's got his man of business with him!' interrupted Dysart, with aplomb. 'In fact, there's no need to tell him I called: came to see her ladyship on a private matter!'

'Just so, my lord,' said Farley, accepting with a wonderful air of unconsciousness the handsome douceur which the Viscount bestowed on him.

'I'll step up to her ladyship's dressing-room, and write a note to her,' said Dysart. 'And you'd better give me my hat again! I don't want his lordship to catch sight of it.'

However, the porter undertook to keep the hat hidden from his master's eyes, so Dysart, quite unembarrassed, told him to see that he did, and, declining escort, went off up the broad stairway.

'As bold as Beauchamp, that's what he is,' remarked the porter, carefully setting the hat down under his huge chair. 'Down as a hammer, up like watch-boy! Got some new bobbery on hand from the look in his ogles. Ah, well! he ain't one of the stiff-rumped sort, that's one thing, and it don't matter to him if he's swallowed a spider: you won't catch him forgetting to tip a cove his earnest! There's plenty as wouldn't give me more than a borde for hiding their tiles, but you mark my words if he don't fork out a hind-coachwheel! What did he drop in *your* famble, Mr Farley?'

But Farley, revolted by such vulgar curiosity, merely withered him with a stare before retiring again to his own quarters.

Twenty minutes later the Viscount came lightly down the stairs again, pausing for a moment on the half-landing to make sure the coast was clear. Encouraged by a nod and a wink from the porter, he descended the last half-flight, and handed over a sealed billet. 'Give that to her ladyship, will you, George?'

'Yes, my lord. Thank *you*, my lord!' said the porter, as a large and shining coin followed the billet.

'And if you want a sure thing for the King's Plate at Chester tomorrow,' added the Viscount, setting his high-crowned beaver on his head, and pulling on his gloves, 'put your blunt on Cockroach!'

The porter thanked him again, but with less fervour. A keen student of the Turf, he perceived that his lordship had taken to betting the long odds, and he could only regret his imprudence: if that was his new lay there would be a sad dwindling of the stream of heavy silver coins that fell from his hand.

Nell, eagerly deciphering the scrawl some hours later, in the privacy of her bedchamber, no sooner made herself mistress of its contents than she read it a second time, more slowly, and with a knit brow, unable to decide whether she ought to be consoled by its message, or alarmed.

'*What the devil,*' wrote Dysart, without preamble, '*is the use of setting up a squawk for me to come and see you if the next thing you do is to go jauntering off to a pic-nic? I can't wait to see you, for I'm going out of town for a day or two, but you may as well stop fretting and fuming, because I have hit on a way of setting all to rights, and more besides. I shan't tell you what it is because ten to one you would not like it, for I never knew anyone with more buffleheaded scruples. I daresay you would have tried to throw a rub in the way, had you been at home, so I am just as glad you are not. If that hog-grubbing mantua-maker of yours starts dunning you again before I get back to town tell her she shall be paid before the week's out. Now, don't be in a pucker, my dear Sister, for we shan't fail this time, and don't get to wondering if I've sold your precious sapphires, or anything else you doat on, for I have not. Your affectionate brother, Dysart. P.S. I greased Farley in the fist not to tell Cardross I was in the house, and your porter too – at least, I shall – so don't go blurting it out to him like a ninny-hammer.*'

Having read this twice, Nell's spirits rose a little. There seemed to be no doubt that Dysart really had discovered a way of paying her debt, though what it could be she had not the remotest guess. It made her uneasy to read that she would not like it; but since he had been indignant with her for supposing that he would play the highwayman in earnest, and had now assured her that he had not taken her jewels, she did not think it could be anything very bad. He wrote with such certainty that her first sharp fear died: even Dysart would not have stated so positively that they would not fail this time had the matter rested on the turn of a card, or the fall of the dice. The worst would be if he had backed himself to perform some crazy exploit, and his going out of town made this appear rather probable. Nell knew that he had jumped his horse over that famous dinner-table because someone had betted heavily against his being able to perform the feat. She knew also that no dependence could be placed on his refusing a dangerous wager, because he was so much a stranger to fear that his anxious relatives had more than once entertained the unnerving suspicion that he was incapable of recognizing peril, even though it stared at him in the face. Vague but hideous possibilities began to suggest themselves to her, but before she had made herself quite sick with apprehension common sense reasserted itself, and she thought what a fool she was to suppose that even the most totty-headed of his cronies would offer him a wager the acceptance of which would put him in danger of breaking his neck.

For twenty-four hours she hung between hope and fear, and then a blow more crushing than any she had thought possible almost annihilated her. She had come in to find a message awaiting her that called for an immediate answer, and taking it upstairs with her, sat down at the tambour-top writing-table in her dressing-room to scribble a reply before ringing for Sutton to dress her for dinner. She had just signed her name and was about to shake the pounce-box over the single sheet of paper, when the door opened behind her, and Sutton's voice said: 'Oh, my lady!'

Sutton sounded agitated. Thinking that she must suppose herself to have been sent for long since (for the only thing that ever ruffled her stately calm was the degrading suspicion that she had fallen short of her own rigid standard), Nell said cheerfully: 'Yes, I am come home, but I had not pulled my bell, so don't be thinking you are late! The India mull-muslin with the short train will do very well for tonight.'

'It's not that, my lady!' Sutton said. 'It is the necklace!'

'The necklace?' Nell repeated uncomprehendingly.

'The necklace of diamonds and emeralds which your ladyship never wears, and which we placed for safety in this very cupboard!' said Sutton tragically. 'Between the folds of the blue velvet pelisse your ladyship wore last winter, where no one would think to look for such a thing! Oh, my lady, it is more than an hour since I made the discovery, and how I have found the strength to keep me on my feet I know not! Never in all my years of service has such a thing happened to any of my ladies! Gone, my lady!'

Nell sat turned to stone. As the appalling implication flashed into her brain she found herself unable to move or to speak. The colour drained away from her very lips, but her back was still turned to her dresser, and Sutton did not see how near she was to fainting.

'I took your ladyship's winter garments out to brush them, and be sure there was no moth crept in, which is always my practice, for too often, my lady, and particularly when a garment is trimmed with fur, will it be found that camphor does not prevail! The case the necklace was laid in was there still, but when I lifted it I thought it felt too light, and the dreadful suspicion came to me – My lady, I opened it, and it was empty!'

A voice which Nell knew must be her own, for all it did not seem to belong to her, said: 'Good God, what a fright you put me into, Sutton!'

'My lady?'

Sutton sounded startled. Nell set the pounce-box down with a shaking hand, her underlip gripped between her teeth. She had overcome her faintness: one must not faint in such an extremity as this. 'But surely I told you, Sutton?' she said.

'*Told* me, my lady?'

She was beginning to see her way: not more than a few steps of it yet. 'Did I not? How stupid! Yet I thought I had done so. Don't – don't be afraid! It hasn't been stolen.'

'You have it safe, my lady?' Sutton cried eagerly.

'Yes. That is – no, it – I took it to Jeffreys.'

'You took it to Jeffreys, my lady?' Sutton repeated, in an astonished tone. 'Indeed you never told me! And to remove it from the case – ! Never say you stuffed it into your reticule! My lady, it is not my place to say so, but you should not! Why, you might have dropped it, or had it snatched from you! It gives one palpitations only to think of it!'

'Nonsense! It was safer by far in my reticule. I hope you may not have told anyone – any of the other servants – that it was stolen? If you have, it must make them very – very uncomfortable – in case they should be suspected of having taken it!'

'Not to a living soul have I opened my lips!' declared Sutton, drawing herself up rather rigidly. 'I should think it very improper, my lady, to make such a disclosure to anyone other than your ladyship.'

'I am so glad! The thing is, you see, that I have some notion of wearing it – at our own ball here. I thought, perhaps, with the pale green gauze I might not dislike it. So – I put it on, to see how it would be – yes, on Thursday last, when you went to visit your sister! – and it seemed to me that the clasp was not quite safe. That is why I took it to Jeffreys.'

'Well, my lady,' said Sutton, rapidly recovering her poise, 'it is a prodigious relief to me to know that my alarm need not have been. I am sure I was never nearer in my life to suffering a spasm.'

She then folded her lips tightly, dropped a stiff curtsey, and withdrew to the adjoining room to lay out the evening-gown of India mull-muslin.

Nell tried to rise from her chair, found that her knees were shaking, and sank back again. She had staved off immediate discovery, but what to do next she had no idea, nor could she, for many minutes, force her stunned mind to think. Only pictures as useless as they were unwelcome presented themselves to her: of herself, taking the necklace from its hiding-place to show it to Dysart – oh, months ago! of Dysart, seated at this very desk, and writing to tell her that he had not taken her sapphires, or anything else she doted on; of Cardross's face, when he had spoken to her so harshly about Dysart, and then, quite suddenly, had checked himself. She uttered a stifled moan, and covered her eyes with her hand. Dysart knew she didn't like the Cardross necklace, but how could he have supposed that it was hers to dispose of at will? Or didn't he care?

It was fruitless to ask herself such questions as that: no answer could be forthcoming until Dysart himself gave it to her. And that at once raised another question, and a far more urgent one: where was Dysart? It seemed to her at first incomprehensible that he should have left London; but presently it occurred to her that it might be very dangerous to sell the necklace to any London jeweller or pawnbroker. She knew very little about such matters, but she believed it was quite a famous piece; and certainly there could be no mistaking it, if once one had seen it. It had been made a long time ago, in the time of Elizabeth, as a wedding-gift from the Cardross of that age to his bride, and it figured in more than one family portrait. It was, moreover, of unusual workmanship, for the jewels were set in the semblance of flowers and foliage, and every flower trembled on the end of a tiny spiral of gold. Nell had worn it once only, at a Drawing-Room, but although it had excited a good deal of admiration, and not a little curiosity (for no one could imagine what held the jewel-clusters quite half an inch clear of Nell's breast, or what caused them to nod and quiver with every movement she made), she knew that it did not really become her; there were too many clusters, too much twisted gold in the foundation from which they sprang, too many leaves of flashing emeralds. She had once told Cardross that he ought to lend it to a museum, but although he had agreed that the proper place for it was in a glass case he liked her to wear it on state occasions, and so it had never gone to a museum. But even though it had not been publicly shown she supposed it must be well enough known to make Dysart seek a buyer for it in the provinces. She wondered hopelessly how he expected her to conceal the loss, whether he had found some craftsman skilled enough to copy the necklace, or whether (and this was the best she could hope) he had not sold, but pledged it.

She became aware of Sutton, coughing discreetly in the adjoining room. It was growing late, and though one might stand on the brink of a deep chasm of disaster one was still obliged to dress for dinner. She got up, steadier now, but with so white a face and such a look of strain in her eyes that Sutton, when she saw her come into the bedchamber, exclaimed that she was ill. She glanced at her own reflection in the mirror, and was startled to see how hagged she looked. She forced up a smile, and said: 'Not ill, but I have had the headache all day. You must rouge my cheeks a little.'

'If I may say it, my lady, I had as lief see you laid down in your bed. I am sure none knows better than I what it is to have the migraine.'

Nell shook her head, but she consented to swallow a few drops of laudanum in water, feeling that even though she had no migraine she had never stood in more urgent need of a composer.

The finishing touches had just been put to her toilette when Cardross sought admittance to the room. A sudden terror that Sutton might mention the disappearance of the necklace to him darted through Nell's mind, and made her tongue cleave to the roof of her mouth; but Sutton did not speak. Her face was always rather immobile, and in Cardross's presence it became mask-like. She dropped a slight curtsey, and at once withdrew, according to her correct practice. Nell remembered that she held men in abhorrence, and could breathe again.

Cardross was still habited in his morning-dress, and the sight of his blue coat and tasselled Hessians made Nell recollect, with relief, that he was not dining at home that evening. She said, with an effort at lightness: 'Ah! Daffy Club, I collect!'

He smiled. 'No: Cribb's Parlour! You have no engagement for tonight?'

'No, none. I am quite thankful for it! I have had the headache all day, and am not rid of it yet.'

'For several days, I think.'

Her eyes flew to his, at once startled and wary. 'No – but I own I am worn to a bone with dissipation!'

'By something, at all events.' He spoke very evenly, but his expression alarmed her. 'I could almost suppose you to be love-lorn – as love-lorn as Letty!'

She looked rather blindly at him. A tragic little smile wavered on her lips, but she turned her head away, not answering.

'I can only wish you a speedy recovery,' he said. 'Who is the man so fortunate as to have hit your fancy? No doubt some dashing sprig of fashion?'

'I think you must be trying to joke me,' she said, her face still averted. 'It is not kind – when I have the headache!'

'You must forgive me.' After a slight pause, he added: 'I came to tell you – and I trust it may relieve your headache – that I learned today that Allandale has gone into the country for a couple of nights, on a visit to an uncle, or some such thing. You may relax your vigilance – and I would he might remain out of town until he sets sail!'

'I can't blame you for that. I know you have had a great deal to vex you?'

'Do you?' he said. 'Well! it is something that you should own it, I suppose!'

Eleven

*T*he night, though she spent the better part of it in desperate thought, brought Nell no counsel, and certainly no comfort. While Dysart remained out of her reach there seemed to be nothing she could do. There was no way, even, of finding him, for though they might know, at his lodgings, where he had gone, she could not follow him. Yet of all things that was the most important, to find Dysart before he had sold the necklace. She wondered, since that could not be done, whether he would be able to recover it for her. Lavalle's bill suddenly became a matter of little significance: so much so that she was vaguely surprised she should have thought it so impossible to tell Cardross about it. It seemed a trivial thing, set beside the loss of the necklace, and far too trivial a thing to have led to the disaster which now confronted her. The maxims of her childhood reproached her; almost she could see Miss Wilby's grave countenance when she lectured her charges on the awful consequences of trying to conceal a fault. Miss Wilby had had plenty of examples to cite, but not even the awe-inspiring tale of the abandoned character whose dreadful end upon the scaffold could be traced back, through a series of crimes, to the fatal day when he had stolen the jam from his mother's cupboard, and denied it, was more terrible than the consequences of Nell's attempt to deceive Cardross. She had been afraid that confession would make it impossible for him to believe that she had married him for love, and not for his fortune; and now it seemed dreadfully probable that he would not care any longer whether she loved him or not. She had made him suspicious of her; there was a hard look in his eyes; and not once, since his return from Merion, had he attempted to do more than kiss her hand. If his love were not already dead, the discovery of her black wickedness would surely give it its *coup de grâce*.

She fell asleep with the dawn, but suffered uneasy dreams, and woke to full sunlight with heavy eyes, and a heavier heart.

She received no morning visit from Cardross, and he had left the house before she emerged from her room, looking, according to his sister, a perfect quiz, in a blue and yellow striped waistcoat, and a spotted cravat. From this unflattering description Nell realized that it must be one of the days when the Four-Horse Club met in George Street, and drove out to dine at Salt Hill. 'Very likely!' said Letty. 'Though why they have to make such figures of themselves I cannot conceive!'

She then informed Nell that her cousin Selina had sent a note round to beg her to go with her in her mama's carriage to choose a wedding-gift for Fanny. She added, with the light of battle in her eyes, that she supposed there could be no objection to that scheme.

Nell was glad to be able to acquiesce. She had no great liking for Miss Selina Thorne, but if Mr Allandale had gone into the country it was hard to see what harm could come of allowing Letty out of her sight for an hour or two. She did indeed suggest, when she saw that Mrs Thorne had not sent a maid with her daughter, that Martha should accompany the young ladies, but Letty scoffed at her for a prude; and Selina exclaimed rather pertly that of all odious things a servant listening to one's private conversations was the worst. Nell had a momentary vision of the cousins with their heads together, giggling over secrets, and thought, not for the first time, that Selina would have been the better for a course of Miss Wilby's discipline. She said no more, however; and after arguing for a few minutes about the nature of the gifts to be chosen, the girls went away, their first objective, Nell guessed, being the Pantheon Bazaar, in which fascinating mart, though they might not discover a suitable wedding-gift, they would certainly fritter away a good deal of money on ingenious trifles for themselves. Nell was too glad to see Letty in better spirits, and too anxious to be left to the indulgence of some quiet reflection, to raise any objection to this programme.

Her quiet reflection did nothing to raise the tone of her own spirits; but when Letty returned, much later in the day, she was seen to be in a sunnier humour than she had been for some time. As Nell had expected, she was laden with parcels, most of which were found to contain such doubtful purchases as a pair of perkale gloves, which it had seemed a pity not to buy, since they were so cheap, but which, on second thoughts, Letty thought she would give to Martha; a stocking-purse; several faggots of artificial flowers, one of which she generously presented to Nell; a gauze apron; two muslin handkerchiefs; a box of honeysuckle soap; and a Turkish lappet, which had hit her fancy at the time, but which, now that she saw it again, was quite hideous. For Fanny she had purchased a gold armlet and ear-rings, a handsome gift which made Nell exclaim: 'Good gracious! I had not thought you could afford anything so dear!'

'No, but I asked Giles, and he said I might purchase what I liked,' replied Letty unconcernedly.

This seemed to indicate that a truce had been declared. The impression was strengthened by Letty's next words, which were uttered after a thoughtful pause. 'He says it is true that he told you that you might invite Jeremy to dine here.'

'Of course it is true!'

'Well, I thought very likely it was a hum, but if it was not I expect it was your notion, and you coaxed him into it. I am very much obliged to you! When will you write to Jeremy?'

'Whenever you wish,' Nell replied. 'Now, if you desire me to.'

'Oh, no, there is no occasion for you to do so now! He is gone to visit his uncle, you know, and he did not expect to be in London again until tomorrow evening. I was thinking, love, that if we were to go to Almack's on Friday I daresay we should meet him there, and then, don't you think? we could discover when it would be convenient for him to come to us.'

It was evident, from this speech, that an assignation at Almack's had already been made. Nell did not feel equal to giving a promise that she would attend the Assembly, but she said that she would do so if she felt well enough, and with this Letty, after a little more coaxing, was obliged to be content. In the state of wretchedness she was in Nell could not think of taking part in such a frivolous entertainment without a shudder, but she did manage to extract a grain of comfort from the reflection that the first fury of Letty's passionate despair had worn itself out, and she was not contemplating any immediate act of imprudence.

The more compliant mood lasted. Letty was able to see Cardross again without ripping up; and although her spirits were languid, and her manner lacked its usual liveliness, there could be no doubt that she was making a serious endeavour to mend her temper.

The hope that Dysart would come to her kept Nell at home on the following day. Cardross was to have escorted both his ladies to a Review in Hyde Park, but in the end only Letty went with him. She had said at first that she was in no humour for it, but upon Nell's appealing to her to bear Cardross company so that she herself might nurse a headache at home she at once agreed to go. She was too much absorbed in her own troubles to perceive that her sister-in-law was looking far from well until her attention was directed to this circumstance, but when Sutton told her that she was quite in a worry over her mistress, she was instantly ready not only to do what was asked of her, but a great deal that was not asked, such as placing cushions behind Nell's head, a stool under her feet, and a shawl across her knees, bathing her brow with vinegar, offering her all manner of remedies from hartshorn to camphor, and enquiring every few minutes if she felt a degree better. Nell endured these ministrations patiently, but Cardross, coming to see how she did, exclaimed: 'Good God, Letty, don't fidget her so! Enough to drive her into a fever!'

Letty was inclined to take affront at this, but he pushed her out of the room without compunction, telling her to go and put her hat on, since his curricle would be at the door in five minutes. 'And if you want me to let you handle the ribbons, take that pout from your face!' he recommended. He turned, and went back to Nell's chair, and held her wrist in his hand for a moment. Under his fingers her pulse was flurried enough to make him say: 'If you are not better by the time we return I'll send for Baillie.'

'Oh, no, pray do not! Indeed I am not ill! Only I still have the headache, and it seems foolish to go out in this hot sun,' she replied quickly. 'I shall be perfectly well presently.'

'I hope you may be,' he said, laying her hand down again. He glanced at Sutton. 'Take care of her ladyship!'

An extremely dignified curtsey was all the answer vouchsafed to his behest. From the dresser's downcast eyes and lifted brows he might have inferred that she was deeply offended, but he did not look at her again. His gaze had returned to his wife's face; his expression seemed to her to soften; and after hesitating for a moment he bent over her, and lightly kissed her cheek. 'Poor Nell!' he said.

He was gone before she could say a word, leaving her with an almost overpowering inclination to cry her heart out. She managed to overcome it, and to assure Sutton, with very tolerable composure, that she was already better, and needed nothing to restore her to her usual health but to be left to rest quietly for an hour or so. She believed that she might fall asleep if no one came to disturb her.

It would have been well for her had she done so, but sleep had never been farther from her. She tried to interest herself in a new novel, and discovered that she had read three pages without taking in the sense of one word; every vehicle heard approaching in the square below brought her to her feet and hurrying to the window; and when she took up her embroidery, determined to employ herself rather than to pace about the room, a prey to most harrowing reflections, she found that her hands were so unsteady as to make it impossible for her to set a stitch.

Dysart did not come, and so severe was her disappointment that it took all the resolution of which she was capable to enable her to meet Cardross upon his return with a calm countenance. Her training stood her in good stead: no one could have supposed from her demeanour that her brain was in a turmoil; and when it was suggested to her that she might prefer not to go to the Italian Opera that evening she laughed away this solicitude, telling her husband and sister-in-law that they must not try to wrap her in cotton.

Dysart walked in on her, unannounced, just before noon on the following morning. She was sitting with Letty in the drawing-room, endeavouring to soothe feelings very much ruffled by a visit from Miss Berry. The good lady had called a little earlier to enquire after her state of health, but upon Letty's coming into the room had speedily infuriated that injured damsel by entering with great earnestness into a discussion of her affairs. What she said held excellent common sense, and did honour to her heart as much as to her judgement, but her manner was unfortunate. A trick she had of repeating over and over again some catch-phrase could only irritate; she had a way of talking in a hurried, over-emphatic style; and the caresses and exaggerated terms of affection she employed in trying to win more confidence than was voluntarily reposed in her served only to set up Letty's back. She had not long left the house when Dysart entered it; and when he walked into the drawing-room the angry flush had not faded from Letty's cheeks.

'Dysart!' Nell cried, springing up from her chair.

'Hallo, Nell!' he responded, with cheerful nonchalance. 'I hoped I should find you at home.' He looked critically at Letty, and enquired in a brotherly fashion: 'What's put *you* in a miff?'

'If nothing else had *you* would!' retorted Letty, with spirit, but a distressing want of civility. 'No doubt, dearest Nell, you would like to be private with your detestable brother! *I* would as lief converse with the muffin-man, so I will go and sit in the library until he has gone away again!'

'Well, if ever I saw such a spitfire!' remarked the Viscount, mildly surprised. 'What have *I* done to set you up on the high ropes?'

Deigning no other answer than a withering look of scorn, Letty swept out of the room with her head in the air. He shut the door behind her, saying: 'Too hot at hand by half!'

'Oh, Dy, thank God you are here at last!' Nell uttered, with suppressed agitation. 'I have been in such distress – such agony of mind!'

'Lord, you're as bad as that silly chit!' said Dysart, diving a hand into his pocket, and bringing forth a roll of bank-notes. 'There you are, you goose! Didn't I promise you I wouldn't make a mull of it this time?'

She would not take the roll, almost recoiling from it, and crying with bitter reproach: 'How *could* you? Oh, Dy, Dy, what have you done? You cannot have supposed that I would accept money obtained in such a way!'

'I might have known it!' ejaculated Dysart disgustedly. 'In fact, I did know it, and I took dashed good care not to tell you what I meant to do! When it comes to flying into distempered freaks, damme if there's a penny to choose between you and Mama!'

'Distempered freaks!' she repeated, gazing at him in dismay. 'You call it that? Oh, *Dysart!*'

'Yes, I dashed well do call it that!' replied his lordship, his eye kindling. 'And let me tell you, my girl, that these Methody airs don't become you! Besides, it's all slum! I may have to listen to that sort of flummery from Mama, but I'll be damned if I will from you! What's more, it's coming it a trifle too strong! Let me tell you, my pious little sister, that if Felix Hethersett hadn't thrown a rub in your way you'd have borrowed the blunt from that Old Pope in Clarges Street!'

'But, Dy – !' she stammered. 'The cases are not comparable! Perhaps it was wrong of me – indeed, I know it was wrong! – but it was not – it was not *wicked*!'

'Oh, stop acting the dunce!' he said, exasperated. 'Of all the fustian nonsense I ever heard in my life – ! What the devil's come over you, Nell? You were never used to raise such a breeze for nothing at all!'

'I can't think it nothing! *Surely* you do not?' she said imploringly. 'I had rather have done anything than lead you into this! I never dreamed – Oh, if I had but told Cardross the truth!'

'Well, if you meant to kick up such a dust as this I'm dashed sorry you didn't tell him!' said Dysart. 'I always knew you had more hair than wit, but it seems to me it's worse than that! Queer in your attic, that's what you are, Nell! First you plague the life out of me to raise the recruits for you – and where you thought I could lay my hand on three centuries the lord knows! Then, when I hit on a way of doing the thing neatly you've no more sense in your cock-loft than to cry rope on me; and now, when I hand you a roll of soft you ain't even grateful, but start reading me a damned sermon! And when I think that I came posting back to town the instant the thing came off right because I knew you'd fall into a fit of the dismals, or go off on some totty-headed start, if I didn't, I have a dashed good mind to let you get yourself out of your fix as best you can!'

'It is all my fault!' she said mournfully, wringing her hands. '*I* was in such desperate straits, and begged you so *foolishly* to help me –'

'Now, don't put yourself in a taking over that!' he interrupted. 'I don't say I was best pleased at the time – and now that all's right I don't mind owning to you that there was a moment when I thought I was at a stand – but *I'm* not complaining. There's no saying but what if you hadn't kept on teasing me to dub up the possibles I mightn't be standing here today pretty well able to buy an abbey!'

'Dysart, *no!*'

'Well, no, it ain't as much as that,' he acknowledged. 'As a matter of fact I had thought it would be more. Still, it's enough to keep me living as high as a coach-horse for a while, and that will be a pleasant change, I can tell you! Lord, Nell, I was so monstrously in the wind that I'd not much more than white wool left to play with! Six thousand and seven hundred pounds is what I've made out of it! And that's not counting my debt to you, and the monkey I owed Corny!'

She grasped the back of a chair for support, for her knees were shaking under her. From out a white face her eyes stared up at her beloved brother in horror; she felt as though she were suffocating, and could only just manage to say: 'Don't! Dy – oh, Dy, you *could* not! Not money gained in *such* a way!'

The thought of his sudden affluence had banished the frown from his brow, but at this it descended again. 'Oh?' he said ominously. 'And why could I not?'

'Dysart, you must *know* why you cannot!' she cried hotly.

'That's where you're out, my girl, because I don't know! And there's something else I don't know!' he said grimly. 'Perhaps you'll be so obliging, my lady, as to tell me what you did with the blunt you won at Doncaster last year! Very pretty talking this is from a chit who backed three winners in a row! You weren't blue-devilled then, were you? Oh, no! you were in high croak!' He shot out an accusing finger at her. 'And don't you try to tell me you didn't go to Doncaster, because I was there myself! Cardross took you to stay at Castle Howard, with the Morpeths, and you drove over there with a whole party of people! It's no use denying it: why, I remember how you told me that the only thing you didn't like at Castle Howard was the old Earl, because there was so much starch in him that he frightened you to death! Now, then! How do you mean to answer that, pray?'

Utterly bewildered, she stammered: 'But – but – I don't understand! What has that to say to anything? I remember perfectly! But –' she broke off suddenly, and gave a gasp. 'Oh, can it be possible that – ? Oh, Dy, dearest, *dearest* Dy – did you *win* that money?'

'Well, of course I did!' he replied, in the liveliest astonishment. 'How the devil else was I to do the trick?'

She sank down on the sofa, wavering between tears and laughter. 'Oh, how *stupid* I have been! I thought – Oh, never mind that! Dy, has the luck changed at last? Tell me how it was! Where have you been? How – Oh, tell me *everything*!'

'Chester, for the King's Plate,' he replied, eyeing her uneasily.

She seemed to him to be in queer stirrups, and he was just about to ask her if she felt quite the thing when a happy explanation occurred to him. 'I say, Nell, you haven't sprained your ankle, have you?' he demanded, grinning at her.

'Sprained my ankle? No!' she answered, a good deal surprised.

'What I mean is – in the family way?'

She shook her head, colouring. 'No,' she said sadly.

'Oh! Thought that must be it.' He saw that her face was downcast, and said bracingly: 'No need to be moped! Plenty of time yet before you need think of setting up your nursery. I shouldn't wonder at it if you were like Mama.'

'Yes, that is what she thinks, but – Oh, never mind that! Tell me how this all came about!'

He sat down beside her. 'Lord, it was the oddest thing! A fifteen to one chance, Nell! And I'd no more notion of laying my blunt on it than the man in the moon! Well, I didn't know the horse existed, and as for backing it – ! Anyone would have laid you odds there was only one horse entered that could beat Firebrand, and that was Milksop. But what do you think happened to me?' She shook her head wonderingly, and he gave a chuckle. 'Sort of thing that only comes to a man once in a lifetime. It was on Saturday night that it started. I thought I might take a look-in at the – well, it don't signify telling you the name of the place: you wouldn't know it! It's a club I go to now and again. Anyway, I called for a tankard there, drank it off, and damme if there wasn't a great cockroach in the pot!'

'Ugh!' exclaimed Nell, shuddering.

'Yes, I didn't like it above half myself,' agreed the Viscount. 'But the queer thing about it was that it wasn't dead! Seemed a bit lushy when I tipped it out on to the table, but, dash it, what could you expect? It got quite lively after a while, and so we matched it against a spider that – a friend of mine – picked off its web.'

'Cockroaches and spiders?' interrupted Nell, aghast.

'Oh, lord, yes: dozens of 'em! The place is full of them!'

'But, Dysart, how *very* shocking! It must be a sadly dirty house!'

'Yes, I expect it is,' he agreed. 'In fact, I know it is, but that don't signify! The thing is, most of the company fancied the spider. Well, I did myself, to tell you the truth, for it was a stout-looking runner, with a set of capital legs to it. I didn't back it, of course, because the cockroach was my entry, but I never thought to see the cockroach win.'

'And it *did*?' Nell asked anxiously.

'Won by half the length of the course!' said the Viscount. 'That was the table. We had 'em lined up, and I must say I thought my entry was still a trifle bosky, and I daresay he was, but no sooner did I give him the office – with a fork – than off he went, in a fine burst, straight down the course for the winning-post! Mind you, the spider had it in him to beat him: devilish good mover, I give you my word! The trouble with him was that he was a refuser. If he didn't fold his legs up under him, he went dashing off in circles. Now, young Johnny Cockroach jibbed a trifle, but every time I used my persuader on him, off he went again at a slapping pace, and always straight ahead! You wouldn't have thought, to look at him, that he was such a good mover. A daisy-cutter, is what *I* thought, and so he was, but a regular Trojan, for all that!'

'Oh, Dy, how absurd you are!' Nell exclaimed, laughing. 'And you won all that money on the creature?'

'No, no, of course I didn't! That was only funning! I didn't win much more than a pony on him.'

'What happened to him?' Nell could not help asking.

'How should I know? Went back to his stable, I daresay: I wasn't paying much heed to him. Or to any of it, if it comes to that. Well, what I mean is, never thought another thing about it, once the race was won. There wasn't any reason why I should. *But*, Nell, when I went to bed on Sunday night, I pulled back the clothes, and damme if there wasn't a cockroach right in the middle of the bed! How I came to be such a gudgeon as not to see *then* what it meant still has me in a puzzle. I didn't. It wasn't till Monday that it fairly burst on me. I went just to see how they were betting their money at Tatt's, and who should be there but old Jerry Stowe? No, you don't know him – not the kind of fellow you would know, but he's a mighty safe man at the Corner, I can tell you. Did him a trifling service once: no great matter, but to hear him you'd think I'd saved his life! Well, the long and short of it was that he told me in my ear to put all my blunt on Cockroach for the King's Plate at Chester! That fairly sent me to grass, I can tell you! I hadn't even heard of the tit: didn't mean to bet on the race at all, because I've no fancy for an odds-on chance, and to my mind there wasn't a horse entered, barring Milksop, that could beat Firebrand. But, of course, as soon as Jerry tipped me the office that settled it: taking one thing with another, I could see Cockroach was a certainty. The only trouble was, how the deuce was I to raise enough mint-sauce to make the thing worth while?' He paused, frowning. The amusement was quenched in Nell's eyes, which were fixed on his face in painful enquiry. 'Did something I've never done before, and never thought I should do,' he said, shaking his head. 'Too damned ramshackle by half! Mind, if I hadn't known the horse *couldn't* lose I wouldn't have done it!'

She smiled faintly: 'What did you do, Dy? Tell me – pray!'

'Borrowed a monkey from Corny,' he replied briefly.

'O-h-h!' It was a long sigh of unutterable relief. 'Is that all? I thought you meant you had done something. – something shocking!'

'Well, if you don't know that it's shocking to go breaking shins amongst your friends it's time someone told you!' said the Viscount severely. 'What if the horse hadn't won? A pretty Captain Sharp I should have looked!'

'Yes, yes, but I am persuaded Mr Fancot wouldn't have thought so, or cared a jot!'

'No, of course he wouldn't, but that don't make it any better! Worse, in fact. I don't mind owing blunt to the regular brags, or to a parcel of tradesmen, but I'm not the sort of rum 'un that sponges on my friends, I'll have you know!'

She was abashed, and docilely begged his pardon. He regarded her frowningly, and suddenly said: 'If you didn't kick up all that dust because you knew I'd won the money at Chester races, how *did* you think I'd come by it?'

She hung her head, blushing. 'Oh, Dysart, I have been so foolish!'

'I daresay, but that don't tell me anything! What made you fly into that odd rage? You aren't going to tell me you thought I'd held up a coach and robbed some stranger?'

'No – worse!' she whispered, pressing a hand to one hot cheek.

'Don't be such a sapskull! I should like to know what you imagine would be worse than that!' he said impatiently.

'Oh, Dysart, forgive me! I thought you had taken the necklace!'

'No, you didn't. I particularly told you I hadn't made off with your precious jewels, so stop bamming me!'

'Not *my* jewels – the Cardross necklace!'

'*What?*'

She quailed involuntarily.

'You – thought – I – had – stolen – the Cardross necklace?' said the Viscount, with awful deliberation. 'Are you run quite mad, girl?'

'I think I m-must have run m-mad,' she confessed. 'It was because you held me up! I never should have thought it if you hadn't meant to seize my jewels, and sell them for me! I thought –'

'I want to hear no more of what you thought!' interrupted Dysart terribly. 'Good God, are you going to sit there telling me you believed me capable of making off with something that don't belong to either of us?'

'No, no! I mean – I wondered if perhaps you thought it *was* mine! And you knew I didn't care for it, so –'

'– so I prigged it while you were out of the way – a thing worth the lord only knows how many thousands of pounds!' he cut in wrathfully. 'Just to pay your trumpery debt, too! Oh, no! I was forgetting! *Not* just to pay your debt, was it? I gave you three centuries – devilish handsome of me, by God! – and pouched over seven thousand! Do you happen to know what I did with the thing? Did I sell it to some fence or other, or did I lodge it with a spouter? I don't wonder at it that I found you in such a grand fuss! The only thing that I wonder at is how I've contrived to keep out of Newgate!'

He had sprung up from the sofa, and was striding about the room, in a black rage that made her quake. She dared not approach him, but she said imploringly: 'It was very bad of me, and indeed, I *beg* your pardon, but if you knew how it was – oh, Dysart, don't be so angry with me! Everything has been so dreadful, and I fear my mind is less strong than I had believed it! I knew how much I had teased you, and when I read your letter my first thought was that you had backed yourself to win some reckless wager. I didn't entertain the least suspicion *then*! It was when I knew the necklace had gone – and you had written the letter in the very room where it was hidden, and I remembered that I had shown you once – Oh, it was unpardonable of me, but –'

He had stopped his pacing, and was standing staring down at her, an arrested expression in his eyes. 'Just a moment!' he interrupted sharply. 'You don't mean that, do you? That the necklace has gone?'

'Yes, I do mean it. That was what overthrew my mind, Dy!'

'My God!' he ejaculated, turning a little pale. 'When did you discover this?'

'The next day – on Tuesday. It wasn't I, but my dresser who discovered it. She told me immediately, and that was when it flashed into my mind that – If I had had time to think, perhaps I should not – But I hadn't, I hadn't!'

'Never mind that! What did you say to your woman?'

'That I had taken the necklace to Jeffreys to have the clasp mended. She assured me she hadn't spoken of the loss to a soul, and I told her not to do so, and I am persuaded she has not.'

'Cardross doesn't know?'

'No, no! How could you think I would tell him when I thought it was you who had taken the necklace?'

He drew an audible breath. '*That's* the dandy, isn't it?' he said with blighting sarcasm. 'It's been missing for three days, and your damned dresser knows it, and you haven't seen fit to tell Cardross or to make the least push to recover it! Famous! And *now* what do you mean to do, my girl?'

Twelve

For perhaps half a minute Nell sat staring up at the Viscount, the colour slowly draining from her face. In the flood of relief that had swept over her her only thoughts had been of thankfulness that Dysart had not taken the necklace, and of remorse for having so misjudged him. But his words brought her back to earth with a jarring thud. She lifted a hand to her brow. 'Oh heavens!' she said, in the thread of a voice. 'I hadn't considered – Dysart, what must I do?'

'*I* don't know!' he replied unhelpfully.

'Someone did indeed steal it. But who? This is dreadful! It must have been one of the servants. Someone who knew where it was hidden, and how can I tell who may have known of it? The chambermaid whom Mrs Clopton turned off a month ago? I cannot think it!'

'Oh, can't you?' said his lordship acidly. 'Much obliged to you, my lady!'

'Don't Dy!' she begged. 'If you had taken it I knew you had done it only for my sake! But *now* – ! It might have been any one of them, at any time! It was not necessary to know where it was kept: it must be known to them all that I have it, and never wear it, and only think how many opportunities there must be for persons living in this house to search for the hiding-place! And when they had found it they would guess that I should not discover the loss for months, perhaps. Had it not been for Sutton's care, in taking out my winter clothes to brush them, I might have known nothing!'

'It ain't a bit of use talking about what *might* have happened,' said Dysart. 'It's what *did* happen that has put you in the basket. Unless you can stop your dresser's mouth, it's bound to come out that you knew the necklace had been stolen three days before you said a word about it to Cardross. Well, you know the woman better than I do! Can you bribe her to tell the same story you mean to tell?'

'I don't know,' she said slowly. 'It's of no consequence, however: I will not do it!'

'I daresay you're right,' he agreed. 'Too damned risky! She'd be bound to guess there was something havey-cavey afoot, and once she knew you was scared of Cardross's getting wind of it she'd very likely bleed you white! Lord, there'd be no end to it!'

'I don't think it. It is not for that reason! Dysart, all this trouble has come upon me because I set out to deceive Cardross, and it has grown and grown until –' She broke off with a shudder. 'I must tell him the truth. I must tell him *immediately*!'

She got up as she spoke, but the Viscount said dampingly: 'Well, you won't do that, because he ain't in. Told Farley he wouldn't be back till five or thereabouts.'

'Not till five! Oh, if my courage does not fail!'

'Do you want me to see him with you?' he demanded.

'You? Oh, no! I must see him alone.'

'Well, it's my belief the thing will come off a dashed sight better if you do,' he said frankly. 'It ain't that I mind seeing him, because now the dibs are in tune again there's no reason why I should, but for one thing I'm pledged to Corny, and for another Cardross won't like it if you take me along, like a dashed bodyguard! That's the way to get his back up at the very start. Besides, you don't need a bodyguard. I don't say he isn't going to be devilish angry, because it stands to reason he's bound to be, but you needn't be afraid he won't come round. He will – and all the quicker if I'm not there! He don't love me, but he loves you all right and tight!'

She said nothing; and after a moment he held out the banknotes to her again. 'Take 'em! No need to mention the mantua-maker's bill to him, unless you choose. You may put the whole on to me: I had three centuries from you, and I've now paid 'em back. I daresay that will surprise him more than if you told him I'd prigged his damned heirloom!'

At these biting words, she flung her arms round his neck, vehemently asserting that no one could ever believe such a thing of him, and again begging him to forgive her.

'Yes, very well, but you needn't think I'm pleased with you, for I'm not!' responded Dysart, disengaging himself from her embrace. 'It's not a bit of use hanging round my neck, and playing off your cajolery: *I'm* not Cardross! And mind this! the next time you run into trouble, don't you come to me to drag you out of it!'

'No,' Nell said meekly.

'I'll be off now,' he announced. 'No getting into high fidgets, Nell!'

She shook her head.

'And no turning short about either!' he warned her.

'No, I promise you I mean to tell Cardross as soon as he returns.'

'Well, see you do!' he said, relenting sufficiently to bestow a brief hug upon her. 'I suppose I ought to stay to bring you up to scratch, but I haven't seen Corny yet, and I must. Besides, it's his birthday, and we mean to make a batch of it.'

With that he went off, leaving her to solitude and her melancholy thoughts. She roused herself presently from these to send Sutton to pay Madame Lavalle's bill, and thought, as she gave the bank-notes into her dresser's hand, how happy it would have made her, only four days earlier, to have been able to do this. She could still be thankful that she would not now be obliged to lay the debt before Cardross, but that seemed a very small alleviation of the ills that beset her. The sight of her dresser brought one of these most forcibly to her mind. It would be necessary to tell Sutton that the necklace was not in the hands of Cardross's jeweller, but indeed lost; and how to account for her own prevarication was a problem to which she could discover no answer. Letty might pour out her troubles to her maid; to Nell it was unthinkable that she should admit Sutton into her confidence.

The thought of Letty made her ask Sutton suddenly where she was. The dresser replied that she believed her to have gone with Martha to Owen's in Bond Street, to purchase fresh ribbons for the gown she meant to wear at Almack's that evening. She availed herself of the opportunity to enquire of Nell which gown she herself wished laid out in readiness; but Nell, who had forgotten the engagement, exclaimed: 'Almack's! Oh, no! I cannot go there tonight!'

Sutton merely said: 'Very well, my lady,' and went away. Letty (if she had indeed arranged to meet her lover at the Assembly Rooms) would scarcely be so acquiescent.

As the day drew towards five o'clock Nell began to feel a little sick. Her spirits had been getting steadily lower for some time, and were not improved by the prospect beyond the window. The day had been dull, and the sky had now become so overcast that the drawing-room, which should have been full of sunshine, had put on a mournful twilight air. It even seemed to be a little chilly, but perhaps that was only her fancy.

Cardross came in shortly after five, but when Nell, bracing herself to face the ordeal in store, went downstairs, it was only to learn from the porter that his lordship was engaged with someone who had called to see him on a matter of business. Knowing that Cardross was dining out that evening, and feeling that her courage would be entirely dissipated if she were forced to remain on the rack for many more hours, she said: 'It is very vexatious, for I particularly wish to speak with his lordship before he goes out again. Who is it who must come to see him on business at such an hour? Not Mr Kent, surely?'

'No, my lady. It's a Mr Catworth. He called this morning, and seeing as he said his business was private, which he wouldn't disclose to Mr Kent, nor anyone, I told him it was no manner of use for him to wait, because his lordship wasn't expected till five. And back he came, my lady, but I would have put him in the office if I'd known your ladyship was wishful to see my lord. Because my lord give his orders when he come in just now that when Sir John Somerby calls he's to be taken to the library straight, my lady.'

'And he may arrive at any moment, I daresay!' Nell exclaimed. 'George, if he should do so before this person who is now with his lordship has gone away, show him into the saloon, if you please, and desire him to wait! And – inform his lordship that I wish to see him before he goes to Sir John!'

'Yes, my lady: never fear!' said George, in a reassuring tone that gave her clearly to understand that he had by this time realized that there was something unusual afoot. 'I'll tip the – I'll drop a word in Farley's ear, my lady!'

She thanked him, flushing a little, and retreated again to the drawing-room, there to pass another miserable half-hour, wondering how much longer the obstructive Mr Catworth meant to linger, and why providence, so falsely called merciful, had not seen fit to remove her from the world when, at the age of five, she had contracted scarlet fever. And yet, when, looking down from the window, she saw a neat individual descending the front steps, and knew that Cardross was at last at liberty, she at once wished that she might be granted just a few more minutes in which to recruit her forces.

But if the dreaded interview were not to be postponed until the morrow there was all too little time left to her; so she went quickly downstairs before a craven panic could wholly master her.

George, his foot on the bottom stair, drew back, saying that he had been on the point of coming to tell her that his lordship was now alone, and ready to receive her. He went before her to hold open the door into the library. He would have liked to have said something encouraging to her, because she looked so young and so scared, and put him in mind of his daughter, but that, of course, was impossible. It was as plain as a pikestaff she was in trouble, poor little thing: it was to be hoped his lordship would let her down easy, but he wasn't looking any too amiable.

He was looking very far from amiable. The instant she had crossed the threshold Nell knew that she had chosen her moment badly. He was standing beside his desk, his countenance very set, and he neither smiled nor moved forward to meet her. She had never before seen so sombre an expression in his eyes; her own eyes dilated a little in sudden alarm; she said involuntarily: 'Oh, what is it?'

It was a moment or two before he spoke, and then he said in a very level tone: 'I understand you particularly wish to speak to me. I am expecting a visit from Somerby, however, so unless the matter is of immediate importance it would be better, perhaps, if this interview were postponed until the morning.'

The cold formality of this speech struck her to the heart; she was only just able to say: 'It is of – most immediate importance! I must, I must tell you at once!'

'Very well. What is it?'

It was not encouraging, but she could not draw back. She said: 'The necklace – the Cardross necklace! It has gone!'

She thought he stiffened, but he did not speak. Frightened and perplexed, she stammered: 'You don't – I think you cannot have understood me!'

'Oh, yes! I understood you!' he said grimly.

'Cardross, pray – ! You are very angry – shocked –'

'Both! Too much to discuss it with you now! I will see you in the morning. I may be able to speak to you then with more moderation than is yet at my command!'

'Oh, say what you wish to me, but don't look at me so!' she begged. 'Indeed, indeed I didn't lose it through any carelessness! It has been *stolen*, Cardross!'

'I didn't suppose that you had mislaid it. Are you suggesting that some thief contrived to enter the house without anyone's being aware of it, or do you mean to accuse one of the servants?'

'I don't know, but I am dreadfully afraid it must have been one of the servants!' she said worriedly. 'They could have searched for it, but a stranger would not have known where to look, or – surely? – have thought it necessary to make it seem as though no one had been to my rooms, or stolen anything. I – I had no suspicion, you see! It might have been months before I discovered the loss, for it was hidden amongst the clothes Sutton put away in camphor.'

'And how does it come about that you have discovered it?' he asked. 'That is puzzling me a trifle, you know.'

'I didn't – it wasn't I who discovered it! Sutton found the case empty when she went to look over my winter clothes.'

'I see. How very disconcerting, to be sure!'

There was a derisive note in his voice, which made her stare at him in bewilderment. 'Disconcerting?' she repeated. 'Good God, it was far, far more than that, Cardross!'

'I am sure you were excessively shocked. I collect that Sutton did not make this unwelcome discovery until today?'

She did not answer him immediately. She had known that full confession would be difficult, but not that he would make it as difficult as this. She had to overcome an impulse to acquiesce, for it now seemed beyond her power to tell the whole of her tangled tale to this stranger who watched her with such merciless eyes, and spoke to her in so biting a tone. But the inward struggle lasted only for a minute. She drew a shuddering breath, and said faintly: 'No. I – I have known – since Tuesday. I must explain to you – try to explain to you – why I haven't told you – until today.'

'For God's sake, *no*! At least let me be spared that!'

She was startled, for the words had burst from him with savage violence. Her eyes leaped to his, and she recoiled instinctively from the blaze of anger she saw there. 'Cardross – !'

'Be silent!' He flung round towards his desk, and wrenched open one of its drawers. 'You need explain nothing to me – as you perceive!'

She stood staring in utter amazement, almost unable to believe her eyes, for what he had taken from the drawer and tossed contemptuously on to the desk was the Cardross necklace.

From a whirl of conjecture nothing coherent emerged; she was so much at a loss that she could only gasp: '*You* have it!'

'Yes, Madam Wife, *I* have it!' he replied.

Relief swept over her. 'Oh, how thankful I am!' she cried. 'But how – why – I don't understand!'

'Don't you? Then I will tell you!' he said harshly. 'It was brought to me not an hour ago by an astute little jeweller whose son – neither as astute, nor, I fancy, as honest as himself! – had bought it, yesterday, for the sum of two thousand pounds! I imagine he must have blessed himself for his good fortune: it cannot be every day that such easy clients present themselves! He would be obliged to cut the necklace up, of course, but even so it is worth a trifle more than two thousand, you know. No, you *don't* know, do you?'

She hardly heard the bitter, jeering note in his voice, or grasped the implication of his words. She was staring at him with knit brows, rather pale, and with her breath coming short and light. 'Yesterday,' she repeated. '*Yesterday*? Who – Did he tell you – *who*?'

His lips curled disdainfully. 'No, he didn't tell me that. His fair client – understandably, one feels! – was heavily veiled.' He caught the tiny sigh of relief that escaped her. 'Nor am I quite such a flat as to have wished for further information on that head!' he said, the savagery again rampant in his voice. 'A lady – unquestionably a lady! A *young* lady, dressed in the first stare of fashion, who would not disclose her name – how should she, indeed? – or accept a banker's draft in payment! Do you suppose, when I had been told *that*, that I catechised Catworth?'

'Catworth?' she said quickly. 'The man who came to see you – came twice to see you – has just been with you?'

'Exactly so! If only you had known! – Is that what you are thinking, my sweet love? How should you have known? It was not he who bought the Cardross necklace for a song! *You* met the son – quite a knowing one, in his way, I should suppose, but by no means as downy as the father! If my new-found acquaintance is to be believed, he had never seen or heard of the Cardross necklace. Well; it may be so! I am much in debt to the father, and should be reluctant to disbelieve him. After all, I have never dealt with a Cranbourn Alley jeweller. Perhaps young Catworth is not fly, but green! It is otherwise with the elder Catworth. *He* recognized the necklace the instant it was shown him, and saw his duty clear before him! I must always regret that I was not just in the humour to enjoy the scene as it deserved to be enjoyed! So discreet, he was! so virtuous! Not an ungentlemanly word spoken throughout! He did not even permit himself to hope for my future patronage, and he accepted without a blink every whisker that I uttered! An admirable man – I must certainly place a little business in his way! How very shabby it would be if I did not!'

He paused, but she did not speak, or move. There was a queer, blank look in her eyes: had he but known it, she was less concerned with the injustice of what he had said than with the realization of what must be the true story.

He picked up the necklace, and put it back in the drawer. Turning the key in the lock, and removing it, he said sardonically: 'You will forgive me, I trust, if henceforward I keep it in my own charge! I am persuaded you must, for you have never admired it, or wished to wear it, have you? You should have discovered its worth, however, before you set out to dispose of it. I cannot have my wife so easily gulled, Lady Cardross!'

At that, she blinked, and half lifted one hand in a beseeching gesture. 'Ah, no! Giles, *Giles*!'

It did not move him. 'Oh, don't waste your cajolery on me, my pretty one! You will catch cold at that now! I was a bigger flat than you, but, believe me, the game is up! You hoaxed me wonderfully: bowled me out with that sweet face, and those innocent ways! I thought I was up to every move on the board, but when I saw you – when you put your hand in mine, and looked up at me, and smiled –' He broke off, and seemed to make an effort to master the rage that was consuming him. 'You must pardon me! I had not meant to open my lips on this subject until I had had time to recover, in some sort, from the chagrin of having every suspicion, forced on me during the few months of our marriage, confirmed! Well! I have come by my deserts! I should have known better than to have been taken in by that lovely face of yours, or to have believed that under your charming manners you had a heart to be won! To be sure, you never gave me reason to think it, did you? How unjust of me to blame you for that! I will engage not to do so again, but must try to fulfil better *my* side of the bargain. It has been brought home to me how lamentably short of expectation I have fallen, but that can be mended, and shall be. Tell me, my sweet life, at what figure do you set your beauty, your dutiful submission, your admirable discretion, and your unfailing politeness?'

She had stood quite still, neither flinching from the ugly shafts aimed at her, nor making any further attempt to speak. She was very white, but although she heard what was being said to her she hardly attended to it. He was saying such terrible things, but he did not know the truth: he was saying those things to some creature who did not exist, not to her. It hurt her that he could so misjudge her, but she never thought of blaming him. Just so had she misjudged Dysart, and with far less cause.

'Well? Why do you hesitate? Or don't you know what I'm worth?'

She looked at him, and saw a stranger. She couldn't tell him all the truth while this black mood held him, much less disclose to him the shocking suspicion in her own heart. In the end he might have to know that too, but it was not certain yet. But if a worse disaster than he knew threatened him there might still be yet time to avert it. Only she must not waste precious moments in trying to justify herself, or expose Dysart and Letty to the white heat of his anger. Later she would tell him, but not now, when her own part in the affair had suddenly become a matter of very little importance beside what might well prove to be Letty's.

She tried to speak, and found that she had too little command over her voice. He was still watching her with those hard, angry eyes. That hurt her, and made tears spring to her own. She winked them away, and managed to say, with a pathetic attempt at a smile wavering on her lips: 'I can't answer you, you s-see. Later, I will. Not now!'

She went rather blindly towards the door. His voice checked her, even startled her a little. 'No, come back! I didn't mean it, Nell! *I didn't mean it!*'

He took a quick stride towards her, only to be brought up short by the opening of the door, and the entrance of his butler.

'I beg your lordship's pardon!' Farley said apologetically.

'Well, what is it?' Cardross snapped.

'I thought you would wish to know, my lord, that Sir John Somerby called to see your lordship ten minutes ago. He is waiting in the saloon.'

'Tell him I will be with him presently!'

'No, please go to him now!' Nell said gently, and left the room without again looking at him.

She went swiftly up the stairs, past her own rooms, and up another flight to Letty's. Martha, running up two minutes later, in answer to the summons of a bell clanging so wildly that it was plain its pull had been tugged with peremptory vigour, found her standing in the middle of the room, and quailed under the sternly accusing look in her eyes. 'Oh, my lady! I didn't know it was your ladyship!'

'Where is your mistress, Martha?'

With the instinct of her kind to admit nothing, Martha said defensively: 'I'm sure I couldn't say, my lady.'

'Indeed! Then will you come down, if you please, to his lordship,' Nell said calmly, gathering up her half-train and moving towards the door.

That was enough to induce Martha, in a panic, to tell all she knew. It was not very much. She had indeed accompanied Letty to Bond Street that afternoon, where they had met Selina Thorne. Letty had sent her home then, saying that she would go with her cousin to Bryanston Square, and her aunt would convey her home later in the carriage.

'Was Mrs Thorne with Miss Selina?' Nell demanded.

'Oh yes, my lady!' Martha said, a little too glibly.

'Did you see her?'

Martha hesitated, but the unwavering blue gaze disconcerted

her, and she muttered that Miss Selina had said she was in Hookham's.

'I see. At what hour was this?'

'I – I don't know, my lady! Not to say precisely! It was when my Lord Dysart was with your ladyship that we stepped out.'

'Lord Dysart left this house before two o'clock. It is now half-past six, but Lady Letitia hasn't returned, and you felt no anxiety?'

'I thought – I thought it was her ladyship that rang for me!'

Nell's eyes swept the room. 'But you have not laid out her ball-dress?'

'Her ladyship said – perhaps she should not go to the Assembly, my lady! She said – not to get in a pucker if she was late, or to say anything to anyone, except that she was gone to Mrs Thorne's, but she didn't tell me more! On my truth and honour she didn't, my lady!'

'You must have known, however, that she didn't mean to return. No, don't tell me lies, if you please! Lady Letitia does not take her brushes and combs and her toothpowder when she goes shopping.'

Martha burst into tears, sobbing that she had not known, that her ladyship had given her a parcel to carry, saying it contained some things she meant to give to Miss Selina. Yes, it was quite a large bundle, but she didn't know what was in it; her ladyship had packed it herself, and never told her; and she would happily lay down her life for her ladyship, particularly when the dear angel was being made so miserable as never was, and not a soul to turn to but one who had served her from the cradle, as it were.

'That will do. I think you have acted this part with the intention of doing your mistress a service, and did not mean to help her to do anything that would bring down the most dreadful consequences on her. But if she has indeed eloped you will have done her the worst turn that lay in your power. I hope she has not – indeed, I believe that Mr Allandale has a greater regard for her reputation than you have shown. I don't know what I may be obliged to tell his lordship: that must depend on whether I can find her ladyship, and bring her safely home. And also, a little, on your conduct *now*.'

The terrified Martha, eyes starting from her head, and teeth chattering, began to gasp out promises of abject obedience, but Nell cut short her protestations, saying: 'Stop crying, and listen to me! I am going immediately to Mrs Thorne's, and if I find your mistress there, or can discover from Miss Selina where she may have gone, perhaps no one need know what has taken place today. So you will not speak of this to anyone. Do you understand me? If you should be asked where I am, you must say that you don't know. Now go downstairs again and desire Sutton to come to my bedchamber, if you please!'

Sutton, entering her room five minutes later, in the expectation of helping her to change her dress, found her clad for the street, in her bonnet and a light pelisse. Before she could give expression to her surprise, Nell said coolly: 'Sutton, it is very vexatious, but I am obliged to go out. I don't know how long I may be.' She raised her eyes from the gloves she was drawing over her fingers, and said: 'Perhaps you may guess my errand. I am persuaded I can rely on your discretion, if that is so.'

'Your ladyship may always do so. But if, as I fancy is the case, you are going to find Lady Letitia, I beg you will permit me to accompany you.'

'Thank you. It is unnecessary, however. I – have a particular reason for wishing you to remain here. I am very reluctant to let it be known to anyone – if Lady Letitia has done something foolish which – which perhaps I may be able to mend!'

'I understand you perfectly, my lady. My lips shall be sealed, come what may!' announced Sutton, in prim accents, but with the resolute mien of one bound for the torture chamber.

'Well, I don't think anything very dreadful will come of it,' said Nell, smiling faintly. 'His lordship doesn't dine at home tonight, so perhaps he will not enquire for me. But if he should do so, could you say that you suppose me to have gone out to dinner? He won't ask then where Lady Letitia is, because he will think she must be with me.'

'Certainly, my lady. He shall learn nothing from me.'

'I am very much obliged to you. One other thing: can you, do you think, contrive to draw George out of the hall so that he doesn't see me leave the house? He would think it odd, and perhaps talk of it, you know.'

'Very likely, my lady! I will step downstairs immediately, and desire him to fetch up your ladyship's dressing-case from the boxroom,' said Sutton with aplomb.

'But what in the world should I want it for?' Nell objected.

'That, my lady, is none of George's business!' replied Sutton coldly.

Whatever George may have thought, the ruse proved successful. There was no one in the hall to see Nell slip out of the house; and no one within earshot when she softly shut the front-door behind her. She heaved a sigh of relief, and set off quickly in the direction of the nearest hackney-coach stand.

Thirteen

*M*rs Thorne's butler, opening the door to Nell in time to see the hackney which had brought her to Bryanston Square move slowly away, was very much surprised that her ladyship should have deigned to enter such a lowly vehicle, but she had expected that he would be, and told him in the easiest way that her carriage had suffered a slight accident. He seemed satisfied with this explanation, but when she asked for his mistress he was obliged to tell her that Madam had retired to her room to change her dress for dinner.

'Then, if you please, be so good as to ask your mistress if I may go up to her,' said Nell, as though it were the most natural thing in the world for a lady of quality to arrive in a common hackney half-an-hour before dinner-time, wearing a morning-dress, and coolly demanding to be taken up to her hostess's bedroom. The butler looked doubtful, but he went to deliver this message, returning almost immediately to beg her ladyship to step upstairs.

Mrs Thorne was seated before her dressing-table, enveloped in a voluminous wrapper, and with her hair only half-pinned up into the elaborate fashion of her choice. She was a stout, goodnatured looking woman, and when she rose to greet Nell she seemed rather to surge out of her chair. 'Oh, my dear Lady Cardross, pray come in, and forgive my receiving you in such a way! But I would not keep you waiting while I scrambled on my clothes, and so I told Thomas to bring you to me straightaway.'

'It is very kind of you. I should not be troubling you at such an awkward time,' Nell said, shaking hands. 'May I talk privately to you for a few minutes?'

'Oh, my dear! Yes, yes, to be sure you may! Go and see if Miss Fanny is dressed yet, Betty! I will ring for you when I want you back again. Set a chair for her ladyship before you go! Do, pray, be seated, Lady Cardross!' She herself sank back into the chair before the dressing-table, saying, almost before her maid was out of the room: 'Tell me at once, my dear! When Thomas came to say that you were below, *such* a presentiment shot through me! And I can see by your face I was right!'

'I don't know – I hope not! Mrs Thorne, has Letty been with you today?'

'Oh, my goodness gracious me!' cried Mrs Thorne. 'If I didn't know it! No, my dear, I haven't seen Letty since she visited us last week. Don't tell me she has gone off with young Allandale! Wait! Where are my smelling-salts? Now tell me everything!'

Clutching the vinaigrette, and warding off a series of palpitations by frequently sniffing its aromatic contents, she managed to listen to the story Nell unfolded without succumbing to the various nervous ills which threatened to prostrate her. She was very much shocked, interrupting the tale with groans, and horrified ejaculations, but there was nothing she could do to help Nell, because she knew nothing. She had never encouraged Mr Allandale: girls liked to flirt, and there was no harm in that; but when she had learnt that Letty considered herself engaged to a young man without a penny to bless himself with, and no prospects worthy to be mentioned, she had never been more upset in her life.

Nell was obliged to break in on her volubility, and to beg that Selina might be sent for. Mrs Thorne was perfectly agreeable, but she could not think that Selina would be able to throw any light on the mystery of her cousin's whereabouts. When she was told of the meeting that afternoon in Bond Street, she could scarcely be brought to believe that such a thing could have happened. 'Selina going off to Bond Street! Oh, you don't mean it, Lady Cardross! I never heard of such a thing! To be sure, girls aren't kept so strict now as they were when I was young – why, not a step outside the house could I take unless my mother, or the governess was with me! And very irksome it was, I can tell you! I made up my mind I wouldn't use *my* girls so, and nor I have, but as for letting any of them go jauntering about town without one of her sisters, or Betty, to go with her, that would be quite beyond the line! Good gracious, whatever would people say? It doesn't bear thinking of, and if I find Martha was telling you the truth, which, however, it's very likely she wasn't, I declare Selina shall go to Miss Puttenham's seminary, say what she will! It was what Mr Thorne said she should do, when Miss Woodbridge left us, but she pleaded so hard against it – well, there! But that Martha would say anything! Depend upon it, my dear Lady Cardross, Selina knows no more than the man in the moon where her cousin may be!'

But when Selina presently came into the room it was evident even to her fond parent that she knew very well why she had been sent for. She was in fine feather, and perfectly ready to be martyred in her cousin's cause. Hers had not been the chief rôle in the delightful drama, but she had been able easily to convince herself that without her self-abnegating offices the interested parties would by this time have been obliged to resign themselves to their equally disagreeable fates. Letty (if she did not go into a decline, and expire within the year) would have been ruthlessly forced into marriage with a titled Midas of evil disposition, at whose hands she would have suffered brutal ill-usage; and Mr Allandale, unaccountably forgotten by his superiors, would have worn out his life in a foreign land, always carrying his lost love's likeness next to his heart, and dying (in circumstances of distressing neglect and anguish) with her name on his writhen lips.

Until she found herself confronting Nell, of whom she stood in a good deal of awe, this affecting story had seemed to her so probable as to border on the inevitable. She had several times rehearsed the elevating utterances she would make, if called upon to account for her actions; and in these scenes every effort made by Letty's persecutors to drag from her the secret of her whereabouts failed. Sometimes she remained mute while the storm raged over her devoted head; but in general she was extremely eloquent, expressing herself with such moving sincerity that even such worldly persons as her father and Lord Cardross were often brought to see how false and mercenary were their ideas, and emerged from the encounter with changed hearts, and the highest opinion of her fearlessness, nobility, and good sense.

But in these scenes the other members of the caste spoke the lines laid down for them; in real life they said things so very different as to throw everything quite out of joint. In the event, Selina pronounced only one of her rehearsed speeches. Asked by her mother if she knew what had become of Letty, she clasped her hands at her breast, and declined to answer the question. She then invited the two ladies to threaten her as much as they chose, to do with her what they would; but warned them that they would find it impossible to force her to betray her cousin.

Mrs Thorne should then have conjured her daughter on her obedience to divulge the truth; instead, and with a lamentable lack of histrionic ability, she begged her irritably not, for goodness sake, to start any of her play-acting; and before Selina could recover from this set-back Nell completed her discomfiture by saying in a tone of grave reproof: 'Indeed, Selina, you must not make-believe over this, for I am afraid it is much more serious than you have any idea of.'

After that, there could be no recapturing the dramatic flavour of the piece. Selina did say that she wouldn't tell anything, but even in her own ears this sounded very much more sulky than noble; and when Mrs Thorne, heaving herself out of her chair, declared her intention of hailing her immediately before her papa, who would know how to deal with such impertinence, instead of behaving like a heroine, she collapsed into frightened tears.

It took a little time to drag the whole story out of her and the effect of her revelations on Mrs Thorne was severe enough to make Nell feel profoundly sorry for the poor lady. She was so much stunned by the discovery that when she had believed Selina to have gone under the escort of her maid to a dancing-class, or a music-lesson, that abandoned damsel had been setting forth by stealth for the most fashionable quarter of the town, alone, and for the purpose of aiding and abetting her cousin in conduct that, if it were to become known, would disgrace them both for ever in the eyes of all persons of ton, that she could do nothing but reproach Selina, and wonder how she came to have a daughter so lost to all sense of propriety. It was left to Nell to question Selina, which she did with a gentle coldness that overawed her far more than did her mother's scoldings.

Letty had sold the necklace to Catworth on the day that she had gone with her cousin to choose a wedding-gift for Fanny. They had dismissed the carriage outside the Pantheon, telling the coachman to call for them at Gunter's, in Berkeley Square, considerably later in the day. After purchasing a couple of thick veils, they had set out in a hack for Cranbourn Alley, having discovered the existence of the firm of Catworth and Son through the simple expedient of asking the jarvey on the box to recommend them a jeweller not patronized by persons of quality. While Letty had transacted her business with the younger Catworth, Selina had remained in the hack, because the jarvey, when instructed to wait outside the shop, apparently suspecting them of trying to give him the slip, had expressed a strong wish of being paid off then and there.

After the sale of the necklace, only one thing was needed for an elopement, and that was the bridegroom, who was then still out of town.

At this point, Mrs Thorne exclaimed: 'Never tell me Allandale was ready to take her with no more than two thousand pounds!'

'My dear ma'am, you cannot suppose that Mr Allandale was a party to such a thing!' Nell said.

'No, he wasn't,' corroborated Selina. 'Letty said she would tell him she had it from her godfather, in case he should think she ought not to have taken the necklace.'

The two girls had met that afternoon by prearrangement, and

as soon as Martha had been got rid of, which was done because Letty wished, with rare consideration, to protect her from blame, they had purchased such necessities as Letty had been unable to pack in her bundle, and brought them to Bryanston Square, to be bestowed in an old cloak-bag belonging to Papa. Finally, Letty had departed in a hackney for Mr Allandale's lodging in Ryder Street. 'But you won't catch them,' Selina said, with a last flicker of defiance, 'because that was *hours* ago, and you may depend upon it they are many miles away by now!'

This seemed all too probable to Mrs Thorne, sinking back in her chair with a groan of dismay, but Nell was more hopeful. When Selina had been dismissed to bed, with the promise of bread and water for her supper, an interview with Papa on the morrow, and incarceration for an unspecified length of time in a Bath seminary for young ladies, she rose to her feet, saying that she would go at once to Ryder Street.

'But what is the use, my dear?' wailed Mrs Thorne. 'You heard what that wicked child of mine said! They're off to Gretna Green, depend upon it!'

'I cannot credit it! No doubt that was Letty's plan, but I shall own myself astonished if it was Mr Allandale's. Oh, he would not do such a thing! I am quite confident he would not!'

'Good gracious, Lady Cardross, where else could they go? They couldn't be married in England, what with Letty's being under age, and special licences, and I don't know what beside! Surely to goodness he wouldn't have let her run away to him if he didn't mean to marry her immediately?'

'I don't believe he knew anything about it,' declared Nell. 'Only consider, ma'am! He is a respectable man of superior sense, and with extremely nice notions of propriety. I am persuaded he would not entertain for an instant the thought of eloping with a child of Letty's age. Her expectations, too! Oh, no, he couldn't do it! If his own good feeling did not prevent him, the knowledge that he would be thought to have behaved like a most unprincipled fortune-hunter surely would!'

'Ay, there is that,' agreed Mrs Thorne, a little doubtfully. 'He would lose his employment, too, I daresay. But, you know, my dear, when a man falls head over ears in love there's no saying what he may do. And you aren't going to tell me Letty ran off to elope with him without him knowing she meant to do it!'

'Yes, I am,' Nell said, on a tiny choke of laughter. 'It would be exactly like her to do so!'

'Well!' gasped Mrs Thorne. 'Of all the brazen little hussies! A nice surprise it will be for Allandale when he goes home from the Foreign Office, thinking of nothing but his dinner, as I don't doubt he will be, and finds that naughty girl in his lodging, as bold as brass, and expecting him to set out with her for Scotland! Well, I hope it will be a lesson to him, that's all! Only, if that's the way it was, why didn't he bring her back to you long since?'

'I've thought of that,' Nell said. 'It does seem strange, but if he were kept late at his work – ? Then, too, it would take him a little time, you know, to persuade Letty to give up the scheme. In fact, the likeliest chance is that she fell into one of her hysterical fits of crying, and the poor man could not have the least notion how to stop her! Oh, I must go to Ryder Street at once!'

The conviction that she would arrive at Mr Allandale's lodging to find him endeavouring to soothe his would-be bride grew steadily upon Nell as she was bounced and jolted there in yet another hack, and she began to be quite buoyant again, feeling that if she could only restore his sister to Cardross with her reputation unblemished she would have done much to atone for the follies and extravagances of the past weeks. But when the hackney turned out of St James's Street into Ryder Street, she suffered a check. The coachman pulled up his aged horse, and clambered down from the box to discover what was the number of the house she wished to visit; and it suddenly occurred to Nell that she did not know it. Nor did the coachman. Asked if he was perhaps familiar with Mr Allandale, he said he wasn't one to bother his head over the names of the gentlemen who patronized him, and surveyed his fair passenger with unwelcome interest. She was put a little out of countenance by this, and had, indeed, been feeling a trifle uneasy from the moment the hack turned into St James's Street, and she had seen all the clubs' windows lighted up, and several gentlemen of her acquaintance strolling along the flagway. This quarter of fashionable London, which lay between Pall Mall and Piccadilly, belonged almost exclusively to the Gentlemen, and it was not considered good ton for a lady to be seen within its bounds. Nearly all the clubs were to be found in St James's Street; and the streets which led from it abounded in bachelor lodgings and gaming-halls. The coachman was plainly wondering whether he had been mistaken in the social status of his fare, and Nell was beginning to feel rather helpless and extremely uncomfortable when she providentially remembered that Mr Hethersett also lived in Ryder Street, and would no doubt be able to direct her to Mr Allandale's abode, if she were fortunate enough to find him at home. So she told the coachman to drive her to Number 5. It did not seem probable that Mr Hethersett would be at home, for it was now past eight o'clock, but fortune favoured her. Just as she was searching in her reticule for her purse the door of No 5 was opened, and Mr Hethersett himself came out of the house, very natty in knee-breeches and silk stockings, a waistcoat of watered silk, a swallow-tailed coat, and a snowy cravat arranged by his expert hands in the intricate style known as the Mathematical Tie. Set at a slight angle on his oiled locks was an elegant chapeau bras, and hanging from his shoulders was a silk-lined cloak. He carried a pair of gloves in one hand, and an ebony cane in the other, but perceiving the unusual spectacle of a lady engaged in paying off a hackney-coachman at his very door, he transferred the gloves to his right hand so that he could raise to one eye the quizzing-glass that was slung about his neck. At just this moment, Nell turned to mount the few steps to his door, and uttered a joyful exclamation. 'Felix! Oh, how glad I am to have caught you!'

The jarvey, observing that the expression on Mr Hethersett's face was of profound dismay, clicked his tongue disapprovingly. In his view, Nell – as dimber a mort as he had clapped eyes on in a twelvemonth – was worthy of a warmer greeting than the startled: 'Good God!' which broke from Mr Hethersett.

'What the deuce brings you here?' demanded Mr Hethersett, alarmed out of his usual address. 'Cardross hasn't met with an accident, has he? Or –'

'Oh, no, no! nothing like that!' she assured him. 'I shan't keep you above a moment – are you on your way to a party? – but I have most stupidly forgotten the number of the house Mr Allandale lodges in!'

Disappointed in this conversation, the jarvey adjured his lethargic steed to get up, and drove slowly off.

'Thank the lord he's gone!' said Mr Hethersett. 'You know, cousin, you shouldn't be driving about in a hack, and coming here to ask for Allandale's direction! I mean – not my business, but it ain't at all the thing! Cardross wouldn't like it. Besides, what do you want with Allandale?'

'Well, that isn't your business either!' Nell pointed out. 'And if Cardross knew I was here he would have not the least objection, I assure you, for I am here for a very sufficient purpose. So will you, if you please, tell me the number of Mr Allandale's lodging, and then you may go to your party, and not trouble your head over me any more?'

'No,' said Mr Hethersett, with unexpected firmness. 'I won't! Well, I should be bound to trouble my head over you: stands to reason! Because it seems to me you're up to something dashed smoky, cousin. And as for saying Cardross wouldn't object to your paying calls in a hack at this time of day – well, if that's what you think, you can't know him! What I'm going to do is take you home.'

'No, you are not!' said Nell indignantly. 'Now, Felix, just because you met me in Clarges Street that day does *not* give you the right to try to bully and hector me over this!'

'Never mind that! – By the by, I hope all's right about that business?'

'Yes, yes, Dysart settled it for me.'

'He did, did he?'

'Yes, for he has won a great deal of money on a horse called Cockroach. It was not very handsome of you to have betrayed me to him, however!'

'No, I know it wasn't. Best thing I could think of, though. What we want now is another hack.'

'No – though I hope it is what I may want in a very little time. I suppose I shall be obliged to tell you what has happened,' she sighed.

'Good God, cousin, do you take me for a flat?' demanded Mr Hethersett. 'If you're searching all over for Allandale, it means that Letty is up to her tricks. What's she done? Eloped with the fellow?'

'I very much fear it.'

'Eh?' he said incredulously. 'No, no, not the sort of fellow to do a scaly thing like that! I was only funning!'

But when he had heard all that Nell saw fit to tell him of the day's events he looked a good deal taken aback, and acknowledged that the affair bore all the appearance of an uncommonly rum set-out. 'What's more, if Allandale's made off with her – yes, but dash it, cousin, that won't fadge! I mean, it wouldn't be up to the rig, and though I can't say I like him above half there's nothing of the queer nab about him!'

'No, indeed! and that is what makes me very hopeful of finding them still here,' she explained. 'So pray will you direct me to the house?'

'Yes, but where's Cardross?' he demanded. 'He can't have gone out of town again, because I saw him at White's this afternoon! It's his business to find Letty, not yours.'

'He – he is dining out tonight, and then, too, he had Sir John Somerby with him, you see.'

'What you mean,' said Mr Hethersett severely, 'is that you haven't told him.'

'No,' she confessed. 'I – I haven't.'

'Well, you ought to have done so. Very unwilling to offend you, cousin, but you've got no right to play the concave suit with Cardross over that chit. Dash it, she's his ward! Daresay you're fond of her, but it won't do to be hoaxing Giles about today's business.'

'No,' she agreed. 'Indeed, I don't mean to, Felix! Only the thing is that – he – he is very much vexed today. Something occurred that put him sadly out of temper, and I particularly don't wish to be obliged to break this news to him when – when perhaps he would be quite dreadfully angry with Letty!'

'Good thing if he was!' said Mr Hethersett unfeelingly. 'If you want to know what I think, it's my belief that the sooner you're rid of that resty girl the better it will be. Unsteady, that's what she is. Maggotty, too: never know where to take her, or what she'll be up to next!' He glanced fleetingly at Nell, but it had grown rather too dark for him to be able to see her face very clearly. However, he had drawn certain conclusions which he was pretty sure were accurate, so he added, in a careless way: 'Shouldn't be surprised if it was her starts that had put him out of temper.'

Nell said nothing in reply to this. The lamplighter was coming down the street, with his ladder carried between him and the boy who followed at his heels. Nell, who was tired of standing outside Mr Hethersett's house, pointed this circumstance out to him, saying: 'Won't he think it excessively odd that we should be standing here?'

'Yes, but we ain't going to stand here,' replied Mr Hethersett. 'It don't look to me as though Allandale's at home, but we may as well enquire for him.'

'Do you mean to say that he lives next door to you?' demanded Nell.

'Yes. Well, no reason why he shouldn't!' said Mr Hethersett, surprised at the indignant note in her voice. 'What I mean is, he don't trouble me: hardly ever see him!'

'And you have kept me standing outside all this time! It is a great deal too bad of you!' said Nell, treading up the steps to the door, and grasping the heavy brass knocker.

'I was trying to think what I should do with you while I did the trick here. Trouble is there ain't anywhere for you to go, but you oughtn't to be asking for Allandale, you know! Leave it to me, cousin!'

She was quite ready to do this, but when the door was opened, and Mr Hethersett asked the proprietor of the establishment if Mr Allandale was at home, and was told that he was not, he seemed so much inclined to withdraw without pursuing his enquiries any farther that she felt obliged to intervene. Disregarding a horrified murmur of protest from Mr Hethersett she boldly asked if Mr Allandale had gone out alone, or accompanied by a lady.

'Would it be Mr Allandale's sister you was referring to, ma'am?' asked the man cautiously.

'Yes,' said Nell, with great promptness.

'Ah!' said the proprietor, stroking his chin in a ruminative way. 'That's what *he* said, I don't deny, but it wasn't what *she* said, which puts me in a fix, in a manner of speaking, because if it was his sister you was wishful to see I couldn't say it was her as was here today, not to take my oath on it, I couldn't. The young party as came here asking for Mr Allandale told Mrs Shotwick, which is my good lady, as how she was engaged to be *married* to him. Which is different.'

'Well, that is the lady I wish to find,' said Nell.

'Ah!' said Mr Shotwick, still caressing his chin. '*I've* no objection, but the question is, *can* you, ma'am? Because she ain't here. Nor hasn't been, this three hours and more. Which I'm just as glad she hasn't, on account of all the bobbery there was.'

'Oh, dear!' Nell said, her heart sinking. 'What – what *sort* of bobbery?'

'No, dash it, cousin – !' expostulated Mr Hethersett, by this time in a state of acute discomfort.

At this point Mr Shotwick was struck by the happy idea of inviting them to step inside so that they might discuss the delicate matter with the mistress of the establishment. Nell readily agreed to this, Mr Hethersett not so readily, and they were ushered into Mr Allandale's parlour, on the right of the front door, and left there while Mr Shotwick went off to summon his wife on to the scene.

'Oh, Felix, what can have happened?' Nell said. 'Gone for more than three hours! When that man said they were not here I thought at first that perhaps Mr Allandale had taken Letty home, and I should find her there when I return. But three hours! Where can she be, if they have not eloped together?'

'I don't know where she can be,' said Mr Hethersett. 'I know where we are, however, and it ain't where I want to be. I'm dashed sure this fellow knows who *I* am, and the next thing we shall find is that he's twigged who *you* are. It'll be all over town before the cat's had time to lick her ear.'

'Well, if you don't like to be seen in my company, you may go away!' said Nell, with spirit.

'I *don't*,' said Mr Hethersett frankly. 'Particularly in this rig, when you ain't dressed for the evening. Not at all the thing: looks dashed peculiar! We shall have all the quizzes wondering what the deuce we were doing. Can't tell 'em we were looking all over for Letty!'

Anxious as she was, she could not help laughing at this. She said mischievously: 'It is very bad, for *your* credit is so good that I am persuaded no one would believe for an instant that you had done anything that was not good ton!'

'Yes, but this is not time for funning, my dear Lady Cardross! Besides, there's no saying what people will believe. The thing is, we're going the quickest way to work to get it set about that that wretched girl has gone clean beyond the line. What's more, Cardross will be as mad as fire with the pair of us for making cakes of ourselves, instead of telling him what had happened.'

She felt that this indeed might be true, but before she could reply Mr Shotwick had come back, with a stout dame in a mob-cap, whom he introduced as his good lady.

From the somewhat involved story that issued from Mrs Shotwick's lips it became apparent that the eruption of Letty into her hitherto ordered existence had disarranged her mind quite as much as it had shaken her faith in her favourite lodger. 'For, not to deceive you, ma'am, what to think I did not know, nor don't!'

Her first impulse, on learning from her spouse that a beautiful young lady, with a cloak-bag, had taken possession of Mr Allandale's parlour, with the expressed intention of remaining there until he returned to his lodging, had been to eject so bold a hussy immediately; but when she had sailed into the room to accomplish this desirable object she had suffered a check. She beheld Quality, and one did not turn Quality out of one's house, however respectable one might be. But she had been on the watch for Mr Allandale, and she had waylaid him on his entering the house, and had given him to understand that Goings-on under her roof she would not allow. It had struck her forcibly that upon hearing of his betrothed's presence in his parlour he had looked queer – to put it no higher.

'Queer as Dick's hatband,' corroborated Mr Shotwick.

'I should think he dashed well would look queer!' said Mr Hethersett, impatient of this circumstantial history.

'Ah!' said Mr Shotwick. ''Specially if he was trying to tip her the double, which was what we suspicioned, sir.'

'I'll thank you not to use that nasty cant, Shotwick!' said the wife of his bosom sharply. 'No such thought crossed *my* mind, not then it didn't!'

'Not till the kick-up started,' agreed Mr Shotwick. 'Lor', how she did take on! I thought we should have the neighbours in on us.' He shook his head mournfully. 'You couldn't help but compassionate her. But what has me fair flummoxed is the way he slumguzzled *us*! Because a quieter, nicer-behaved gentleman you couldn't find, not if you was to look from here to Jericho! But he tipped her the rise, no question!'

'That'll do!' said his wife. She looked significantly at Nell, and said darkly: 'Not a word shall pass *my* lips with a gentleman present, but I ask you, ma'am, what is anyone to think when a sweet, pretty young thing carries on like she was desperate, and begs and implores a gentleman – if such you can call him! – to marry her?'

'Crying five loaves a penny, in course,' said Mr Shotwick helpfully.

'Yes, never mind that! What I mean is, no such thing!' intervened Mr Hethersett, devoutly trusting that this expression was unknown to Nell. Not that there was any chance that she hadn't understood the gist of Mrs Shotwick's remarks: she was looking aghast, as well she might! 'All I want to know is, did they leave this house together, and did you hear where they were bound for?'

'That I cannot say,' replied Mrs Shotwick. 'Leave it they did, in a post-chaise and pair.'

'A post-chaise!' Nell echoed, in a hollow voice.

'A post-chaise it was, ma'am, as I saw with my own eyes, and which Mr Allandale stepped out to bespeak his own self,' nodded Mrs Shotwick. 'And this I will say: whatever he's done, he means to do right by that poor young thing now, for when I asked him what was to be done he answered me straight out there was only one thing he could do. I don't say he looked like he wanted to, but he was very resolute – oh, very resolute he was! He didn't say anything more to me, but turned sharp about and came back into this very room, where Miss was laid down on that sofa, looking that wore out as never was. But what he said to her I don't know, for he shut the door. All I do know is that whatever it was it had her up off of the sofa in a twinkling, and as happy as a grig! Then he went off to hire a chaise, and Miss called to me to help her pack his valise, and not another tear did she shed!'

'No need to worry about her, then,' said Mr Hethersett, making the best of a bad business. 'I'm much obliged to you!' He then requested Mr Shotwick to step out in search of a hack, and cast an uneasy glance at Nell. She was looking quite stricken, but, to his relief, she did not speak until Mrs Shotwick had curtseyed herself out of the room. He said curtly: 'Going to take you home. Nothing to be done. Too late. Very scabby conduct of Allandale's, but I'm bound to say I'm dashed sorry for him!'

'Oh, could he not have brought her back to her home?' Nell cried, wringing her hands.

'Not if she was screeching in hysterics,' said Mr Hethersett, with considerable feeling. 'What's more, I don't blame him!'

'I blame myself! If I had told Cardross of my suspicion! He might have been able then to have overtaken them, but *now* – ! I was so certain Mr Allandale would not – I thought I should be able to set the wretched business to rights, but I have only helped to ruin Letty!'

'Don't see that at all,' he replied. 'Plenty of time for Cardross to catch 'em, if he wants to. Only travelling with a pair of horses. Wouldn't make much difference if they had four. Give Cardross his curricle, and four good 'uns, and I'd back him, over the distance, if they'd had twice as long a start of him. You ever seen Giles with a four-in-hand? Well, he's top-of-the-trees, give you my word! Knows how to keep strange horses together, too.'

'Oh, do you think they could still be overtaken?' she said eagerly.

'Lord, yes! All we have to do – *Now* what is it?'

She had uttered a chagrined: '*Oh!*' and she now said: 'Cardross is not at home. He was dining out, and I don't know where!'

'No need to get into a taking over that,' replied Mr Hethersett calmly. 'Farley will know.'

This made her feel rather more cheerful, and upon Mr Shotwick's coming back to announce that a hack was waiting to take them up she started up, begging Mr Hethersett to make haste.

There was certainly a hack standing in the street: a large and dilapidated vehicle, whose body, hanging drunkenly between two old-fashioned perches, showed by tarnished silverwork, and an almost obliterated coat of arms, that it had descended a long way in the social scale since the days when, with a powdered coachman on the box, and two Knights of the Rainbow standing up behind, it had been the town chariot of a nobleman. It was not at all the kind of carriage any person of fashion would now choose to ride in, but Nell and Mr Hethersett, emerging from the house, found that their temporary possession of it was not to be undisputed. Two gentlemen were arguing with the jarvey on their right to claim it, and this worthy man had apparently found it necessary to come down from the box to preserve it from invasion.

Mr Hethersett, after one glance, tried to obscure the scene from Nell's view, saying tersely: 'Better step inside again till I've got rid of 'em!'

'But it's Dysart!' said Nell.

'Yes, I know it is, but we haven't any time to stand talking to him!' said Mr Hethersett.

'No, of course not, but he is trying to hire our hackney, and he must not!' said Nell, trying to push him out of the way.

'For the lord's sake, cousin, go back into the house!' begged Mr Hethersett. 'He ain't alone!'

'No, but the other is only Mr Fancot, and I *think*,' said Nell knowledgeably, 'that they are both of them a trifle foxed. Dysart!'

The Viscount, upon hearing himself addressed, turned. The light from the near-by street-lamp enabled him quite plainly to recognize his sister, but he knew better than to trust his eyes when he was (in his own estimation) a little above par. He called upon his companion for assistance. 'Corny, that ain't my sister Cardross, is it?'

'No,' said Mr Fancot obligingly.

'What a horrid creature you are, Dy!' remarked Nell, descending the steps. 'You cannot drive off in that coach, because it was brought for me, and I must have it. I am in the greatest haste, so do, pray, stop disputing with that poor man, and go away!'

'By God, it *is* my sister Cardross!' exclaimed the Viscount, thunderstruck.

'Yes,' agreed Mr Fancot, smiling vaguely but with immense affability at Nell.

'Well, there's no need to shout it all down the street!' said Mr Hethersett tartly.

The Viscount looked intently at him, while he wrestled silently with a problem. 'It's you, is it?' he said, a certain kindling in his eyes, and a brooding note in his voice. 'You, and my sister!'

Mr Hethersett, who had foreseen from the start that something like this would happen, said soothingly: 'Escorting her ladyship home!'

'Oh, you were, were you?' said the Viscount, showing signs of rising choler. 'We'll see that! Because it seems to me – Corny! Where *are* we?'

'Watier's,' said Mr Fancot, after a moment's thought.

'No, we ain't!' said his lordship, irritated.

'*Going* to Watier's,' amended Mr Fancot.

'*I'll* tell you where we are!' announced the Viscount, in menacing accents. 'We're in Ryder Street!'

'That's right, sir: Ryder Street it is,' said the jarvey encouragingly. 'You don't want no 'ack to take you to Watier's!'

'Ryder Street,' said the Viscount. '*Now* I know whose house you were coming out of! *Now* I know what made you take such an uncommon interest in my sister's affairs! By God, if I don't cut your liver out for this! As for you, my girl –'

'That'll do!' interrupted Mr Hethersett. 'You can cut my liver out in the morning, but for the lord's sake stop making such a damned kick-up in the street!'

'Not liver,' said Mr Fancot positively, his wandering attention recalled by this word. 'Duck. That's what we said, Dy. Got a way of cooking it at Watier's I like.'

'Well, you take Dysart there!' recommended Mr Hethersett.

''E can *take* him, but 'e won't never get 'im past the porter, guv'nor, not as lushy as what they both are!' observed the jarvey sapiently.

'Yes, I will,' said Mr Fancot. 'It's my birthday.'

'Get into the hack!' Mr Hethersett said to Nell. 'No, not you!'

Mr Fancot, hauled off the step of the coach by the jarvey, called upon the Viscount to come and give this individual one in the bread-basket, but the Viscount had more important matters to attend to. Addressing himself to Mr Hethersett, he commanded that harassed exquisite to name his friends.

Alarmed by his evident intention to force a quarrel on to Mr Hethersett, Nell laid a hand on his arm, and said: 'Dy, *pray* don't be so gooseish! You quite mistake the matter, you know! Indeed, it is abominable of you to think such horrid things, besides being excessively embarrassing!'

'Don't you try to bamboozle me!' replied her brother, shaking off her hand. 'Are you going to name your friends, sir, or are you not?'

'You wouldn't remember 'em if I did. What you need is a damper: you're as drunk as a brewer's horse!'

'Oh, no, I'm not! I'll tell you what *you* are! A damned loose fish! A regular hedge-bird! A man-milliner, by God! *Cowhearted!*'

'If you ain't stale-drunk in the morning, come round to my place, and I'll dashed well show you how cowhearted I am!' promised Mr Hethersett, stung by these opprobrious terms. 'It'll be bellows to mend with you, what's more! I've seen you sport your canvas at Jackson's, and when it comes to handy-blows you ain't any better than a moulder!'

'Now, by God – !' ejaculated the Viscount, squaring up to him. The jarvey called out approvingly: 'A mill, a mill!' Nell flung herself between the two incensed gentlemen; and Mr Fancot, who had been standing wrapped in thought, suddenly announced his intention of driving to Watier's in the hack, and disappeared round the back of the coach.

'Dysart, how dare you be so uncivil!' Nell said hotly. 'Pray don't heed him, Felix! I was never so mortified! Dysart, if you say another word to Felix –'

'It don't signify!' interrupted Mr Hethersett, who had had time to recollect the impropriety of engaging in fisticuffs in a lady's presence. 'Forgot myself!' he looked at the Viscount. 'If you want to fight, you can tell me so tomorrow! I'm going to escort her ladyship home now.'

'Oh, no, you ain't!' retorted the Viscount. '*I* am going to take her home! Yes, and I'm dashed well going to tell Cardross what sort of a May-game you've been playing, my buck!'

'Oh, dear, what are we to do?' said Nell distractedly. 'Felix, there are a couple of men coming towards us!'

'Good God! There's nothing for it: we shall have to take him along with us. Get into the hack, cousin!'

'Take him with us! But if Cardross sees him in this shocking state – !'

'Lord, Giles knows what he is!' said Mr Hethersett impatiently.

'Good heavens!' said Nell rather faintly. 'Then that must have been what he meant! How very dreadful!'

'Here, wait a bit!' suddenly said the Viscount. 'Where's Corny? Can't leave Corny behind: it's his birthday!'

'Well, thank goodness *he* has gone at least!' said Nell, as Mr Hethersett handed her up into the coach. 'If only we could persuade Dy – *Oh!*'

'Good God, what's the matter?' demanded Mr Hethersett, as she recoiled from the vehicle.

'He *hasn't* gone!' said Nell despairingly. 'He's inside, and I think he's fallen asleep!'

'Well, I'll be gormed!' exclaimed the jarvey, peering into the coach. ''E must have crope round when I wasn't a-watching of 'im, and got in by t'other door. Now we'll 'ave to 'aul 'im out again!'

'No, no, pray don't!' begged Nell, hurriedly getting into the coach. 'Only let us go away from here!'

'But I can't let you drive about the town with a couple of ensign-bearers!' expostulated Mr Hethersett. 'Oh, my God, if it ain't Bottisham bearing down on us! Well, that settles it: we can't stay here another moment! Here, Dysart, stop looking for Fancot *under* the hack! He's *in* it!' With this, he thrust the Viscount into the coach, gave a hurried direction to the jarvey, climbed into the coach himself, and slammed the door.

Fourteen

*I*t seemed at first as though the drive to Grosvenor Square was to be enlivened by a brawl, for although the Viscount's mind had been diverted by the loss of his friend, this aberration was but of short duration. No sooner had he satisfied himself that Mr Fancot was still with them than he discovered that Mr Hethersett was also with them, and took instant exception to his presence. However, before he could attempt to carry out his promise to throw him out Mr Fancot, roused by the jolting of the wheels over the cobblestones, woke up, and demanded to know where he was.

'Never mind that!' said the Viscount. 'Here's this curst fellow, Hethersett, got in with us! Help me to throw him out, will you?'

'No, no, can't do that!' said Mr Fancot, who was filled with a large tolerance. 'Very good sort of a man! Didn't know I'd invited him, but very glad he came.'

'You didn't invite him! Nobody invited him!' said the Viscount.

'Must have,' said Mr Fancot. 'Wouldn't have come if I hadn't. Polite to a point! Happy to take a glass of wine with him.'

'Well, if ever I saw old Corny so castaway!' exclaimed Dysart. 'Dashed if he ain't as drunk as a wheelbarrow!'

'Yes, but at least he is perfectly amiable!' said Nell. 'He doesn't say outrageous things, or try to throw people into the street!'

This unfortunate remark reminded the Viscount that his purpose was still unaccomplished, but just at that moment Mr Fancot began to warble an entirely unintelligible ditty. Since he was apparently afflicted with tone-deafness this musical interlude was a severe trial to the rest of the company, and caused the Viscount to forget Mr Hethersett again. 'Stop it, Corny!' he said indignantly.

'Chip-chip, cherry-chip, fol-di-diddle-di-dee!' sang Mr Fancot.

'*That's* not right!' said Dysart scornfully. 'It don't even make sense!' He then upraised his powerful baritone, and favoured the company with the correct version, which, as far as his sister could discover, differed hardly at all from his friend's. But Mr Hethersett, unmoved by Mr Fancot's outburst, was powerfully affected by the Viscount's. No sooner did the refrain of *Chip-chow, cherry-chow, fol-lol-di-riddle-low* break upon his ears than Nell felt him stiffen, and heard him utter an exclamation under his breath.

The Viscount beguiled the rest of the way with song, and was still singing when Cardross's astonished butler admitted the party into the house.

But it did not appear to be Lord Dysart's condition that surprised Farley. It was the sight of his mistress that made his eyes widen. He exclaimed involuntarily: 'My lady!'

'Yes, did you not know that I had been obliged to go out?' said Nell, with an attempt to carry the situation off unconcernedly. 'Pray show Lord Dysart and Mr Fancot into the library! They – they have come to take supper with me!'

'My birthday,' said Mr Fancot affably. 'Celebrating it! Blackbeetle, too.'

'*I* see, sir,' responded Farley, gently removing the hat from his grasp.

'Blackbeetle be damned!' said the Viscount. 'Cockroach! Where's his lordship?'

'His lordship is not at home, but he will be in directly, my lord,' replied Farley, consigning the visitors into the care of the footman who had followed him into the hall.

Mr Fancot was easily shepherded into the library, but the Viscount was recalcitrant. 'It ain't a bit of use trying to fob me off,' he told his sister sternly. 'I'm not letting you out of

225

my sight, Nell, so don't think it! Not with that fellow in the house!'

'Dysart, for heaven's sake – !'

'You'd better go with him, cousin,' advised Mr Hethersett. 'No sense in starting him off again on his high ropes! Much better leave this to me.'

Since Dysart had acquired a firm grip on her arm, there really seemed to be nothing else she could do, so, with a low-voiced entreaty to Mr Hethersett to lose no time in setting forth in search of Cardross, she retired to the library.

Here she was made welcome by Mr Fancot, happy in the belief that he was entertaining friends under his own roof. He shook her warmly by the hand, and offered her a glass of wine. She declined this, which distressed him; but Dysart, who had discovered glasses and a decanter set out on a side-table, said: 'No use pressing her: only two glasses!'

Mr Fancot was shocked. 'Only two glasses?' he repeated. 'That's absurd, Dy! No other word for it: absurd! Stupid fellow of mine misunderstood. Ring for more glasses!'

'We don't need any more glasses,' replied Dysart, lavishly pouring wine into the two that stood on the table.

'Yes, we do,' insisted Mr Fancot. 'Can't give a party with two glasses: stands to reason!'

'Well, it ain't a party. It ain't your house either.'

'It ain't?' Mr Fancot said incredulously. He subjected his surroundings to a keen, if somewhat owlish scrutiny. 'By Jove, Dy, so it ain't! Dashed if I know whose house it is! You know what, dear boy? Come to the wrong house! Better go.'

'No, we haven't. Came here to see Cardross,' said Dysart with a darkling look.

Mr Fancot thought this over profoundly. 'No,' he pronounced at last. 'Not sure why we came here, but we don't want to see Cardross. Nothing against him, mind! Not particularly acquainted with him, but capital fellow! Bang up to the mark. Honoured to meet him, but the thing is, not what we set out to do. Tell me this, Dy! Have we *dined*?'

'To hell with dinner! I'm going to see Cardross!' said Dysart obstinately.

'Oh, Dysart, I wish you will go away!' Nell exclaimed. 'You don't want to meet Cardross! you know you don't!'

'That's what I said,' nodded Mr Fancot, gratified. 'Not what we set out to do. Besides, he ain't here. Go to Watier's!'

'Not till I've seen Cardross. Got something to say to him. No business to let that fellow dangle after my sister! I'm going to tell him so.'

'Which fellow?' enquired Mr Fancot.

'Hethersett,' replied the Viscount, tossing off the wine in his glass. 'You know what he is, Corny? A damned Man of the Town! And there's Cardross, letting him make up to my sister, while he goes off like a regular Care-for-Nobody! What I say is, he's got no business to neglect her, and so I shall tell him!'

'He doesn't neglect me!' said Nell hotly. 'And if you were not so odiously foxed, Dy, you wouldn't say such detestable things!'

'Yes, I should,' he retorted. 'In fact, the more I think of it the more I can see he's too high in the instep by half! Took a pet because I held you up. Very well! if he didn't want me to hold you up, why didn't he do it himself? Tell me that! Who brought the dibs in tune for you? *I* did! Who stopped you getting into Jew King's clutches? –'

'Felix Hethersett did!' she intervened crossly, taking off her bonnet, and running her fingers through her flattened curls.

'Yes, by Jove, so he did!' exclaimed the Viscount, his eyes kindling. 'Like his damned impudence!'

Fortunately, since his mood was becoming increasingly belligerent, he was diverted by Mr Fancot, who suddenly offered to set him a main. He turned to find that his amiable friend, losing interest in the conversation, had seated himself by the table in the middle of the room, produced a dice-box from his pocket, and was engaged in throwing right hand against left. Drunk or sober, the Viscount was not the man to refuse a challenge of this nature. He instantly sat down on the other side of the table, and, to Nell's relief, became absorbed in his ruling passion. From this he was momentarily disturbed by the entrance of the footman, who came in bearing two tankards, which he silently set down at either gentleman's elbow. Dysart, staring at them, demanded to know what the devil he thought he was doing, and told him to bring in a bottle of brandy. The footman bowed, and withdrew, saying: 'Very good, my lord,' but he did not remove the homely tankards. Nor did he return to the library, but as the Viscount immediately struck a run of amazing and most unaccustomed good fortune his failure to bring in the brandy went unnoticed, both gamesters refreshing themselves with draughts of porter, and Dysart, having rapidly relieved Mr Fancot of his ready money, beginning to amass a number of notes of hand which that well-breeched young gentleman scrawled somewhat illegibly but with the greatest goodwill on leaves torn from his pocket-book.

Meanwhile, Mr Hethersett, to whose thoughtful offices they owed a beverage well-known for its sobering quality, had suffered a check. Farley was unable to tell him where his master had gone when he had left the house earlier in the evening.

Mr Hethersett eyed him. 'Dashed discreet, ain't you? Did he go off with Sir John Somerby?'

'No, sir, although I had understood that such was his intention. A meeting at the Daffy Club, sir, I fancy. But his lordship cried off.'

'Well, there's no need to make a mystery of it!' said Mr Hethersett, irritated. 'Where *did* he go?'

'That, sir, I cannot say, his lordship not having informed me. He had his whisky brought round, but he didn't take his groom with him, nor yet his Tiger, and when I ventured to ask him if he would wish supper to be prepared for him he said that he didn't know when he should be returning. His lordship appeared, sir, to be in quite a fret, if I may say so. Not at all like himself.'

The mystery was now plain to Mr Hethersett. In his experience it was a foolish waste of time to attempt to hoodwink one's servants. He had not for a moment imagined that the supposed secret of Letty's flight was not known to every member of the household, so he had no hesitation in saying bluntly: 'Set off after Lady Letitia, did he? Oh, well, if that's so, no need for me to find him!'

'No, sir,' replied Farley. 'His lordship was not aware that her ladyship had not returned to the house. I was not myself aware of it, until Miss Sutton – my lady's dresser, sir – informed me that Lady Letitia was gone to spend the night with Mrs Thorne. His lordship did not enquire for Lady Letitia. It was my Lady Cardross which his lordship was anxious to find.' He coughed delicately. 'No doubt some urgent matter which he wished to discuss with her ladyship,' he said, gazing limpidly at Mr Hethersett. 'Being as they were disturbed by Sir John Somerby, and her ladyship, in consequence, leaving the book-room rather hastily, sir.'

'Oh!' said Mr Hethersett, looking at him very hard.

'Yes, sir. So, as soon as he was rid – as soon, I should say, as Sir John left the house, his lordship went upstairs to find her ladyship, which, not being able to do, vexed him a trifle. Quite put out, he was, which was not to be wondered at, because it seems her ladyship forgot to inform him she was obliged to go out quite suddenly. And, of course, his lordship couldn't help but be in a fidget when he found that my lady's carriage had not been sent for. Very understandable, I am sure, sir, that his lordship should have felt anxious, for it was going on towards dinner-time, and naturally he wouldn't like to think of my lady's going out in such a way. Particularly,' he added, in a disinterested voice, 'if she was going on a journey.'

'Is that what he thought she was meaning to do?' demanded Mr Hethersett.

'Well, sir, that is not for me to say,' replied Farley carefully. 'But when his lordship questioned George, it came out that her ladyship had sent down to have her dressing-case taken up to her room. Just after she had parted from his lordship, that would have been.' He looked Mr Hethersett firmly in the eye, and said: 'What I thought, sir, was that very likely her ladyship had had word brought her that my Lord Pevensey was lying on his deathbed, perhaps – which would account for her going off like she did. Being quite distracted, which no one could wonder at.'

'Yes, well, you can stop pitching your gammon!' said Mr Hethersett indignantly. 'Dashed well ought to know better! Must know I ain't such an easy cove as to swallow all that humdudgeon! *I* know what you thought, and it was a bag of moonshine!'

'Yes, sir,' said Farley, bowing. 'I am very glad of it. I apprehend that her ladyship went in search of Lady Letitia, but on that subject I shall not presume to open my lips.'

'Well, see you don't!' recommended Mr Hethersett.

He then repaired to the library, where the Viscount, intent upon throwing a difficult chance, did not at first notice him. Nell, seated on the sofa at the end of the room, was a good deal dismayed to see him come walking in, for she had supposed him to have gone in search of Cardross. It was evident, since he had shed his cloak, that he had no immediate intention of leaving the house, and she could not help looking reproachfully at him, as he came towards her.

'No use,' he said, in an undervoice. 'Floored at all points. Farley don't know where Cardross is. Seems to me he's making a dashed cake of himself. In fact, it wouldn't surprise me if he's gone off to Devonshire.'

'Gone off to Devonshire?' she echoed, in amazement. 'Nonsense, why should he do such a thing?'

'Chasing after you,' he said. 'Shouldn't think he'd be such a gudgeon as to set off in a whisky, but he may have hired a chaise. Left the whisky at the posting-house.'

Quite bewildered, she said: But why should he think I had gone to Devonshire? Oh, Felix, are *you* foxed too?'

'No, of course I ain't! Been talking to Farley. No wish to pry into what don't concern me, but collect you had a turn-up with Cardross.' He added hastily, as the colour rushed into her cheeks: 'Not my business! The thing is, Giles found you wasn't in the house. Couldn't discover where you was gone, and, by what I can make out, was thrown into a rare taking. Silly gape-seed of a porter told him some farradiddle about taking your dressing-case up to your room. Sounds to me as if he was pitching it pretty rum, but can't be surprised it put Cardross in the devil of a pucker.'

'Oh, good God!' she exclaimed guiltily. 'That was only to draw George out of the hall! How *could* he suppose – ?' She stopped, and turned apprehensive eyes towards him. 'Did – did the servants think I had run away?'

'Lord, yes! Bound to!' he replied. 'However, it don't signify. What I mean is, you hadn't.'

'No, indeed! But to have caused such a commotion – set them all gossiping – Oh, do you think he will be very angry with me?'

'No, no! Might be in a miff, I daresay, but he'll come about,' he said soothingly. 'Must see you meant it for the best. Not your fault you made a mull of it.'

This well-meant consolation caused her to spring up, wringing her hands. 'Letty!' she uttered. 'Felix, it *is* my fault! Oh, if I had but told him! He will never forgive me!'

The Viscount, his attention jerked from the bones by her unguarded movement and raised voice, looked round. 'What the deuce – Well, by God, if that fellow Hethersett hasn't come sneaking back!'

'What are you still castaway?' said Mr Hethersett disgustedly. 'I wish you'd take yourself off!'

'Oh, you do, do you?' countered his lordship. 'Well, I'm not going to stir from this house while you're in it, my buck, and that you may depend on!'

Mr Fancot, with hazy recollection of earlier events, looked puzzled, and said: 'But you don't like him, Dy! You said you was going to throw him out.'

'Felix!' said Nell, too lost in agitated reflection to heed this interchange. 'There is nothing for it but for me to go after them! It may not be too late!'

'Good God, cousin, you can't do that!' said Mr Hethersett, shocked.

'If I went in our own chaise, and you were so very obliging as to go with me?' she urged. 'It may be hours before Giles returns, and then –'

'Well, upon my soul!' ejaculated the Viscount, rising with such hasty violence as to overset his chair. 'If that don't beat all hollow!' He seized his sister by the shoulders, and shook her. 'Have you taken leave of your senses?' he demanded. 'Go off in a chaise with that fellow? Not while I'm here to stop you!' He rounded suddenly on Mr Hethersett, an ugly look on his face. 'What damned cajolery have you been playing off on her?' he said fiercely.

'For the lord's sake, Dysart, go and dip your head in a bucket!' begged Mr Hethersett.

'Oh, listen!' Nell said sharply, her face turned towards the door.

A quick stride was heard approaching; the door was flung open, and Cardross stood on the threshold. There was a hard, anxious look on his face, and he had not stayed to put off his long, many-caped driving coat. His eyes swept the room, and found his wife. He went quickly forward, totally ignoring the rest of the company, saying in a shaken voice which she hardly recognized: 'Nell! Thank God! Oh, my darling, *forgive* me!'

'Giles! Oh, no! it was all my fault!' she cried, casting herself into his arms. 'And it is much, much worse than you know! Letty has gone with Mr Allandale!'

'*Damn* Letty!' he said, folding her close. 'You have come back to me, and nothing else is of the smallest consequence!'

Mr Hethersett, averting his eyes with great delicacy from the passionate embrace being exchanged, began to polish his quizzing-glass; the Viscount stared in thunderstruck silence; and Mr Fancot, after blinking at the extraordinary spectacle offered him, rose carefully to his feet, and twitched his friend's sleeve. 'Think we ought to be taking leave, Dy,' he said confidentially. 'Not the sort of party I like, dear boy! Go for a toddle to the Mutton-walk!'

'Damned if I will!' replied Dysart. 'I want a word with Cardross, and I'm going to have it!'

Recalled to a sense of his surroundings, Cardross looked up. Flushing a little, he let Nell go. 'By all means, Dysart: what is it?'

'I'll tell you in private,' said the Viscount, in whom the effects of his potations were beginning to wear off.

'Well, I don't know why you should suddenly wish to be private!' said Nell, with unusual asperity. 'When you have been saying the most abominable things without the least regard for anyone, even the hackney coachman! Besides trying to call poor Felix out in the most insulting way! Oh, Giles, pray tell him he must not do so!'

'But why in the world should he wish to?' asked Cardross, startled, and considerably amused.

'Silly clunch saw her ladyship coming away from Allandale's lodging with me, and would have it that it was *my* lodging,' said Mr Hethersett tersely, responding to the laughing question in his cousin's eye.

'Oh, that's the tale is it?' said the Viscount. 'Well, it won't fadge! Didn't think to tell *me* that, did you? Why not? That's what I want to know! *Why not?*'

'Because you were a dashed sight too ripe to attend to a word anyone said to you!' replied Mr Hethersett, with brutal frankness.

'And in any event there was no need for you to behave in such an outrageous way, Dy,' interpolated Nell severely. 'Even if it *had* been Felix's house, which it might as well have been, because I had the intention of calling on him, on account of my not knowing the number of Mr Allandale's. Only, by good fortune, he chanced to be coming out just as I was paying off the hack.'

'Yes, you have that mighty pat, haven't you, my girl?' said Dysart. 'And I daresay you think it makes all right! Well, it don't! Pretty conduct in a female of quality to be paying calls on every loose fish on the town, I must say! In a common hack, too! Well, that may suit your notions of propriety, Cardross, but it don't suit mine, and so I'll have you know!'

'Dy, how can you be so absurd?' protested Nell. 'No one could possibly think poor Mr Allandale a *loose fish*!'

'Dash, it, cousin!' exclaimed Mr Hethersett indignantly.

'My dear Dysart, do let me assure you that I honour you for such feelings, and enter into all your ideas on the subject!' said Cardross. 'You may safely leave the matter in my hands.'

'That's just what it seems to me I can't do!' retorted Dysart. 'Yes, and that puts me in mind of another thing I have to say to you! Why the devil don't you take better care of Nell? Did you get her out of a silly scrape? No, you didn't! *I* did! All you did was to put it into her head you thought she only married you for your fortune, when anyone but a gudgeon must have known she's too big a pea-goose to have enough sense to do anything of the kind. So when she finds herself under the hatches she daren't tell you: *I* have to pull her out of the River Tick! A pretty time I had of it! Why, I even had that fellow Hethersett hinting it was *my* fault she was being dunned for some curst dress or other!'

Mr Hethersett blushed. 'Misapprehension! Told you so at the time!'

'Well, it was my fault!' said Dysart furiously. 'I daresay if I hadn't borrowed three centuries from her *you* wouldn't have had to snatch her off Jew King's doorstep, but how was I to know it would put her in the basket? Besides, I've paid it back to her!'

'Nell, my poor child, how *could* you think – Did I frighten you as much as *that*?' Cardross said remorsefully.

'No, no, it was all my folly!' she said quickly. 'I thought that shocking bill from Lavalle had been with those others, only it *wasn't*, and when she sent it me again it seemed as though I *couldn't* tell you! Oh, Dysart, *pray* don't say any more!'

'Yes, that's all very well, but I am going to say something more! I've a pretty fair notion of what your opinion of me is, Cardross, but I'll have you know that it was not I who prigged that damned necklace of yours!'

'Eh?' ejaculated Mr Hethersett, startled.

'You have really no need to tell me that, Dysart,' Cardross replied, his colour heightened, and his eyes fixed on Nell's face.

'Well, it's what my own sister thought!' said Dysart bitterly.

'Good God, Giles, you've never lost the necklace?' Mr Hethersett demanded.

'No,' answered Cardross, holding Nell's hand rather tightly. 'It isn't lost. If it were, I should not imagine for one instant that you had taken it, Dysart.'

'Much obliged to you!'

'I must say, that's the outside of enough,' observed Mr Hethersett. 'Whatever made you take a notion like that into your head, cousin?'

'It was very, very foolish of me!'

'Well, I call it a dashed insult!' declared the Viscount.

'Yes, Dysart: so do I!' said Cardross, raising Nell's hand to his lips. 'I hope you have begged his forgiveness, Nell – as I beg for yours!'

'Oh, Giles, pray *hush*!'

The Viscount, having frowned over this for a moment, exclaimed: 'What, did you think *she* had sold the thing? If that don't give you your own again, Nell!'

'That's all very well,' objected Mr Hethersett, 'but you said it *wasn't* lost, Cardross!'

'It was lost, but it has been restored to me. I suppose I now know who stole it – and should have known at the outset! Not your sister, Dysart, but mine! Was that it, Nell?'

'Well, yes, it was,' she confessed. 'But you mustn't be out of *reason* cross with her, because indeed I believe she would never have thought of doing such a thing, only that Dysart put it into her head!'

'What?' exclaimed Dysart. 'No, by God, that's too much! I never did so!'

'Yes, Dy, you did! Oh, I don't mean to say that it was what you intended, but I have been thinking about it, and I am persuaded it was your holding me up that night, with Mr Fancot – good gracious, where *is* Mr Fancot?'

'Yes, by Jove! Where is he?' exclaimed Dysart.

'No need to worry about him,' said Mr Hethersett, nodding to where Mr Fancot was peacefully sleeping in a large wing-chair.

'Wouldn't have let you all talk in that dashed improper way if he'd been listening to you!'

'If ever I knew anyone like Corny for dropping asleep the instant he gets a trifle above oar!' remarked the Viscount, eyeing his friend with tolerant affection.

'Don't wake him, I beg of you!' said Cardross. 'What, my darling, had that hold-up to do with this affair?'

'Yes, *what*?' demanded Dysart.

'Well, you see, Giles, when I wouldn't sell any of the jewels you gave me – and I *still* think it would have been the most odiously deceiving thing to have done, Dy, however tiresome you may have thought it of me! – Dysart hit upon the notion of pretending to be a highwayman, and taking them from me in that way. Only I recognized him, so it came to nothing. But the thing was that Letty thought it had been a famous notion, and I am very sure that *that* was what put it into her head to sell the Cardross necklace!' She broke off, as a thought occurred to her. 'Good heavens, *Letty*! What are we about, wasting time in this way? Cardross, we discovered, Felix and I, that they set out with only a pair of horses! It is true that they have several hours start of you, but Felix seems to think that you might easily overtake them before they can reach the Border!'

'I daresay I might – if I were to make the attempt,' he agreed.

'But won't you?' she asked anxiously.

'No. I have had my fill of driving this evening! Allandale is welcome to her!'

'Yes, but to be married in such a way! Giles, only think what the consequences must be! I shouldn't wonder at it if it ruined him as well as her! Indeed, I was never more astonished in my life than when I learned he had yielded to her persuasions! I had not thought it of him! And for you, too, how disagreeable must it be! Oh, do, pray, go after them, and bring her back!'

'Dashed if I would!' remarked the Viscount.

'Giles!'

He laid his hand over the small one insistently tugging at the lapel of his coat. 'Hush, my love! This is where we must be guided by the judgement of that arbiter of all matters of taste and ton. Well, Felix?'

Mr Hethersett, impervious to the quizzical look in his cousin's eye, took snuff in a meditative way, his brow creased. 'Don't fancy it will make much difference,' he pronounced at last, restoring the box to his pocket, and flicking a few grains of King's Martinique from his sleeve. 'Bound to be a deal of gossip whatever you do. Can't suppose it won't leak out, if you go careering off after Letty. Devilish nasty scene, too, if you force her to come home. Seems to have gone into strong hysterics when Allandale tried to get her to do that. Not the sort of thing *I* should care for.'

'No, my God!' said Cardross, with feeling.

'Better make the best of it,' decided Mr Hethersett. 'Think I'll be going now. Daresay, you'll like to be left alone.'

Nell held out her hand to him. 'I have quite ruined your evening!' she said contritely. 'Indeed, I am sorry, and so very much obliged to you!'

'No, no, happy to have been of service!' he replied, bowing with exquisite grace over her hand. 'Besides, no such thing! Only on my way to White's, before taking a look-in at the Seftons' ball. Night's young yet!'

'Yes, by Jove, so it is!' said the Viscount. 'Here, Corny, wake up!'

Mr Fancot, urgently shaken, opened his eyes, smiled upon the company, and began to hum softly and unmelodiously to himself.

'Now, for the lord's sake, Corny, you ain't as dead-beat as that!' said the Viscount. 'Don't start singing again, because you know dashed well you can't do it!'

'It's my birthday,' stated Mr Fancot.

'Well, that's got nothing to say to anything! Come along! Time we were going!'

'I can sing on my birthday,' said Mr Fancot. 'I can sing *Sing old rose, and burn the bellows*, and I can sing your song, and I can –'

'*Chip-chow, cherry-chow?*' interrupted Mr Hethersett.

'That's the one!' nodded Mr Fancot, pleased. 'You know it too?'

'I've heard it,' replied Mr Hethersett, rather grimly. He met the Viscount's challenging gaze, and held it. 'You've called me a few names this night, Dysart! Now I'll take leave to tell you that you're the biggest cod's head *I* ever knew!'

'What the devil do you mean by that?' the Viscount shot at him, flushing.

'You know dashed well what I mean! You learned that song from Cripplegate!'

'What if I did?' demanded Dysart.

'*I'll* tell you that, Dysart,' interposed Cardross. He nodded dismissal to his cousin, and looked Dysart over. 'Beggars' Club, eh? Well, I thought as much! A Hussar regiment should suit you: it would be a pity to waste your horsemanship. Well?'

'Oh, to hell with you! I've told you I can't!' Dysart said.

'You'll find you can, I promise you.'

'By Jove, what wouldn't I give to be out there!' Dysart said impulsively.

'You going to join, Dy?' enquired Mr Fancot, who had been following this conversation with great interest. 'That's a devilish good notion! Let's go and join at once!'

'Well, we can't,' said Dysart shortly. 'Besides, you don't want to join!'

'Yes, I do,' asserted Mr Fancot. 'Can't think why I didn't hit on the notion before! There's nothing left to do here, except walk backwards to Brighton, and I don't fancy that above half.'

'Who shall blame you?' agreed Cardross, shepherding him kindly but firmly into the hall.

'That's just it,' explained Mr Fancot. 'I may have to. Never refused a challenge in my life, and I've a notion Willy means to try me with that one. You know Willy?'

'No, but I should lose no time in leaving the country.'

'You're a sensible man,' said Mr Fancot warmly. 'Very happy to have met you!'

'The pleasure has been all mine,' said Cardross, putting his hat into his hand, and opening the front door.

'Not at all, not at all!' responded Mr Fancot, ambling down the steps.

'Lord, if ever I saw him in such prime and plummy order before!' said the Viscount. 'Now I shall have him going all over town, trying to find the Horse Guards!' He picked up this own hat, and hesitated, looking at Cardross.

Cardross smiled. 'You're a damned fool, Dysart, and a damned nuisance besides – but too good a man to be wasting your talents cutting up cork-brained larks! Don't tease yourself about your mother! I'll make all right in that quarter.'

He held out his hand, and the Viscount took it, grinning ruefully. 'I wish you might!'

'I will.'

'Devilish good of you. Got something else to say to you, and it ain't easy. From what Nell told me, when she found herself in that fix – Well, the long and the short of it is she didn't know till I told her that you were in love with her. Thought you'd married her as a matter of convenience, and had too much civility to let her see it.' He gave a crack of laughter. 'Convenience! Lord, what a silly little greenhead!'

'Are you serious?' Cardross demanded. 'It isn't possible!'

'Ain't it? You don't know my mother, Cardross!' said Dysart. 'Good-night! Must go after Corny!'

He went down the steps, waved, and went striding off. Cardross stood looking after him for a moment, and was just about to go back into the house when a post-chaise swept round the angle of the square, and drew up below him. From this vehicle Mr Allandale jumped down, and turned to give his supporting hand to his betrothed.

'But what a charming surprise!' said Cardross blandly.

Fifteen

*M*r Allandale, having paid off the postilion, took his love in one hand and Mr Thorne's cloak-bag in the other, and trod up the steps to the front-door. Here he paused and looked Cardross squarely in the face. 'I have brought her home, sir,' he said.

'I see you have,' replied Cardross. 'Most understandable, I am sure!'

Letty cast a scared, resentful look up at him, but said nothing.

'An explanation is due to you,' said Mr Allandale. 'But first I must beg of you most earnestly that whatever wrath you may feel – and I do not deny that it is a just wrath! – you will visit upon my head alone!'

'I fail entirely to see why I should visit my wrath on your head, but if you suppose me to be contemplating a violent revenge on Letty do let me hasten to reassure you!'

'You see, love?' said Mr Allandale tenderly.

'I'm n-not afraid of Cardross!' said Letty, in a small, resentful voice.

'It would have been very much better for you, and all of us if you had been,' said Cardross. 'Come into the house, but leave your heroism outside!' He led the way into the hall, and saw Farley standing in the middle of it with his mouth at half-cock. 'Just so!' he remarked.

'I heard a carriage drive up, my lord!' explained the butler, staring at Letty.

'Yes, Lady Letty decided after all she would not spend the

night in Bryanston Square,' said Cardross ironically. 'You may come into the book-room, both of you.' He walked to the door and held it wide. Across the room Nell's eyes met his, a startled question in them. 'Giles, I thought I heard –'

'You did, my love. Can you conceive of anything more delightful? Dear little Letty is once more in our midst!'

'I *hate* you!' said Letty passionately, and burst into tears.

'Letty! Oh, Letty, thank God you've come back!' cried Nell, hurrying forward.

'I wish I hadn't! I wish I were dead!' sobbed Letty.

'No, no, you mustn't say that!' Nell told her, putting an arm round her, and stretching out her other hand to Mr Allandale. 'Mr Allandale, how *glad* I am that I wasn't mistaken in you! I couldn't think it possible that you would do such an improper thing as to elope with her!'

He kissed her hand punctiliously, and said: 'I wish that I could find the words to express to your ladyship the sense of obligation I feel. But when I consider the circumstances, and what cause you have had (the whole truth not being known to you) to think me infamous, I am rendered tongue-tied.'

'Not noticeably,' said Cardross dryly.

Nell bit her lip, and drew Letty to the sofa. 'Come, love, sit down beside me, and try to compose yourself!' She saw how anxiously Mr Allandale was watching Letty, and smiled at him reassuringly. 'She will be better directly: don't pay any heed to her!'

He looked grateful, but turned with a resolute air to Cardross. 'Sir, I have a duty to discharge. I speak on behalf of Lady Letitia, and I shall be brief, merely imploring you to remember that she is young, and in the greatest distress, and has thrown herself upon your mercy. What I have to disclose to you cannot but shock you deeply. You do not yet know the worst, and it is my painful duty to inform you of it.'

'Oh, yes, I do!' replied Cardross. 'You are about to tell me that Letty stole the Cardross necklace.'

Letty raised her head from Nell's shoulder. 'It *wasn't* stealing!

It *wasn't*!' she declared. 'It didn't belong to Nell, and she didn't even like it! It belonged to the *family*, and so it was just as much mine as yours, Giles!'

'My love, you are forgetting that I have several times explained to you that that is not so,' said Mr Allandale gravely.

'Yes, but it *is*! And anyway Giles won't let me have my fortune, so what else could I do?'

Mr Allandale looked pained, but apparently decided that the moment was not ripe for argument. Drawing a package from his pocket, he laid it on the table before him, and said: 'That is the sum the necklace realized, my lord. Had I been able, I would have done my utmost to recover the necklace itself. It was not in my power, however: I have not been at liberty to repair to the jeweller to whom it was sold. I will furnish your lordship with –'

'Let me set your mind at rest!' Cardross interrupted. 'The jeweller brought it to me earlier today, and I have already redeemed it.'

'Sir, you have removed a weight from my mind!' said Mr Allandale earnestly.

'Yes, I expect I have,' agreed Cardross. 'I wish you will satisfy the curiosity in mine! Was it the discovery that your bride had stolen the necklace which made you abandon your flight to Gretna Green? At what stage did you turn back?'

'There was no such flight, my lord.'

'No, of course not!' Nell said. 'But – where *did* you go to, Mr Allandale?'

'I was guilty of practising deception,' he said heavily. 'I need not, I hope, assure you that such a course was of the utmost repugnance to me. To deceive one so dear to me, and one who, moreover, placed the most implicit trust in my integrity, was more painful than I can describe. But when I found that no words of mine could avail to persuade my darling to return to her home, when I saw her in such agony of grief and despair –'

'Yes, I've seen Letty in hysterics,' said Cardross. 'You have no need to describe the scene to me! I pity you sincerely. What, in fact, did you do?'

'Fearing that if I compelled her to return to this house she might put a period to her existence, I agreed to fly with her to the Border,' said Mr Allandale. 'She believed that we were on our way north, but it was not so. I did not carry her to Gretna Green, but to Wimbledon.'

There was a moment's astonished silence. 'To Wimbledon!' said Cardross, in a voice that shook. 'I expect you had an excellent reason for your choice.'

'Why, to be sure he had!' exclaimed Nell, bestowing a warm smile upon Mr Allandale. 'You mean you took her to your mother's house! How *very* wise of you!'

He bowed. 'It seemed to me, ma'am, the only course open to me. In my mother's judgement I could repose complete confidence, for her understanding is superior, her mind of an elevated order, and her firm yet tender command over my sisters such as encouraged me to hope that over my darling also her influence would prevail.'

'And we perceive that it did!' said Cardross. 'My dear Allandale, why have I never been privileged to meet your mother?'

'I would like to *kill* you!' choked Letty.

'My mother, sir, seldom goes into society,' said Mr Allandale stiffly.

'But I hope she may be persuaded to receive me, nevertheless.'

'I am at a loss to understand your lordship,' said Mr Allandale, more stiffly yet. 'I apprehend, however, that you are in funning humour!'

'No, I am not funning,' Cardross replied. 'Oblige me by telling me, in all frankness, whether or not my sister's want of conduct, her excessive sensibility, and the unscrupulous means she does not hesitate to use to attain her ends have convinced you that she is totally unfitted to be your wife?'

'Giles, *don't*!' begged Nell, as Letty broke into renewed weeping.

'Sir,' said Mr Allandale, very pale, but steadily meeting

Cardross's eyes, 'I do not attempt to condone her faults, though I can perceive excuses for them, but I love her, and must always do so, whatever she is, or whatever she does.'

Letty looked up, her tears arrested, awe in her face. 'Jeremy!' she said. 'Oh, *Jeremy!*'

Cardross turned his head. 'You are not worthy of that, Letty.'

'No,' she said forlornly. 'I know I am not, but – oh, I *wish* I were!'

He smiled wryly. 'Well, I daresay there may be hope for you. You had better marry her, Allandale.'

It seemed for several moments as though neither of the interested parties could believe that they had heard him correctly. It was Letty who found her voice first. 'Giles – do you mean *now*? Before he sails?'

'Yes, that's what I mean.'

'Oh, my dearest brother, how kind you are!' cried Letty, flying up off the sofa and casting herself upon his chest. '*Pray* forgive me for saying horrid things to you! I didn't mean them! Oh, how happy I am! Oh, Jeremy, I *promise* I will never do anything you don't like!'

'Sir,' said Mr Allandale, 'I do not know how to convey to you my sense of your generosity, my gratitude, the –'

'Then don't try!' said Cardross. 'You are a very estimable young man, but I should like you so much more if you would refrain from addressing me in flowing periods! I am going to send you away now, but you may come to see me tomorrow, at noon, if that should be convenient to you, when I will arrange the marriage settlements with you. You may escort him to the front door, Letty, and after you have bidden him good-night, you had better go to bed.'

'Bed at ten o'clock!' she said, by no means pleased.

'Yes, bed at ten o'clock. If you are not exhausted after a day of unbridled passion, you should be! Don't argue with me! My patience won't stand it.'

'Indeed, you should go, love!' Nell urged her. 'You are quite worn out. I will come up to you, and –'

'No, you will not,' Cardross interrupted.

Overawed by this display of cool and sweeping authority the young lovers withdrew circumspectly. Nell showed her husband a laughing countenance. 'Well, *really*, Giles!' she expostulated.

He caught her up from the sofa, and held her a little away from him, looking down into her face with bright, smiling eyes. 'Yes, *really*, *Giles*!' he retorted. 'How much longer did you think I would wait to get you to myself?'

She did not answer him, but blushed a little, meeting his gaze shyly but very openly.

'There's so much to say to you, Nell – and, God forgive me, so much to unsay! My darling, I wish I had cut my tongue out before –'

'No, there is nothing to unsay, because you didn't say those things to me,' she intervened. 'They hurt me only a very little – not as much as I deserved, perhaps! For I am afraid I have been extravagant, and – and deceitful, and very foolish!'

'And above all very foolish,' he agreed, turning her words into a caress. 'It seems I have been a great deal too easy with you, Madam Wife! *That* will not happen again! So you thought I offered for you because I wanted a wife, and saw nothing in you to disgust me, did you? Nell, how *could* you be such a goose?'

The blush deepened; she hung her head. 'Mama said – that you were disposed to be *fond* of me, and considerate, and she warned me not to hang on you, or – or appear to notice it if – perhaps – you had Another Interest.'

'I am obliged to Mama! And did it seem to you that I had Another Interest?'

'No. But I knew,' she said simply. 'The first time we met Letty said that I was prettier than your mistress.'

'She was right. I wish I could think that Allandale would beat her regularly every week, but I fear he won't. The lady with whom I enjoyed an agreeable connection for several years need never have troubled you. We parted without regret or ill-will, and when we meet in company today it is with the indifferent pleasure of old acquaintances. From the moment I saw you, Nell, you have had all my heart. That is the truth.'

'Dysart said that. He said that everyone knew it, too.'

'I infinitely prefer your brother to my sister. But why, my foolish little love, did you then keep me at an even greater distance?'

She looked up again. 'You see, I owed Lavalle more than *three hundred pounds*, so how could I do anything else, until that dreadful debt was paid? With that on my conscience I couldn't tell you that I had been *agonizingly* in love with you from the very beginning; and if you had discovered the debt you would never have believed me. But I was, Giles.'

Farley, quietly entering the room at that moment, beheld his mistress locked in a crushing embrace, and with instant presence of mind stepped noiselessly back into the hall. There he remained for some few minutes, after which, with a little fumbling with the door-handle, he entered the book-room for the second time. My lord, before the mirror above the fireplace, was pensively absorbed in some delicate adjustment to the folds of his cravat; my lady, a trifle dishevelled, but otherwise a model of fashionable decorum, was seated in a large armchair. 'I don't know how it comes about, my lord,' she said, in a light, languid voice, 'but we do not increase our covers for guests tonight.'

'But why, my love, did you not inform me of this circumstance earlier?' enquired my lord reproachfully. 'I should then have used my best endeavours to have persuaded your brother and his amiable friend to have given us the pleasure of their company.'

'Yes, indeed! How – how stupid of me!' said my lady, with very creditable command over her voice.

'And Allandale,' pursued my lord ruthlessly, 'in case the conversation should have flagged.'

Pained to see such a want of chivalry in my lord, Farley came to the rescue of his sorely-tried mistress, and, in a few dignified and well-chosen words, put an end to this scene 'Supper, my lady, is served!' he announced.

Welcome to the world of

Georgette Heyer

We hope you have enjoyed Georgette Heyer's world of spirited heroines, brooding heroes, and perfect period detail.

Discover more of Georgette Heyer's unique storytelling skills in further novels in this collection.

Why I love *Georgette Heyer*

A Q&A with bestselling author Katie Fforde

When did you first discover Georgette Heyer?

I first discovered Georgette Heyer when the eldest daughter of a visiting family left behind her copy of *Friday's Child*. I'm not sure how old I was but I know I couldn't read all the words. But oh the story, the characters! I can never decide what I love most about her books – her characters or her dialogue. I so admire the way you can tell who's talking by their manner of speech, use of language, etc. Just heaven! And because I started reading her so young I found her heroines good role models. I discovered that boys didn't like girls who simpered. I only have a sister (she is just as much a fan) and went to a single-sex school, so learning how to deal with boys was jolly useful.

What do you love most about her books?

I think her books are so enjoyable because the heroines are instantly likeable. Some are beautiful, others less so, some have wealth and fortune, others very little, but they are all intelligent, brave, kind and with an excellent sense of humour. The heroes are all very easy to fall in love with, although I doubt I would have dared speak to them had I been lucky enough to come across anyone so gorgeous when I was young. And they are so funny! And yet the humour isn't shoehorned in; it arises naturally from the circumstances and there is real feeling there too – they are more than just a jolly good laugh. I also love the period detail – the clothes, the hats, the trimmings – and the servants, who are just as finely drawn as the protagonists. Even the animals have character.

One of my particular favourites is Horry from *A Convenient Marriage*. She is positively headstrong in her courage but she uses this trait for the good of the family. She does get into all sorts of scrapes but Rule, the hero, is prepared to put up with a lot because of her huge charm and innate innocence. This book shows Georgette Heyer's ability to write really nail-biting descriptions and proves she's so much more than frills and fa-las. Of course Rule has a sense of humour otherwise he'd never have taken on Horry, but he's prepared to learn from her, too. It's one thing being rich and powerful and good at everything, but unless you can laugh at yourself, you'd end up pretty boring. Not all Heyer's heroes are like Rule, but they all see their faults and change their behaviour once they've fallen in love.

How does Georgette Heyer influence you today?

Someone asked me at almost my first event as a writer whether I was influenced by Georgette Heyer. At first I was confused – I write contemporary fiction – but then I was incredibly flattered. I read her historical novels so often for so long, of course she influenced me! I suspect she influenced my school essays, too – she certainly improved my vocabulary massively. As a novelist, I long for her skills in characterisation and dialogue. Many, many people have tried to emulate her style but, although there are some jolly good efforts, none of them achieve what she does. Maybe I write contemporary fiction because I couldn't aspire to her vast historical knowledge, but how I wish I could!

If you like your escapist fiction to be brilliantly written, highly amusing and completely addictive, look no further. And rejoice because there are over forty Heyer novels to enjoy (although there are many of us who think that isn't nearly enough).

Katie Fforde

YOU ARE CORDIALLY INVITED TO JOIN THE

Georgette Heyer
CLUB

If you wish to receive all the latest news from the most important Heyer circles, find out about competitions, new book releases, and to receive interesting articles, follow us today.

Join us on Facebook:
thecompletegeorgetteheyer

Sign up to our newsletter by visiting:
www.penguin.co.uk/georgetteheyernewsletter

We look forward to welcoming you.